ANNIE

THE CRYSTAL E ...JRDER

Annie Haynes was born in 1865, the daughter of an ironmonger.

By the first decade of the twentieth century she lived in London and moved in literary and early feminist circles. Her first crime novel, *The Bungalow Mystery*, appeared in 1923, and another nine mysteries were published before her untimely death in 1929.

Who Killed Charmian Karslake? appeared posthumously, and a further partially-finished work, *The Crystal Beads Murder*, was completed with the assistance of an unknown fellow writer, and published in 1930.

Also by Annie Haynes

ANNIE HAYNES

THE CRYSTAL BEADS MURDER

With an introduction
by Curtis Evans

DEAN STREET PRESS

Published by Dean Street Press 2015

All Rights Reserved

First published in 1929 by The Bodley Head

Cover by DSP

Introduction © Curtis Evans 2015

ISBN 978 1 910570 80 7

www.deanstreetpress.co.uk

The Mystery of the Missing Author

Annie Haynes and Her Golden Age
Detective Fiction

The psychological enigma of Agatha Christie's notorious 1926 vanishing has continued to intrigue Golden Age mystery fans to the present day. The Queen of Crime's eleven-day disappearing act is nothing, however, compared to the decades-long disappearance, in terms of public awareness, of between-the-wars mystery writer Annie Haynes (1865-1929), author of a series of detective novels published between 1923 and 1930 by Agatha Christie's original English publisher, The Bodley Head. Haynes's books went out of print in the early Thirties, not long after her death in 1929, and her reputation among classic detective fiction readers, high in her lifetime, did not so much decline as dematerialize. When, in 2013, I first wrote a piece about Annie Haynes' work, I knew of only two other living persons besides myself who had read any of her books. Happily, Dean Street Press once again has come to the rescue of classic mystery fans seeking genre gems from the Golden Age, and is republishing all Haynes' mystery novels. Now that her crime fiction is coming back into print, the question naturally arises: Who Was Annie Haynes? Solving the mystery of this forgotten author's lost life has taken leg work by literary sleuths on two continents (my thanks for their assistance to Carl Woodings and Peter Harris).

Until recent research uncovered new information about Annie Haynes, almost nothing about her was publicly known besides the fact of her authorship of twelve mysteries during the Golden Age of detective fiction. Now we know that she led an altogether intriguing life, too soon cut short by disability and death, which took her from the isolation of the rural

English Midlands in the nineteenth century to the cultural high life of Edwardian London. Haynes was born in 1865 in the Leicestershire town of Ashby-de-la-Zouch, the first child of ironmonger Edwin Haynes and Jane (Henderson) Haynes, daughter of Montgomery Henderson, longtime superintendent of the gardens at nearby Coleorton Hall, seat of the Beaumont baronets. After her father left his family, young Annie resided with her grandparents at the gardener's cottage at Coleorton Hall, along with her mother and younger brother. Here Annie doubtlessly obtained an acquaintance with the ways of the country gentry that would serve her well in her career as a genre fiction writer.

We currently know nothing else of Annie Haynes' life in Leicestershire, where she still resided (with her mother) in 1901, but by 1908, when Haynes was in her early forties, she was living in London with Ada Heather-Bigg (1855-1944) at the Heather-Bigg family home, located halfway between Paddington Station and Hyde Park at 14 Radnor Place, London. One of three daughters of Henry Heather-Bigg, a noted pioneer in the development of orthopedics and artificial limbs, Ada Heather-Bigg was a prominent Victorian and Edwardian era feminist and social reformer. In the 1911 British census entry for 14 Radnor Place, Heather-Bigg, a "philanthropist and journalist," is listed as the head of the household and Annie Haynes, a "novelist," as a "visitor," but in fact Haynes would remain there with Ada Heather-Bigg until Haynes' death in 1929.

Haynes' relationship with Ada Heather-Bigg introduced the aspiring author to important social sets in England's great metropolis. Though not a novelist herself, Heather-Bigg was an important figure in the city's intellectual milieu, a well-connected feminist activist of great energy and passion who believed strongly in the idea of women attaining economic independence through remunerative employment. With Ada

Heather-Bigg behind her, Annie Haynes's writing career had powerful backing indeed. Although in the 1911 census Heather-Bigg listed Haynes' occupation as "novelist," it appears that Haynes did not publish any novels in book form prior to 1923, the year that saw the appearance of *The Bungalow Mystery*, which Haynes dedicated to Heather-Bigg. However, Haynes was a prolific producer of newspaper serial novels during the second decade of the twentieth century, penning such works as *Lady Carew's Secret, Footprints of Fate, A Pawn of Chance, The Manor Tragedy* and many others.

Haynes' twelve Golden Age mystery novels, which appeared in a tremendous burst of creative endeavor between 1923 and 1930, like the author's serial novels retain, in stripped-down form, the emotionally heady air of the nineteenth-century triple-decker sensation novel, with genteel settings, shocking secrets, stormy passions and eternal love all at the fore, yet they also have the fleetness of Jazz Age detective fiction. Both in their social milieu and narrative pace Annie Haynes' detective novels bear considerable resemblance to contemporary works by Agatha Christie; and it is interesting to note in this regard that Annie Haynes and Agatha Christie were the only female mystery writers published by The Bodley Head, one of the more notable English mystery imprints in the early Golden Age. "A very remarkable feature of recent detective fiction," observed the *Illustrated London News* in 1923, "is the skill displayed by women in this branch of story-telling. Isabel Ostrander, Carolyn Wells, Annie Haynes and last, but very far from least, Agatha Christie, are contesting the laurels of Sherlock Holmes' creator with a great spirit, ingenuity and success." Since Ostrander and Wells were American authors, this left Annie Haynes, in the estimation of the *Illustrated London News*, as the main British female competitor to Agatha Christie. (Dorothy L. Sayers, who, like Haynes, published her debut mystery novel in 1923, goes unmentioned.) Similarly, in 1925 *The Sketch* wryly noted that "[t]ired men, trotting home at the end of an imperfect day, have been known to pop into the library and ask for an Annie Haynes. They have not made a mistake in the street number. It is not a cocktail they are asking for...."

Twenties critical opinion adjudged that Annie Haynes' criminous concoctions held appeal not only for puzzle fiends impressed with the "considerable craftsmanship" of their plots (quoting from the *Sunday Times* review of *The Bungalow Mystery*), but also for more general readers attracted to their purely literary qualities. "Not only a crime story of merit, but also a novel which will interest readers to whom mystery for its own sake has little appeal," avowed *The Nation* of Haynes' *The Secret of Greylands*, while the *New Statesman* declared of *The Witness on the Roof* that "Miss Haynes has a sense of character; her people are vivid and not the usual puppets of detective fiction." Similarly, the *Bookman* deemed the characters in Haynes' *The Abbey Court Murder* "much truer to life than is the case in many sensational stories" and *The Spectator* concluded of *The Crime at Tattenham Corner*, "Excellent as a detective tale, the book also is a charming novel."

Sadly, Haynes' triumph as a detective novelist proved short lived. Around 1914, about the time of the outbreak of the Great War, Haynes had been stricken with debilitating rheumatoid arthritis that left her in constant pain and hastened her death from heart failure in 1929, when she was only 63. Haynes wrote several of her detective novels on fine days in Kensington Gardens, where she was wheeled from 14 Radnor Place in a bath chair, but in her last years she was able only to travel from her bedroom to her study. All of this was an especially hard blow for a woman who had once been intensely energetic and quite physically active.

In a foreword to *The Crystal Beads Murder*, the second of Haynes' two posthumously published mysteries, Ada Heather-Bigg noted that Haynes' difficult daily physical struggle "was materially lightened by the warmth of friendships" with other authors and by the "sympathetic and friendly relations between her and her publishers." In this latter instance Haynes' experience rather differed from that of her sister Bodleian, Agatha Christie, who left The Bodley Head on account of what she deemed an iniquitous contract that took unjust advantage of a naive young author. Christie moved, along with her landmark detective novel *The Murder of Roger Ackroyd* (1926), to Collins and never looked back, enjoying ever greater success with the passing years.

At the time Christie crossed over to Collins, Annie Haynes had only a few years of life left. After she died at 14 Radnor Place on 30 March 1929, it was reported in the press that "many people well-known in the literary world" attended the author's funeral at St. Michaels and All Angels Church, Paddington, where her sermon was delivered by the eloquent vicar, Paul Nichols, brother of the writer Beverley Nichols and dedicatee of Haynes' mystery novel *The Master of the Priory*; yet by the time of her companion Ada Heather-Bigg's death in 1944, Haynes and her once highly-praised mysteries were forgotten. (Contrastingly, Ada Heather-Bigg's name survives today in the University College of London's Ada Heather-Bigg Prize in Economics.) Only three of Haynes' novels were ever published in the United States, and she passed away less than a year before the formation of the Detection Club, missing any chance of being invited to join this august body of distinguished British detective novelists. Fortunately, we have today entered, when it comes to classic mystery, a period of rediscovery and revival, giving a reading audience a chance once again, after over eighty years, to savor the detective fiction fare of Annie Haynes. *Bon appétit!*

Introduction to
The Crystal Beads Murder

The Bodley Head published Annie Haynes' detective novel *The Crime at Tattenham Corner* just three weeks before the author passed away, on 30 March 1929. Haynes' death from heart failure at the age of 63 likely was not entirely unexpected to those who knew her, given her long illness. However, it presented the publishers with a dilemma. In addition to an eleventh mystery that Haynes had completed before her death (which, under the title *Who Killed Charmian Karslake?*, was published in the UK in the fall of 1929), there was an unfinished manuscript, which concerned a fatal shooting in a summer-house and a broken strand of crystal beads. Haynes at the time of her death having finished not quite fifteen manuscript chapters (about half the story), The Bodley Head was compelled, in order to have one last Annie Haynes mystery to put before her sizable reading public in 1930, to find a crime writer who could complete the book.

Haynes' surviving companion, Ada Heather-Bigg, wrote a moving foreword to *The Crystal Beads Murder*, in which she discussed not only Haynes' struggles against physical adversity but also the matter of the authorship of her final novel. "One of Miss Haynes' friends, also a popular writer of this type of fiction, offered to undertake the work of completion," Heather-Bigg explained, "and it says much for her skill that she has independently arrived at Miss Haynes's own solution of the mystery, which was known only to myself." This author friend has never been formally identified. Prominent English women detective novelists at the time of the completion of *The Crystal Beads Murder* in 1929-30 included Agatha Christie, Dorothy L. Sayers, Anthony Gilbert (Lucy Beatrice Malleson), A. Fielding (Dorothy Feilding), Molly Thynne and Margaret Cole. Agatha Christie and Dorothy L. Sayers seem unlikely candidates, given that had either woman done the deed it would likely be known by now. However, there are certain clues to the mystery woman's identity.

Stylistically, the use in the second half of the novel of the phrase "flotsam and jetsam" suggests to me that the author might be Lucy Beatrice Malleson (still at this time a relatively inexperienced crime writer), "flotsam and jetsam" being a term Malleson recurrently used in her fiction. After writing two non-series mysteries, published in 1925 and 1927 under the pseudonym J. Kilmeny Keith, Malleson launched her Anthony Gilbert pseudonym in 1927 with *The Tragedy at Freyne*. Remaining single all her life, Malleson wrote authoritatively about the lives of England's so-called "superfluous women," a subject that would have been of interest to Annie Haynes and Ada Heather-Bigg as well. My suggestion is conjectural, to be sure, yet whoever completed *The Crystal Beads Murder*, she made good work of her effort.

The novel opens with the orphaned Anne Courtenay being pressured by a debauched swine, William Saunderson, into acceptance of an unwanted marriage proposal. Her brother Harold Courtenay is in deep financial debt to Saunderson, a familiar presence in horseracing circles, though "[n]obody knew exactly who he was or where he came from." For their part, the Courtenays are impecunious but well-connected socially, being cousins of Lord Medchester. Anne in fact is engaged to Lord Medchester's horse trainer, Michael Burford, "second son of old Sir William Burford and half-brother of the present baronet"; but Saunderson has no intention of letting that fact stand in his way.

When Saunderson is found murdered in the summer-house of Holford Hall, Scotland Yard's Detective-Inspector William Stoddart and his redoubtable assistant Alfred Harbord are called into the case by the Loamshire constabulary. They confront a sizeable cast of suspects, including Lord Medchester's wife, Minnie, said to have had "a distinct penchant for Saunderson." But what of the three white crystal beads, linked by a thin, gold chain, that Harbord finds in Saunderson's overcoat pocket? Lady Medchester scoffs at the idea that she might have owned such a cheap trinket, "though so many people wear this sort of thing nowadays"; and Anne Courtenay produces for police inspection her own crystal bead necklace, quite unbroken. Just what are Stoddart and Harbord to make of the cryptic crystal beads?

Annie Haynes' half of *The Crystal Beads Murder* is composed in the author's best vein, with intriguing plot complications and interesting characters capturing the readers fancy. In Joseph Wilton, the "clean-looking, clean-shaven" Holford Hall gardener in "whole and tidy" working clothes who discovered Saunderson's corpse in the summer-house, one glimpses sturdy Victorian-era Midlanders who worked for the author's Scottish-born grandfather Montgomery Henderson, the highly-respected superintendent of the gardens at Coleorton Hall in Leicestershire. The novel's summer-house crime setting also recalls England's infamous Edwardian-era Luard murder case. Two decades previous to the composition of *The Crystal Beads Murder*, before her crippling rheumatoid arthritis made such activity unthinkable, Haynes had cycled some thirty miles from her home near Hyde Park in London to Ightham, Kent, to inspect "La Casa," the summer-house where in 1908 Caroline Luard was found, like the fictional Robert Saunderson, slain by a single gunshot wound.

Haynes lived long enough to introduce the colorfully vulgar variety performer Tottie Delauney to readers of *The Crystal Beads Murder*, and she nearly completed the inquest scene in chapter fifteen. In the last eleven chapters of the novel, however, the keen Haynes reader may detect certain differences in narrative style, such as a comparatively greater reliance on authorial voice rather than dialogue. Nevertheless, the new author accurately deduced Haynes's intended murderer, as Ada Heather-Bigg noted in her foreword to the novel, and she finished her challenging task quite creditably. Haynes' final mystery is, as one reviewer noted, "uncommonly well-constructed"; and it stands as a fitting tribute to the career of a Golden Age mystery writer who overcame tragic physical limitation to achieve true distinction in her chosen form of fictional endeavor. "She wrote in pain, and kept her head clear," admiringly observed the British writer and critic Charles Williams of Annie Haynes after her death: "could any genius ask a nobler epitaph."

Curtis Evans

FOREWORD

This, the last of twelve mystery stories written by the late Annie Haynes – who died last year – was left unfinished. One of Miss Haynes's friends, also a popular writer of this type of fiction, offered to undertake the work of completion, and it says much for her skill that she has independently arrived at Miss Haynes's own solution of the mystery, which was known only to myself.

It is not generally known that for the last fifteen years of her life Miss Haynes was in constant pain and writing itself was a considerable effort. Her courage in facing her illness was remarkable, and the fact that she was handicapped not only by the pain but also by the helplessness of her malady greatly enhances the merit of her achievements. It was impossible for her to go out into the world for fresh material for her books, her only journeys being from her bedroom to her study. The enforced inaction was the harder to bear in her case, as before her illness she was extremely energetic. Her intense interest in crime and criminal psychology led her into the most varied activities, such as cycling miles to visit the scene of the Luard Murder, pushing her way into the cellar of 39 Hilldrop Crescent, where the remains of Belle Elmore were discovered, and attending the Crippen trial.

It would be a dark and sombre picture if it were not mentioned how this struggle with cruel circumstances was materially lightened by the warmth of friendships existing between Miss Haynes and her fellow authors and by the sympathetic and friendly relations between her and her publishers.

Ada Heather-Bigg, 1930

CHAPTER I

"My hat! Nan, I tell you it is the chance of a lifetime. Battledore is a dead cert. Old Tim Ranger says he is the best colt he ever had in his stable. Masterman gave a thousand guineas for him as a yearling. He'd have won the Derby in a canter if he had been entered."

"It is easy to say that when he wasn't, isn't it?" Anne Courtenay smiled. "Don't put too much on, Harold. You can't afford to lose, you know."

"Lose! I tell you I can't lose," her brother returned hotly. His face was flushed, the hand that held his card was trembling. "Battledore must win. My bottom dollar's on him. Minnie Medchester has mortgaged her dress allowance for a year to back him. Oh, Battledore's a wonder colt."

"What is a wonder colt – Battledore, I suppose?" a suave voice interposed at this juncture. "Mind what you are doing, Harold. Best hedge a bit. I hear Goldfoot is expected. Anyway, the stable is on him for all it's worth."

"So is Ranger's on Battledore. Old Tim Ranger says it is all over bar the shouting. Oh, Battledore's a cert. I have been telling Anne to put every penny she can scrape together on him."

"I hope Miss Courtenay has not obeyed you," Robert Saunderson said, his eyes, a little bloodshot though the day was still young, fixed on Anne Courtenay's fair face. "It's all very well, young man, but I have known so many of these hotpots come unstuck to put much faith in even Tim Ranger's prophecies. I'd rather take a good outsider. Backing a long shot generally pays in the long run."

"It won't when Battledore is favourite," Harold Courtenay returned obstinately. "He ran away with the Gold Cup. It will be the same."

"H'm! Well, you are too young to remember Lawgiver. He was just such a Derby cert that he was guarded night and day and brought to the tapes with detectives before and behind, but he sauntered in a bad fifteenth."

"Battledore won't," young Courtenay said confidently. "Wait a minute, Nan. There's young Ranger. I must have a word with him." He darted off.

Robert Saunderson looked after him with a curious smile. Saunderson was well known in racing circles and was usually present at all the big meetings. He was sometimes spoken of as a mystery man. Nobody knew exactly who he was or where he came from. But as a rich bachelor he had made his way into a certain section of London society. At the present moment he, as well as the Courtenays, was staying at Holford Hall with the Courtenays' cousin, Lord Medchester.

Rumour had of late credited Lady Medchester with a very kindly feeling for Saunderson. Holford was within an easy driving distance of Doncaster, and the house-party to a man had come over on Lord Medchester's coach and a supplementary car to see the St. Leger run. The Courtenays were the grandchildren of old General Courtenay, who had held a high command in India and had been known on the Afghan frontier as "Dare-devil Courtenay". His only son, Harold and Anne's father, had been killed in the Great War. The Victoria Cross had been awarded to him after his death, and was his father's proudest possession. The young widow had not long survived her husband, and the two orphan children had been brought up by their grandfather.

The old man had spoilt and idolized them. The greatest disappointment of his life had been Harold's breakdown in health and resultant delicacy, which had put the Army out of the question. General Courtenay was a poor man, having little but his pension, and the difficulty had been to find some work within Harold's powers. The Church, the Army and the Bar were all rejected in turn. Young Courtenay had a pretty taste in literature and a certain facility with his pen, and for a time he had picked up a precarious living as a journalistic freelance. For the last year, however, he had been acting as secretary to Francis Melton, the member for North Loamshire.

Earlier in the year Anne Courtenay had become engaged to Michael Burford, Lord Medchester's trainer. It was not the grand match she had been expected to make, but Burford was sufficiently well off, and the young couple were desperately in love.

There was no mistaking the admiration in Saunderson's eyes as he looked down at Anne.

"You could not persuade the General to come to-day?"

Anne shook her head.

"No; it would have been too much for him. But he is quite happy talking over old times with his sister."

"He was a great race-goer in his day, he tells me."

"I believe he was an inveterate one. He still insists on having all the racing news read to him."

Anne moved on decidedly as she spoke. She did not care for Robert Saunderson. She had done her best to keep out of his way since his coming to Holford. Unfortunately the dislike was not mutual. Saunderson's admiration had been obvious from the first, and her coldness apparently only inflamed his passion. He followed her now.

"The Leger horses are in the paddock. What will Harold say if you don't see Battledore?"

Anne quickened her steps. "I don't know. But we shall see them all in a moment. And I must find my cousins."

Saunderson kept up with her, forcing their way through the jostling crowd round the paddock.

"Lord Medchester's filly ran away with the nursery plate, I hear. The favourite Severn Valley filly was not in it," he began; then as she made no rejoinder he went on, "We shall see a tremendous difference here in a year or two, Miss Courtenay. There will be an aerodrome over there" – jerking his head to the right – "second to none in the country, I will wager. And a big, up-to-date tote will be installed near the stand. Altogether we shan't know the Town Moor."

"I heard they were projecting all sorts of improvements," Anne assented. "But it will take a long time to get them finished and cost a great deal of money. Harold is frightfully keen on the tote, I know."

"Ah, Harold!" Saunderson interposed. "I wanted to speak to you about Harold. I am rather anxious about him. I don't like this friendship of his with the Stainers. He ought never to have introduced them to you. They've had the cheek to put up at the 'Medchester Arms' – want to get in touch with the training stables, I'll bet! Stainer's no good – never has been – he is a rotter, and the girl – well, the less said about her the better."

Anne recalled the red-haired girl who had seemed so friendly with Harold just now, but she let no hint of the uneasiness she felt show in her face.

"I am sure Harold does not care for her. Of course she is very good-looking. But why do you trouble about Harold?"

Saunderson looked at her.

"Because he is your brother," he said deliberately.

Anne's eyes met his quietly.

"A very poor reason, it seems to me."

"Then suppose I say, because I love you, Anne?" he said daringly.

Anne held up her head.

"I am engaged to Michael Burford."

"To Burford, the trainer!" Saunderson said scoffingly.

"No; to Burford, the man," she corrected.

A fierce light flashed into Saunderson's eyes. A whirl of sound of cheering, of incoherent cries rose around them. The St. Leger horses were coming up to the post.

"Battledore! Battledore!" Harold's choice was easily favourite. Masterman's scarlet and green were very conspicuous. Under cover of the tumult Saunderson bent nearer Anne.

"Michael Burford. Pah! You shall never marry him. You shall marry me. I swear it."

Anne's colour rose, but she made no reply as she hurried back to the Medchester coach. Most of the party were already in their places, but Lady Medchester stood at the foot of the steps. She was a tall, showily-dressed woman, whose complexion and hair evidently owed a good deal to art. Her mouth was hard, and just now the thin lips were pressed closely together.

"I hope you have enjoyed your walk and seeing Battledore," she said disagreeably.

Anne looked at her.

"I did not see Battledore."

Lady Medchester laughed, but there was no merriment in her pale eyes.

"I can quite understand that. Oh, Mr. Saunderson" – turning to the man who had come up behind her young cousin – "will you show me –"

Anne did not wait for any more. She ran lightly up the steps. Her brother hurried after her.

"I believe one gets a better view from the top of this coach than from the stand," he said unsteadily.

Anne looked at him with pity, at his flushed face, at his trembling hands.

"Harold, if you –"

She had no time for more. Harold sprang on the seat. There was a mighty shout. "They're off! They're off!" Then a groan of disappointment as the horses were recalled. A false start – Battledore had broken the tapes. Bill Turner, his Australian jockey, quieted him down and brought him back to the post.

"Goldfoot was sweating all over in the paddock just now," young Courtenay announced to nobody in particular. "He was all over the place, too, taking it out of himself. Doesn't stand an earthly against Battledore – he's a real natural stayer – isn't a son of Sardinia, a Derby second and Greenlake the Oaks winner for nothing –"

His voice was drowned by a great roar as the horses flashed by, Battledore on the outside.

"Better than too near the rails," Harold consoled himself. "The luck of the draw's been against him, but he doesn't want it. He'll do, he'll do!"

"Battledore! Battledore!" the crowd exulted.

But now another name was making itself heard – "Goldfoot! Goldfoot! Come on, Jim!" – "Goldfoot leads – No – Partner's Pride! – No – Battledore! – Battledore!" Harold Courtenay yelled. "Come on, Bill! He's winning, he's winning! Partner's Pride is nothing but a runner-up."

Followed a moment's tense silence, then a mighty shout: "Goldfoot's won! Well done, Jim Spencer! Well done!"

Anne dared not look at her brother's face as the numbers went up.

"Goldfoot first," a voice beside her said. "Proud Boy second, Partner's Pride third. Battledore nowhere."

Anne heard a faint sound beside her – between a moan and a sob. She turned sharply.

"Harold!"

Her brother was leaning back in his seat on the coach. His hands had dropped by his side, his face was ghastly white, even his lips were bloodless.

Anne touched him. "Harold!"

He gazed at her with dazed, uncomprehending eyes.

"Don't look like that!" she said sharply. "Pull yourself together! It will be all right, Harold. I have a savings box, you know. You shall have it all."

"All!" Harold laughed aloud in a wild, reckless fashion that made his sister wince and draw back hastily. "It means ruin, Anne!" he said hoarsely. "Ruin, irretrievable ruin. That's all!"

The Dowager Lady Medchester was an old lady who knew her own mind, and was extremely generous in the matter of presenting pieces of it to other people. She and her brother, General Courtenay, were too much alike to get on really well together. Nevertheless, they thoroughly enjoyed a sparring match, and looked forward to their meetings in town and country. The house-party at Holford this year was an extra and both of them were bent on making the most of it.

This afternoon the old people were out for their daily drive, and in the smallest of the three drawing-rooms Anne Courtenay and her brother Harold stood facing one another, both of them pale and overwrought.

"Yes, of course we must find the money. My pearls will fetch something, and I can borrow –"

Anne was anxiously watching her brother's white, drawn face.

He turned away and stood with his back to her, staring unseeingly out of the window.

"That isn't the worst. I – I had to have the money, you understand? I was in debt. I put every penny I had on Battledore and – more."

Anne stared at him, every drop of colour ebbing slowly from her cheeks.

"What do you mean, Harold? You put more – you are frightening me."

"Can't you see? I stood to make my fortune out of Battledore. If he'd won I should. I didn't think he could lose, and money of Melton's was passing through my hands. I put it on."

"Harold!" Anne's brown eyes were wide with horror. "You – you must put it back. I – I will get it somehow."

"I have put it back. I had to. I don't know whether Melton suspected, but he talked of going through his accounts, and it had to be paid into the bank." The boy's voice broke. "I went to a money-lender and he lent me money on a bill that didn't mature till next May. He wouldn't give it to me at first. I couldn't wait – the money had to be replaced at once. The bill had to be backed – I knew it was no use asking Medchester, and the money-lender wouldn't take Stainer – else Maurice would have got it for me like a shot."

"I don't like Maurice Stainer," Anne interposed, "or his sister, either. He is no good to you, Harold."

"Well, anyway, the old shark wouldn't look at him and I couldn't wait – or I should face exposure. I knew I could meet the bill all right if Battledore won. He – the money-lender – suggested I should get Saunderson's name. I knew I couldn't – Saunderson's as close as a Jew, but I had to have the money somehow, and I was mad – mad! I wrote the name."

The fear in Anne's eyes deepened.

"You – you forged!"

A hoarse sob broke in her brother's throat.

"I should have met it – I swear I should have met it, and it gave me six months to turn round in. But it is too late. He has found out – Saunderson. He has got the bill and he swears he will prosecute. He will not even hear me."

"But he cannot – cannot prosecute! He is your friend."

"He will," Harold said hopelessly. "He is a good-for-nothing scoundrel and he will send me to gaol and blacken our name for ever – unless you –"

"Yes?" Anne's voice was low; she put her hands up to her throat. "I don't know what you mean. Unless what?"

"Unless you go to him, unless you plead with him." Harold brought the words out as if they were forced from him. "He thinks more of you than anybody."

Anne threw her head back. In a swift, hot flame the colour rushed over her face and neck and temples.

"Unless I ask him – that man? Do you know what that means? I – I hate him! I am afraid of him."

"I know. I hate him. He is a damned brute, but – well, if I blew my brains out it would not save the shame, the disgrace – " Her brother broke off.

A momentary vision of General Courtenay's fine old face rose before Anne, of his pathetic pride in his dead son's Victoria Cross, in the Courtenay name. A sudden, fierce anger shook her. This careless boy should not cloud the end of that noble life with shame and bitter pain.

Harold slipped forward against the side of the window-frame.

"That's the end."

Anne watched him in unpitying silence. Then old memories came back to her – of their early childhood, of the handsome, gallant father who had been so proud of his little son, of the sweet, gentle mother who had dearly loved them both, but whose favourite had always been Harold. Her heart softened. She looked at her brother's head, bent in humiliation. For the sake of her beloved dead, no less than for the living whose pride he was, Harold must be saved at whatever cost to herself.

She went over and touched his shoulder.

"I will do what I can," she promised. "I will ask him; I will beg him. I will save you, Harold, somehow."

CHAPTER II

In her room at Holford Hall Anne Courtenay was twisting her hands together in agony. The Medchesters and their guests were amusing themselves downstairs in the drawing-room, the gramophone was playing noisy dance music. In the back drawing-room her grandfather and his sister were having their usual game of bezique. Anne had pleaded a headache and had gone to her room directly after dinner. The hands of the clock on the mantelpiece were creeping on to ten o'clock. In five minutes the hour would boom out from the old church on the hill. It was no use delaying, that would only make matters worse. She sprang up. Purposely to-night she had worn black. She threw a dark cloak round her, and picking up a pull-on black hat crushed it over her shingled hair. Then she unlocked a small wooden box on her dressing-table and took out a piece of notepaper. Across it was scrawled in Robert Saunderson's characteristic bold black writing: "To-night at the summer-house at ten o'clock." That was all. There was neither beginning nor ending. Not one word to soften the words that were an ultimatum. Anne's little, white teeth bit deeply into her upper lip as she read.

The summer-house stood in a clearing to the right of the Dutch garden. From it an excellent view of the moors could be obtained with the hazy, blue line of the northern hills in the distance. It was a favourite resort with Lady Medchester for the picnic teas which she favoured. That Anne Courtenay should be giving an assignation there at this time of night seemed to her to show the depths to which she had fallen. Saunderson had left the Medchesters the day after the St. Leger. He had turned a resolutely deaf ear to all Harold's appeals, and his ultimatum remained the same. He would only treat with Anne. Anne herself must come to him, must plead with him. To her alone he would tell the only terms on which Harold could be saved.

Anne drew her cloak round her as she stole quietly down the stairs to a side door. There was a full moon, but the masses of fleecy cloud obscured the beams; little scuds of rain beat in Anne's face as she let herself out. Through the open windows the laughter and the gaiety of her fellow-guests reached her ears. She crept silently by the side of the house into the shadow of one of the giant clumps of rhododendrons that dotted the lawn and bordered the expanse of grass between the house and the Dutch garden.

Anne looked like a wraith as she flitted from one bush to another and finally gained the low wall that overlooked the Dutch garden. A flight of steps led down to the garden and from there, through a hand gate at the side of the rosery, a path went straight to the summer-house.

It all, looked horribly dark and gloomy, Anne thought, as she closed the gate. She waited uncertainly for a minute. All around her she caught the faint multitudinous sounds of insect life that go on incessantly in even the quietest night. Already the leaves were beginning to fall. They lay thick upon the path and rustled under her feet; in the distance she caught the cry of some night-bird. Then nearer at hand there was a different sound. She stopped and cowered against a tree, listening. What was it? It could not be the cracking of a twig, footsteps among the withered leaves, the dead pine-needles that lay thick on the ground? It could not be anybody watching her – following her? Then a sudden awful sense of fear assailed her, a certainty that something evil was near her. For the time she was paralysed as she caught blindly at a low branch. She listened, shivering from head to foot. Yes, undoubtedly she could hear light footsteps, with something sinister, it seemed to her, about their very stealthiness. Yet, as the moon shone out from behind a passing cloud, there was nothing to be seen, no sign of any living thing or any movement. All was quiet, and as she stole softly to the summer-house, casting terrified glances from side to side, she did not see a figure standing up against the trunk of a tall pine near at hand, a face that peered forward, watching her every movement.

She had expected to find Saunderson waiting for her – she told herself that he must be – but there was no one to be seen, and somewhat to her surprise the door of the summer-house was nearly closed. She stopped opposite; there was something sinister, almost terrifying, to her in the sight of that closed door, in the absence of any sound or movement. At last very slowly she went forward, halting between every step. Surely, surely, Saunderson must be waiting for her?

"Mr. Saunderson," she whispered hoarsely, "are you there?"

There came no faintest sound in answer; yet surely, surely she could catch the faint smell of a cigarette?

Very softly, very gingerly she pushed open the door.

"This," said Inspector Stoddart, tapping a paragraph in the evening paper as he spoke," is a job for us."

Harbord leaned forward and read it over the other's shoulder.

"Early this morning a gruesome discovery was made by a gardener in the employ of Lord Medchester at Holford Hall in Loamshire. In a summer-house at the back of the flower garden he found the body of a man in evening-dress. A doctor was summoned and stated that the deceased had been shot through the heart. Death must have been instantaneous and must have taken place probably eight or nine hours before the body was discovered."

"Look at the stop press news." Stoddart pointed to the space at the side.

"The body found in the summer-house at Holford has been identified as that of a Mr. Robert Saunderson, who had been one of Lord Medchester's guests for the races at Doncaster but had left Holford the following day."

"Robert Saunderson," Harbord repeated, wrinkling his brows. "I seem to know the name, but I can't place him. Isn't he a racing man?"

"He would scarcely be a friend of the Medchesters if he wasn't," Stoddart replied, picking up the paper and staring at it as if he would wring further information from it. "Regular racing lot they belong to. Oh, I have heard of Saunderson. A pretty bad hat he was. He had a colt or two training at Oxley, down by Epsom. Picked up one or two minor races last year, but he's never done anything very big. Medchester's horses are trained at Burford's, East Molton. Lord Medchester's a decent sort of chap, I have heard. Anyway, a victory of his is always acclaimed in the North. He generally does well at Ayr and Bogside, and picks up a few over the sticks. Rumour credits him with an overmastering desire to win one of the classic races. His wife is a funny one – I fancy they don't hit it off very well. His trainer, Burford, is a good sort. His engagement to a cousin of Lord Medchester's was announced the other day."

"Not much of a match for her, I should say."

"Oh, quite decent. Burford makes a good thing out of his training. He's a second son of old Sir William Burford and half-brother of the present baronet. This Saunderson was pretty well known in London society too, and I have heard that he was one of Lady Medchester's admirers. I believe he was an American."

"Anyway, so long as he wasn't English, he wouldn't have much difficulty in getting on in London society," Harbord remarked sarcastically. "A bachelor too, wasn't he?"

"As far as anyone knows," Stoddart answered.

A copy of "Who's Who" lay on the table. He pulled it towards him. "'Saunderson, Robert Francis,'" he read. "'Born in Buenos Aires 1888. Served in the Great War as an interpreter on the Italian frontier. Invalided out in May 1917. Clubs, Automobile, Junior Travellers.'"

"H'm! Not much of a dossier – wonder why they put him in?" Harbord remarked.

"No; more noticeable for what it leaves out than for what it puts in," Stoddart agreed.

"Well, I have received an S.O.S. from the Loamshire police, so you and I will go down by the night express to Derby. From there it is a crosscountry journey to Holford. Take a few hours, I suppose."

"I wonder what Saunderson was doing in that neighbourhood when he had left the Hall?" Harbord cogitated.

Stoddart shrugged his shoulders.

"I dare say we shall find out when we get there."

CHAPTER III

"This is the principal entrance, I suppose," Stoddart said, stopping before the lodge at Holford, and looking up the avenue of oaks that was one of the chief attractions of the Hall.

As he spoke a small two-seater pulled up beside them and two men sprang out. One of them Stoddart had no difficulty in recognizing as the local superintendent of police; the other, a tall, military-looking man, he rightly divined to be the Chief Constable, Major Logston.

The Major looked at the two detectives.

"Inspector Stoddart, I presume. I was hoping to catch you. I missed you at the station – had a break-down coming from home. This is a terrible affair, inspector."

"I have only seen the bare account in the papers," Stoddart said quietly. "Before we go any further I should very much like to hear what you can tell us."

"I shall be glad to give you all the details I can," Major Logston said, entering the gates with him and leaving the superintendent to bring up the rear with Harbord in the two-seater.

"Of course we have had quantities of those damned reporters all over the place." the Major began confidentially. "But we have told the beggars as little as possible, and now we are not allowing them within the gates."

The inspector nodded.

"Quite right, sir. Reporters are the very devil, with what they pick up and what they invent. They've helped many a murderer to escape the gallows."

"I entirely agree with you." The Chief Constable paused a minute, then he said slowly, "This Robert Saunderson had been staying at Holford quite recently. He had been one of the house-party for the races, you know, inspector, for the St. Leger. But he left the next day like most of the other guests, and deuce knows why he came back. An under-gardener – Joseph Wilton by name – was clearing up rubbish and such-like for one of those bonfires that always make such a deuce of a stink all over the place at this time of the year. He was round about the summer-house and, glancing inside, was astounded to see a man lying on the floor. He went in, as he says, to find if one of the gentlemen had been 'took ill,' and discovered that he was dead and cold. He gave the alarm to his fellow-gardeners and then he and another man went up to the Hall to acquaint Lord Medchester with his discovery; Medchester went back with them, imagining Wilton had exaggerated, and was amazed and horrified to find not only that Wilton's story was too true, but that the dead man was no other than Robert Saunderson, who had so recently been his guest. Of course they got the doctor there as soon as possible. He said the man had been dead for hours, had probably died the night before the discovery."

"Presumably I should not be here if the case was one of suicide?"

"Out of the question," Major Logston said decidedly. "I can't give you the technical details, but the fellow had been shot through the heart. Death must have been instantaneous. And the revolver cannot be found."

"H'm!" The inspector drew in his lips. "Pretty conclusive, that. Any clue to the murderer?"

The Chief shook his head.

"Not so far. The summer-house is a favourite place for tea with Lady Medchester, so there'll be a maze of finger-prints and what not. Oh, it won't be an easy matter to find out who fired the fatal shot, as things look at present. I don't know whether Dr. Middleton will be any help to you, but he is up at the Hall now. He is attending General Courtenay, an uncle of Lord Medchester's, who had a stroke last night, so you will be able to hear what he has to say at once. Lord Medchester wants to see you too."

"I shall be glad to see him," Stoddart said politely. "But first about the body – I presume you have had it moved?"

"Yes. As soon as the doctor had seen it we had it taken to an outhouse near the churchyard, which has to serve as a temporary mortuary."

"Well, naturally you could do nothing else," the inspector said, staring up at the windows of Holford Hall. "This Saunderson, now, what was he like to look at?"

"Alive, do you mean?" the Chief Constable questioned. "I saw him at Doncaster. Didn't care much for the look of him myself. Big haw-haw sort of brute, don't you know. Pretty bad lot from all accounts – always after the skirts. Well, here we are!"

Stepping inside the big portico that was over the front entrance to the Hall, his ring was answered instantly. The two-seater stood before the door. A young footman flung the door open and announced that his lordship was expecting them. Stoddart joined Harbord and the two went in together.

Lord Medchester received them in his study. The walls were lined with books, but a little inspection showed that the two shelves which had the appearance of being the most used were devoted to racing literature. Lord Medchester was a tall, thin man in the early forties; perfectly bald in front and on the crown, the ridge of hair at the back was unusually thick and had the appearance of having slipped down from the top. He glanced sharply at Stoddart as the detectives entered, and came forward to meet them.

"I am delighted to see you, inspector. This – this is an appalling thing to happen in one's grounds. And our local police don't seem able to grapple with it at all – we look to you to find out who killed the poor beggar."

"I will do my best, Lord Medchester. Will you tell me what you know of Mr. Saunderson?"

"That will be precious little," said his lordship, subsiding into a chair near the fireplace and motioning to Stoddart and Harbord to take chairs close at hand. "I have met him out and about for years. He was staying at Merton Towers for the Derby, and when we were talking about putting a bit on Harkaway he gave me a tip for Battledore for the Cup. The colt ran away with it, you know, and I made a tidy pocketful over him. So, times being what they are, and these damned Socialists not content with screwing every penny they can out of you when you are alive, but dragging your very grave from you when you are dead, I was deuced bucked with my luck and on the spur of the moment I asked Saunderson here for the St. Leger. He rather jumped at it, I thought, and turned up all right. Of course we all put our shirts on Battledore and he let us all down and ran nowhere. So I lost most of what I won at Goodwood. I was a bit rattled, I can tell you. Not that it was Saunderson's fault."

"Did he lose?" Stoddart asked quickly.

"Well, he went down on Battledore of course," his lordship answered, "but he'd hedged on Goldfoot, lucky beggar! At least, I thought he was lucky until this happened."

"He left Holford the day after the races, I understand?" Stoddart pursued.

Lord Medchester nodded. "Yes, he went up to town with Colonel Wynter, another of the men who were staying here."

"And you had no reason to expect him at Holford again?"

"Good Lord, no!" his lordship said impatiently. "You might have knocked me down with a feather when I heard he had been shot in the summer-house; matter of fact, he had no encouragement from me to come again. On further acquaintance I didn't exactly take a fancy to Saunderson. Thought he was a bit of a bounder. Still, I don't want to talk about that now the poor chap's been done in. But you are asking."

"Precisely." The detective glanced at his notes and made a hieroglyphic entry. "Now, I want to know whether he had any sort of a quarrel with any of your other visitors – any woman got a down on him?"

Glancing at him as he answered, Harbord caught a curious, momentary gleam in Lord Medchester's eyes.

"He wasn't exactly a favourite, but they all seemed friendly enough together," he replied, ignoring the latter half of the question. "Besides, most of 'em had gone away. If they had wanted to murder one another, they could have done it in town; no need to come down here."

"Any possible love-affair with anyone at Holford?"

"Oh, Lord, I should think not!" he said with a laugh that sounded a bit forced in Stoddart's ears. "I shouldn't think Saunderson was that sort, getting a bit long in the tooth. Besides, there was nobody here he could have got soppy about. All of 'em married and not the kind that are looking about to get rid of their husbands."

"Nobody unmarried?" the inspector queried. "Not that that matters. The married ones are generally the worst."

"Yes, there I am with you. They are if they take that way. But you are talking about the unmarried ones. The only one in the lot was my cousin, Miss Courtenay, and she is engaged to my trainer, Michael Burford – no eyes for anyone else; damned nuisance sometimes, don't you know! Be a bit more interesting in a year or two. I made the remark to Saunderson, I remember."

"What did he say?"

"Oh, nothing much. Merely laughed. There wasn't much he could say. Anybody could see it."

Stoddart got up. "Well, marriage doesn't make much difference to some of them. I think the best thing I can do is just to have a look round at the summer-house and then at the body. Perhaps you would let me have a list of the house-party later on?"

"I'll have one made," Lord Medchester promised, getting up and taking a position before the fireplace. "And if there's anything else we can do you've only to let us know. It's no joke having a man murdered at the back of your own garden."

That seemed to be all there was to be got out of Lord Medchester and, as Stoddart observed to Harbord, it was not very illuminating.

The doctor could only tell them two things – first, that death had probably occurred some nine or ten hours before the body was discovered, which would place the time round about ten o'clock the preceding evening; and that, secondly, the automatic had not been fired close at hand. The murderer, according to Dr. Middleton, had probably stood outside the summer-house and fired through the open doorway.

Stoddart drew his brows together as he and Harbord walked across the lawn to the Dutch garden.

"Queer case!" the younger man ventured.

The inspector nodded.

"We'll just have a look at the summer-house before it gets too dark, and interview the local superintendent. And then it strikes me we may as well toddle back to town in the morning and investigate Saunderson's doings. I fancy we are more likely to hit on the clue there than here."

"I don't know," Harbord said slowly. "Of course he came here to meet some one."

"Naturally!" the inspector assented. "One hardly imagines that he travelled down for the sole purpose of being murdered. But the two questions that present themselves, and which I fancy we shall have some difficulty in answering are these: who did Saunderson come to meet, and why did he come to Holford for the meeting?"

They were crossing the Dutch garden now. Harbord looked all round before he answered.

"Through that gate at the side I suppose our way lies, sir. With regard to your first question, I think it is pretty obvious the person Saunderson came to meet must be some one in the Hall, either a resident or a visitor. And he came, I should imagine, with some very definite object. If it should be a love-affair it must have been an illicit one. Therefore I should make a few careful inquiries about any married women who may be in the house. As far as I have ascertained they have a pretty good houseful now, as large, if not larger, than the one they had for the St. Leger. If there should be anyone here at the present time who was included in the Doncaster party, I should look up that person's antecedents."

"Well reasoned, Alfred. But" – the inspector looked at him with a wry smile – "we have no proof that the murderer was a woman. As a matter of fact I should say it is quite as likely, if not more likely, to have been a man. Money or love, and in love I include jealousy. As far as my experience goes nine-tenths of the murders committed are committed for one or other of these motives. In this case I think financial difficulties are just as likely to have led to the death as an illicit love-affair."

"I wonder if they searched the place thoroughly?"

Stoddart shrugged his shoulders.

"You don't need me to tell you that when a place is used for tea fairly often anything may be found there. Might be a dozen clues that mean nothing. This is our way, I presume."

He unlatched the gate at the right-hand side of the Dutch garden. They heard voices as they went along the path to the summer-house.

The inspector frowned as he saw the downtrodden grass.

"Done their best to destroy any clue there might have been, of course."

The summer-house stood on a little knoll in the midst of the clearing; all around it the rhododendrons that formed the sides of the Dutch garden had spread and were pressing closely.

Superintendent Mayer and another man, apparently occupied in staring at the summerhouse, turned as the detectives approached.

"I am pleased to see you, Inspector Stoddart," the superintendent began. "This is a terrible job. We can't make anything of it ourselves. 'Tain't believable that anybody hereabouts would have done a thing like this."

"It is pretty obvious that somebody did, superintendent," the inspector said dryly. "Still it is more than likely it was not a native of Holford. This is where the body was found, I suppose. Can you show me just how it lay?"

"Yes, I can." The superintendent stepped into the summer-house. "He lay right on his back, did the corpse. His head was over here," indicating a spot by the nearest leg of the rustic table. "His feet, they were right there in the doorway. Seemed as if he had been standing there, or maybe on the step. And I should say them as he was expecting came right on him, maybe by a way he wasn't looking for them."

The inspector surveyed the place where the dead man had lain in silence for a minute. Then, standing on the step, he looked round.

"It wouldn't have been very difficult for anyone to take him unawares. The rhododendrons come right up on all sides except the front, it seems to me. But it rained last night in town. I expect it was the same here. How did your unexpected assailant see to aim at his victim?"

The superintendent stared at him.

"I don't know. But there was a moon, though it was showery most of the time. The – the murderer must ha' waited till it shone a bit, like, and then the gentleman's shirt front would make a decent target."

The inspector nodded.

"Quite. Down here you say he was lying. Were his feet projecting beyond the doorway?"

The superintendent scratched his head. "Sticking out, like, you mean? No, they didn't. But I think as the murderer had searched through his pockets and maybe been disturbed. The body had got on a light overcoat and one of the pockets looked as if it had been pulled out and pushed in again carelessly. I mean as it wasn't right in like, a bit of it was left pulled out and just here by the side of the pocket there was a notebook lying on the ground and a paper or two, as if them that took them out had been in too much of a hurry to put them back."

The inspector pricked up his ears.

"Where are they?"

The superintendent tramped across the summer-house and, stooping down, drew a small leather attache-case from beneath the seat.

"I put 'em in this and locked 'em up." He felt in his pockets and produced the key. "I thought you'd be wanting to see them or I'd have taken them down to the police station," he said as he unlocked the case and handed a pocket-book and a couple of letters not enclosed in envelopes to Stoddart. "There's a lot of notes in the pocket-book, so it don't look as if robbery had much to do with it."

The inspector glanced at the letters first. One was merely a business communication from a wholesale leather firm saying that Mr. Saunderson's esteemed order should have their earliest attention. The other was a very different affair. The detective's eyes brightened as he looked at it. Written on good paper, it was neither stamped nor dated, but across it was scrawled in large, badly printed letters: "I accede because I have no choice."

That was all. There was no signature. Stoddart turned it over, looked at it from every angle, and even actually smelt it before he handed it back to the superintendent. Then he made no comment, but he turned to his case-book and jotted down an unusually lengthy entry. He opened the dead man's pocket-book and after a rapid glance through it laid it on the table.

"Put this back in your case, superintendent. We will take it back to the police station and go into it all carefully. Now, before we go across to the mortuary, do you know how the deceased got here? As he was not staying at the Hall, and presumably not in the immediate neighbourhood, I mean? Did he come to Holford by train?"

The superintendent shook his head.

"Not to Holford, he didn't. I have asked at the station and nobody answering to his description was seen there last night, and he must have been noticed if he had come, for there's precious few passengers at Holford except the folks from the Hall. There's other stations he might ha' come to, of course, but not hardly within walking distance – seven or eight miles maybe, and cross-country at that. His shoes don't look as if he had come far, either. And yet, if he was in a car, where is the car?"

"H'm – well!" The inspector looked thoughtful. "We will go down to the mortuary at once," he decided.

CHAPTER IV

As the Chief Constable had said, the temporary mortuary at Holford was just an ordinary barn. Some rough trestles had been set up in the middle under the direction of Superintendent Mayer, and Robert Saunderson lay on them. Some one had thrown a white sheet over the body. Superintendent Mayer tramped across and laid it back.

"Looks as if he'd been surprised somehow," he commented, gazing down on the face that, sensual and coarse-looking in life, had gained a certain dignity in death. "Stiff and cold he'd been for hours before we found him," the superintendent went on.

Standing beside him, Inspector Stoddart looked down at the dead man. He glanced quickly over the face and form, then passed to the light overcoat that hung over the bottom of the trestles.

"You have gone through the pockets, you said, superintendent?"

"I have – and there's nothing in 'em to help us," that worthy announced in a tone of assurance that made Stoddart raise his eyebrows. "There's a letter or two, none from anywhere about here, and the money that I showed you before. His wrist-watch too, I left that on."

One of the dead man's arms was lying by his side. Stoddart lifted it up; the watch had stopped at 9.30.

"We get the time of death approximately from that. Probably when he fell the arm hit the ground heavily and stopped the watch."

"It might ha' been a bit fast or a bit slow, though," the superintendent remarked wisely.

Stoddart's smile would have been a laugh but for the quiet presence lying there before him.

Harbord at the side was going through the pockets of the dead man's overcoat with quick, capable fingers. Suddenly he uttered a sharp exclamation. As Stoddart and the superintendent looked at him he held up something that gleamed for a moment in a ray of light that filtered through the shadows of the barn.

Stoddart beckoned him to the door, and while the superintendent replaced the sheet over the dead man the inspector glanced curiously at the object his assistant had in his hand. He saw three crystal beads linked together by a thin, gold chain.

Harbord looked at him.

"It must have dropped there when the pocket was searched."

The superintendent came up and elbowed them apart.

"No, beg pardon, it was not," he contradicted. "That wasn't in the pocket when I searched it this morning. It must ha' been put there since."

Harbord looked at him.

"It was the right-hand pocket beside which you found the book and the notes, wasn't it?"

The superintendent nodded. "Ay, it was the right-hand pocket sure enough, and it was pulled out, like, a bit, but the beads weren't in it then."

"The chain had caught in the lining. That must have been how you overlooked it," Harbord said shortly.

"It wasn't there at all," the superintendent said positively. "I turned that pocket inside out. There was nothing there, I will swear."

"Well, the thing is here now. What possibility is there of getting it into the pocket after you searched it?" Stoddart inquired sharply.

The superintendent scratched his head.

"I don't know. There was nobody but me and Constable Jones went into the hut, not until the ambulance men fetched the body away. I and the constable went across here to the barn to look round the place and give orders about the trestles. The gardeners were seeing to it and got a bit rattled, poor chaps. But we weren't gone more than a few minutes before the ambulance men arrived – but what would they go dropping glass beads about for?"

"Who were the ambulance men?"

"They weren't men as I know," the superintendent said thoughtfully. "Not as to say well, that is. They work at the Cottage Hospital on the hill, the two as brought the ambulance-stretcher, as they call it. It's on wheels. His lordship, he gave it to the hospital. They lifted him" – with a backward jerk at the stark form under the sheet – "the two men and Jones and a gardener that was passing. I gave a hand, steadying the stretcher and helping when they laid it on. But I don't see – I do not see" – pausing and endeavouring apparently to recall the scene – "as any of them had the chance to put those beads in the pocket, even if they wanted to, which don't seem likely."

It did not. As the inspector closed the door of the barn behind them his eyes had a puzzled, far-away look.

"Did you know the gardener who helped you?" Stoddart inquired as they crossed the churchyard and turned in at the private gate into the Holford grounds.

"No, I don't know as I do; he isn't a Holford man," the superintendent said, his broad, red face wearing the look of bewilderment that had come over it when he saw the beads. "He was just working in the rosery and saw them bring the ambulance, and came along to find out if he could help. He were likely enough one of the young men that's here to learn a bit of gardening from Mr. Macdonald, and lives up at the cottage at the back of the glass-houses."

"I see!" The inspector made a note in his book. "We will just have a word with this gardener. Who is that?"

"That" was a young man who had come out of the Hall and was walking a little way down the path across the lawn at a brisk pace. Seeing them, he had hesitated a minute, and then turned off sharply towards the big entrance gates.

The superintendent stared after him.

"That – that is young Mr. Courtenay, his lordship's cousin. I should ha' said he didn't want to see us."

"So should I!" the inspector assented grimly. "But unfortunately, as it happens, since the desire is apparently not mutual, Mr. Harold Courtenay is a young gentleman I particularly wish to interview. I fancy striking over here by the pine trees we shall manage to intercept him."

He set off at a brisk pace, Harbord by his side, the burly superintendent puffing and blowing behind.

They emerged from the grove of trees at the side of the Hall immediately in front of Harold Courtenay.

That young gentleman looked amazed to see them step out on the walk in front of him. The inspector, glancing at him keenly, fancied that he saw discomposure mingling with the surprise.

He went forward.

"Mr. Harold Courtenay, I think? I should be glad if I might have a few words with you."

Harold Courtenay glanced round as if seeking some way of escape, but nothing presenting itself apparently resigned himself to the inevitable.

"Inspector Stoddart, I think, isn't it? My cousin told me you had come down. I am quite at your service, inspector."

"Thank you, Mr. Courtenay."

Young Courtenay was looking very ill, the inspector thought. His face was sickly grey beneath its tan, his eyes had a scared, furtive look, two or three times his mouth twitched oddly to one side as the inspector watched him.

"Just a question or two I wanted to put to you," Stoddart went on. "Later on there may be other things, but now I shall not detain you more than a minute or two."

"That's all right," Courtenay said at once. "If anything I can tell you will help you I shall be only too glad. I am only afraid it won't. I had no idea even that Saunderson was likely to be in the neighbourhood last night." He stopped and swallowed something in his throat. "He was rather by way of being a friend of mine, you know, inspector."

Stoddart nodded, his keen eyes never relaxing their watch on the young man's face.

"So I have heard. When did you last see him, Mr. Courtenay?"

The young man hesitated a moment.

"Oh, just a few days ago," he said vaguely. "The beginning of the week, I think it was. Monday evening, I remember now. I called at his flat."

"Did he tell you he was coming down here in the near future?" the inspector questioned.

Courtenay shook his head. "Never even mentioned Holford so far as I can remember."

"Did he speak of anyone or anything that could have had any bearing on last night's tragedy?"

"Certainly not!" Courtenay said with decision.

"We only spoke on the most ordinary topics."

"Can you remember any of those topics?" the inspector questioned.

Harold Courtenay waited a moment before answering.

"Nothing much," he said slowly. "Most of the time it was about racing. We both of us cursed Battledore for letting us down over the St. Leger. And Saunderson said somebody had given him a tip for the autumn double – Cesarewitch and the Cambridgeshire, you know – White Flower and Dark Mouth; and he said he shouldn't do it, though the chap that told him generally knew what he was talking about. Dark Mouth is French – he'd never fancied a French horse, he said, since Epinard let him down over the Cambridgeshire."

"Did you tell him you were coming here?"

"N–o! I don't think so," the young man said with a momentary indecision that did not escape the inspector's keen eyes. "No, as a matter of fact I don't think I knew that I was coming here myself then."

"When did you come?" the inspector asked. "In the afternoon of Thursday, wasn't it?"

"Yes, by the 3.30 from Derby to Holford." There was a certain relief in Courtenay's tone now. His eyes met Stoddart's openly.

"And Saunderson – when did he come?" the inspector said quickly.

"Saunderson?" Courtenay stared at him. "I don't know. I don't know anything about him. I couldn't believe it when I heard he was lying dead in the summer-house."

"When did you hear?" The inspector looked straight at the young man as he put the question.

"Why, when the gardener came up and told us all." Courtenay looked down and shifted his feet about on the gravel uncertainly.

The inspector brought out his notebook. "Now, Mr. Courtenay, this is just a matter of course. I have nearly finished. What were you doing between nine and ten o'clock last night, and where were you?"

"Ten o'clock last night?" Courtenay repeated, kicking up a big bit of gravel. "Well, the Medchesters had some neighbours in to dinner and of course there were a few of us staying in the house, and afterwards we had a rubber of bridge in the card-room. I meant to take a hand, but I cut out, and after I'd watched the play a bit I went into the billiard-room with a couple of other men and knocked the balls about. Later on I went back to the card-room and had a game. Landed a pound or two, too – my luck was in."

"How long were you in the billiard-room?"

Courtenay, having got up his piece of gravel, kicked it off into the grass.

"Oh, it might have been half an hour or so, or maybe it might have been a bit longer. I couldn't tell you nearer than that," he said carelessly, but his eyes from beneath their heavy lids shot an odd glance at the inspector as he spoke.

Stoddart's quick fingers were making notes. He was not looking at Courtenay now.

"Who were the two men with you in the billiard-room?"

"Sir James Wilson and Captain Maddock," Courtenay said quickly. "Mind, I don't say they were there all the time. We were in and out, you know."

The inspector made no comment.

"Can you give me the names of the card-players?"

"Not all of them right off, I can't," Courtenay said after a minute or two spent apparently in trying to quicken his memory. "Old Lady Frinton was my partner, I know, and the vicar part of the time. The others may come back to me later on."

"Lord and Lady Medchester, perhaps?" the inspector suggested.

Courtenay shook his head.

"I don't think so. Lord Medchester was with us in the billiard-room a bit. Then he went off. I think a few of them were smoking on the veranda."

"And Lady Medchester? Was she playing?"

Courtenay paused a moment.

"No," he said. "I remember she wouldn't, though she is generally pretty keen about it. But I don't think they played high enough for her. She goes in for pretty high stakes in town. She just dodged about, looking after folks. The two old people – the Dowager and my old grandfather – were playing bezique in the small drawing-room. I didn't see much of her."

"I see." The inspector produced the crystal beads from his pocket and held them up. "Have you ever seen these before, Mr. Courtenay?"

Harold Courtenay stared at them, and as he looked the colour which had been coming back to his face ebbed away again.

"I – I don't know," he stammered. "I don't think so."

"Are you quite sure?" The inspector spoke suavely, but there was a look in his eyes which Harbord knew was a danger signal.

Harold Courtenay wriggled uneasily.

"I may have done; I can't be sure. Every woman you meet wears this sort of thing nowadays."

"True enough," the inspector assented, dangling the beads before him. "And these are of no particular value. You can see that at once."

"Where did you find them?" Harold Courtenay asked, his eyes watching them as if fascinated, while the inspector dangled them before him.

A curious, enigmatic smile twisted Stoddart's thin lips.

"Ah! That," he said as he restored the beads to his pocket, "is my secret, Mr. Courtenay – and it will be as well if you say nothing about them at present."

CHAPTER V

"This is a queer case," Inspector Stoddart said slowly. "There is something about it I don't understand, I can't fathom –"

Harbord made no rejoinder. He looked tired and worried. The two men were sitting in the little room the inspector had engaged at the "Medchester Arms." It was a small, unpretentious village inn, and they had been fortunate in securing the rooms vacated that morning by Maurice Stainer and his sister. They had just finished their midday meal – the cold beef and pickles which, with a slice of apple pasty, was all that Holford could produce in the way of luncheon at the end of the week.

A box of cigarettes stood on the table. Stoddart stretched out his hand and took one.

"There's nothing like a smoke for clearing one's brain; to my way of thinking, nothing beats a gasper. Lord Medchester made me take a couple of Egyptians this morning. Very good, but give me my own gold flake."

"Yes, I hate those strong things," Harbord assented. "But I'd smoke 'em fast enough if I thought they'd do my brain any good. It seems to be made of cotton-wool lately. Young Courtenay knows something. I am clear enough about that."

Stoddart drew in his lips.

"So do a good many other people – Lord Medchester for one. But as to what it is, and how much there is to it, I can't make up my mind. How did those beads come in Saunderson's pocket, and who put them there?

"There were those few moments when the superintendent went to look at the barn, but to my mind they must have been there when he searched the body."

Harbord lighted a cigarette and continued:

"As I see things, it must have been a woman who shot Saunderson – probably he had letters from her. He may have been holding them over her, for he seems to have been a tolerably bad hat where women are concerned. Then she searched his pocket – possibly she knew they were there, and the beads look as if they had been part of a chain, one of those long, dangling things women wear to make up for their short skirts, maybe. A chain of white glass beads is common enough. They are always catching on buttons and what not, you know, sir."

"*I* don't," the inspector said with emphasis on the pronoun. "They never get the chance of catching on my buttons, thank the Lord. But there's a snag in your theory, Alfred – the beads were not there when the body was found."

"According to Superintendent Mayer," Harbord corrected. "They were not in the bottom of the pocket, you know, sir. One of the links of the chain had hooked itself in the lining of the pocket. I think it would be quite easy to take papers or anything of that sort out without feeling the beads."

"Only the pocket-book and papers were lying on the floor," the inspector objected. "No use trying to make facts fit in with your theory, Alfred. And don't make the mistake of underestimating the superintendent's intelligence. Because he is fat and ponderous and talks with the accent of Loamshire, you do not give him credit for the brains he possesses."

"Does he?" Harbord questioned sceptically. The inspector nodded.

"Undoubtedly. Medchester isn't much of a place certainly, but a man doesn't become police superintendent even there without a certain amount of ability. As for Superintendent Mayer –" He paused.

"Well?" Harbord said interrogatively.

"Those little pig's eyes of his see further than you think," Stoddart finished. "Oh, there were no beads when he went through the pocket; I feel sure of that."

"Then how did they get there?"

"Ah!" The inspector lay back in his chair and smoked his gasper. "I should very much like to discover that. As I said just now, there is some nasty, hanky-panky work going on here that I don't understand at all."

Harbord was on the point of replying when there was a knock at the door. The landlady of the "Medchester Arms" looked in.

"Joseph Wilton is asking to see you, sir. The gardener that found the poor gentleman dead in the summer-house," she added in an explanatory tone.

The inspector sat up.

"Show him in, please, Mrs. Marlow."

Joseph Wilton was a clean-looking, clean shaven man, probably in the early forties. He was evidently in his working clothes, but they were whole and tidy. About him there clung that indefinable smell that always seems to hang about those who work on the land.

He touched his forehead to the inspector.

"Afternoon, sir."

"Good afternoon, Mr. Wilton," the inspector returned politely. "I hear that it was you who found Mr. Saunderson's body in the summer house."

"It was, sir." The man hesitated a minute. "It was, sir," he said again. "I found the poor gentleman then, and now I ha' found this here." He put one horny hand in his trouser pocket and fumbled for a moment or two; then very slowly he produced something that he dangled before the inspector's amazed eyes – a long chain of crystal beads linked together by a thin, gold chain. It had evidently been broken and the two ends hung loose.

The inspector sprang up.

"That, by Jove! Where did you find it?"

"Down among the rhododendrons hard by the rosery gate, on the right side. I was clearing out there and cutting the rhododendrons back a bit," Joseph Wilton answered, shaking his find before the inspector. "I showed it to Mr. Macdonald, our head gardener, and he said I'd better bring it to you; it might be you'd want to see it, he said."

"So I do," the inspector said, taking the chain in his hand and examining it with care. "It is a thing I have wanted to see very much indeed, Mr. Wilton. Now, should you be able to show us exactly where you found this thing if we went back to the garden with you?"

Wilton scratched his head and looked doubtful.

"Well, maybe I could, and again maybe I couldn't. I dessay I should be within a few yards, anyway."

"That'll do for our purpose." The inspector crossed over to a cupboard that was let into the wall near the fireplace and, opening it, deposited the chain in a small box therein, and carefully locking it dropped the key in his pocket. "Well, we will walk up with you, Mr. Wilson, and you shall show us as near as you can."

"Yes, sir, I'll do my best."

They all three went out of the "Medchester Arms" together and, walking up the village street towards the Hall, Joseph Wilton's pleasure at being seen by his neighbours in the company of his obvious superiors was tempered by fear that they might imagine he had been taken into custody.

"'Twould be easier, like, to cross over there through the paddock to the blue doors and walk up to the rosery from there than to go round by the lodge," he observed at last, pointing to a stile by the side of the road.

"Well, the quicker we are the better," the inspector assented.

He sprang over the stile and the other two followed. The path across the paddock was pretty well defined and quite obviously led to the path at the bottom of the rosery.

"Easily accessible, the Hall gardens," the inspector observed, looking round. "Saunderson would have had no difficulty in getting in."

"N—o!" Wilton, too, looked round. "He could ha' got in right enough, but the keeper's lodge's round there and the dogs are often out at night, and they might go for a stranger. I did hear, though, that they were all out at the Spring Wood that night looking for poachers."

"Oh, indeed! Well, later on we might have a chat with the keeper," Stoddart remarked with a glance at Harbord. "It must have given you a scare, Mr. Wilton, when you saw the man lying dead in the summer-house."

"It did that," Wilton assented. "First when I saw some one lying there the thought come to me that it was some tramp that had got in and maybe gone to sleep. When I saw what it was I turned fair sick."

"I don't wonder. I expect it would turn most of us," the inspector said sympathetically. "Did you move the body at all, or touch it in any way?"

Wilton shook his head.

"I did not, sir. I saw directly I got up to him the gentleman was dead and cold, and I called out to Bill Griggs as was sweeping up leaves outside on the walk, and when he had had a look we both run up to the house to tell his lordship."

"You were one of those who lifted the body on to the stretcher, I understand?" the inspector pursued.

"Ay! That I was, and a nasty job it was," the other agreed slowly. "I dunno as I should care for such another."

"This Bill Griggs you spoke of just now, was he one of the others to lift the body?"

"No, that he wasn't," Wilton said, pausing by an iron railing that ran down one side of the rosery. "There was just the two ambulance men and me. The superintendent he helped a bit, steadying the head and so forth. There wasn't anybody else needed."

"That so?" The inspector looked at him. "Who were the ambulance men? They would be in some sort of uniform, I presume? You would know them?"

"Y—es, I did, in a manner of speaking," Wilton responded slowly. "They was Holford men, the two of 'em. I ha' passed the time of day with them when I've met 'em, which hasn't been often. If you could get over those railings, sir, it'd be the nearest way to the summer-house."

"Oh, I can manage that right enough," the inspector said lightly.

He put his hand on the top rail and vaulted over. Harbord followed suit, then Wilton clambered over.

"You are wonderfully nippy for town gentlemen," he said, gazing admiringly at the detectives.

The inspector laughed.

"Ah, I wasn't always a town gentleman, Mr. Wilton. You've no idea, I suppose, who the owner of the bead necklace might be?"

The man shook his head.

"You're sure?" the inspector pressed. "Never seen it on any of the ladies staying at the house?"

"Ay, I am that!" Wilton said positively. "Not that I'd notice much what they got round their necks. Never saw 'em before so far as I know."

"Bead necklaces are pretty much alike," the inspector said thoughtfully. "I suppose we are getting near the place where you found it?"

Wilton assented as he unlatched the little gate at the side of the rosery and led the way into the Dutch garden. Right in front of them were the rhododendrons that formed the hedge between the garden and the clearing in the midst of which the summer-house stood.

"It was up here." Wilton quickened his step until he had nearly reached the wall forming the northern boundary of the Dutch garden. "I left my shears here, you see. I was cutting back the bushes. Those leaves I brushed up near there and I saw the necklace caught on one of the lowest boughs of that there rhododendron, a fine pink 'un it is in the spring. But I couldn't reach it from here, and there's wire along the lower part to keep the rabbits away from the flower-beds, so I had to go to the summer-house side to get it."

The inspector peered through. The rhododendrons were high and thick and strong with the growth of years. He marvelled how Wilton could have seen anything.

"Tidy distance from the summer-house, isn't it? Looks as if the thing must have been put there on purpose."

"'Tain't so far from the summer-house as you think," Wilton dissented. "Nearly right opposite here it is. And pretty straight across it is. If anybody came down in the dark, side of those rhododendrons, that necklace might easily get caught and pulled off. That's how I look at it; or, again, it might ha' been thrown there by somebody that didn't want it to tell tales," he finished darkly.

"It'll tell tales all right," the inspector muttered as he and Harbord, having marked the spot, walked off.

CHAPTER VI

"Only two women who were in the house-party for Doncaster were staying at Holford Hall last Thursday," Stoddart said, meeting Harbord in the village street outside the 'Medchester Arms.' "One of them is Miss Courtenay, Lord Medchester's cousin, the other is a Mrs. Williamson, the pretty young second wife of a retired Indian colonel, to whom she is apparently devoted."

"That narrows matters down a little," Harbord said consideringly. "Though of course we have no certainty that the person who shot Saunderson was a member of the Doncaster house-party, or of the party last Thursday, for that matter."

"No certainty at all," the inspector assented.

"In fact, there is no certainty about the whole thing except Saunderson's death. He is to be buried to-morrow, by the way. The coroner has given the certificate. I was about to add that four men were included in both parties. Colonel Williamson, Mr. Harold Courtenay – he, of course, is the young gentleman who was so anxious to get out of our way this morning – Captain Maddock and Sir John Linford. All of those must be interviewed to-day. If possible we must see the ladies first."

"Of course," Harbord agreed thoughtfully. "There is also Lady Medchester. Rumour credits her with a distinct penchant for Saunderson."

"Oh, I haven't forgotten her ladyship," Stoddart said quietly. "But Lady Medchester is a lady of a good many affairs – still, you can't say she wouldn't lose her head over Robert Saunderson. However, we will get her first if we can. Lord Medchester says we may interview the folks in the gun-room. But I fancy it will be best to ask for Lady Medchester first and see her wherever she wishes. It is curious that nobody appears to have a satisfactory alibi."

Just inside the lodge gates they encountered Lord Medchester. He greeted them with effusion.

"I was just going down to have a word with the vicar. It's about this funeral of Saunderson's. Nobody seems to know anything about the fellow, and he's left no directions that anybody knows of. I think the poor chap will have to be buried down here."

"Hasn't he left a Will?"

"Haven't been able to get on the track of it if he has," Lord Medchester said discontentedly. "They say at the bank – the United Overseas, you know – that he was joking with the manager a week or two ago about not having made a Will, and said he would when he had anything to leave and anybody to leave it to. Sort of rubbishing joke a chap does make, you know."

"I know," the inspector assented gravely. "Well, perhaps it will be as well to bury him here if he hasn't expressed any wish for anywhere else."

"Well, I can't say I have any wish to be buried anywhere myself," his lordship rejoined. "I'd rather stay above ground as long as I can. And I don't want to be cremated. Beastly business that."

"There is something to be said for and against," the inspector said impartially. "We were just coming up to the Hall. You will understand that, purely as a matter of form, we have to ask every one who was at the Hall that night to account for his or her movements at the time of the murder?"

"What!" His lordship looked aghast. "You don't mean everybody at the Hall? Gardeners and gamekeepers, of course. And, as I said before, the gun-room is at your service if you wish to see 'em indoors; but you can't suspect my guests or the indoor servants!"

"I don't suspect anybody, Lord Medchester," the inspector said gravely. "But I have got to find out who shot Mr. Saunderson, and first of all I have to find out where every one in the immediate neighbourhood was between nine and eleven o'clock last Thursday. Perhaps I might be allowed to begin with you? You would be, I presume, with your guests?"

"Of course I was." His lordship took off his hat and mopped his bald head. "Well, if that is how things are, I'd better walk back with you myself. I expect some of the folks will be a bit rattled when they know what you are up to."

"Oh, I hope not," the inspector dissented. "I shall only keep them a few minutes if they are sensible. You, now, will be able to tell me just who was with you at that time. That will put them out, of course."

"I am sure I don't know that I can." Lord Medchester replaced his hat and turned back up the avenue with them. "Nine o'clock? That would be just after dinner. Well, we didn't stay in the dining-room long – some of 'em started playing auction, but I always find that a bit slow myself, and as there didn't seem much chance of poker or baccarat I went into the billiard-room with some of the others. But I had only just gone in when Mr. Burford – that's my trainer – and Captain Maddock came in and wanted a word with us. Some of the horses were coughing, and he had taken a fancy to have some vet he'd heard of down from town. Well, we didn't quite see it, either of us. It would have meant a pretty pot of money, and we were satisfied with old Tom Worseley, who'd looked after them before. Burford, who is a pretty obstinate chap, was inclined to argue the matter. So we went to smoke our cigarettes and talk things over in the veranda."

"Well, Lord Medchester, you can at least answer for it that neither Captain Maddock nor Mr. Burford was near the rosery during the suspected time." The inspector cast a keen glance at the other's face as he spoke.

"I am sure I don't know that I could," he said in a worried tone. "I was dodging about, you know, in and out from the card-room to the billiard-room talking to one and the other. When a man has guests he can't sit in one place all the evening."

"Of course he can't," the inspector agreed. They were getting near the front door, but Lord Medchester turned off across the grass.

"We'll go in by the side door and to my study. Then I will fetch Lady Medchester."

"Thank you."

"She won't like coming. I dare say you will find her a bit ratty," his lordship observed confidentially. "And I don't think she will be able to tell you anything. But that's that."

He took them in by the conservatory door and straight to his study – an apartment redolent of tobacco and scattered over with racing papers.

Lady Medchester did not hurry herself. Stoddart went over to the bookshelves.

"Who was Lady Medchester, I wonder?"

He took out a Peerage and turned over the leaves rapidly. Then he drew in his lips.

"H'm! Tells its own tale. Richard Frederick, fifth Viscount Medchester... Married Minnie, daughter of Francis, Baron Loamfield...Oh, that may account for a great deal."

Harbord looked puzzled.

"I don't understand."

"Ah, well, you observe she was not the Honourable Minnie. Francis, Baron Loamfield, was about as bad as they make 'em. Lady Loamfield couldn't stand him. But she didn't divorce him, being a Catholic. Loamfield had any amount of mistresses and a large family of illegitimate children. Looked after 'em, too, which is more than some of 'em do. One of 'em is a butcher in Loamby. This Minnie, I have heard of her, though it had slipped my memory till I saw this paragraph. Well, Minnie was running about wild, and she took his fancy, being both pretty and independent; he had her educated and gave her a big marriage portion. But the Loamfield blood's in her, and if she runs straight – well, there isn't much in heredity."

"I wonder if there is?" Harbord hesitated.

They had no time for more. Lady Medchester came quickly across the hall and into the room.

"You want to speak to me?" she said abruptly.

"If you please, Lady Medchester." Stoddart placed a chair for her and closed the door. A glance told him that she was not looking well. Her make-up was not sufficient to disguise the pallor of her face or do away with the dark circles round her eyes, and her lips, scarlet with lipstick, were visibly trembling.

"You remember the night of Thursday?"

Lady Medchester nodded and put her handkerchief up to her trembling lips.

"Of course I do. I – I wish I could forget it. But I can't. I never shall."

"You had a dinner-party that night, I understand?"

"Of course we had. You know that. Lord Medchester told you about it," Lady Medchester returned impatiently. She put down her handkerchief, on which two dabs of lipstick were plainly visible, and started twisting it about in her fingers.

"Could you tell us all you know about Mr. Saunderson?"

"Well, it wasn't so much really," she began, and Harbord wondered whether he was mistaken or whether there really was the shadow of a great fear in the big, pale eyes with their bistre-tinted eyelashes and eyebrows. "I met him in town this last season fairly often, and we stayed in the same house for Goodwood."

"He was an agreeable, pleasant sort of man, I understand?"

"Oh, very. I was quite pleased when my husband asked him to join our party for Doncaster."

Inspector Stoddart consulted his notebook.

"I take it that you found him quite an agreeable visitor? But that when he left you had no particular reason to expect to see him in the neighbourhood again?"

"No, not the least." Lady Medchester's tone was growing more assured now. "I simply could not believe it when I heard he had been found dead in the summer-house," she added.

"You have not the least idea what brought him to Holford?"

"I cannot imagine. The only thing I can think of is" – she stopped and swallowed something in her throat – "that he had some important news for my husband, something about the horses, perhaps, and came down to see him. Perhaps he knew of the short-cut from the village that brings you out by the rosery. Then perhaps some poacher met him and shot him."

"But why should Saunderson be in the village?" Stoddart questioned.

Lady Medchester shrugged her shoulders.

"I don't know. I do not pretend to explain everything. That is the only thing I have been able to think of."

"I see." The inspector consulted his notes again. "Now, Lady Medchester, I am sure you will understand that this is merely a formality – can you tell me just what you were doing between nine and ten o'clock on the night of Thursday?"

Once more there was that odd trembling of the lips, the curious light eyes avoided his.

"I was with my visitors, of course. I don't know that I can tell you any more."

"Perhaps you played bridge?" Stoddart suggested.

"No, I didn't. As a matter of fact, I had rather a headache and I didn't feel quite up to cards. We had some music in the drawing-room and I was there most of the evening. But of course I went backwards and forwards to the card-room and the hall two or three times just to see how people were getting on."

"I wonder whether you could tell me if Mrs. Williamson and Miss Courtenay were playing cards?"

Lady Medchester hesitated.

"I – I think Mrs. Williamson was. Miss Courtenay I know was not. She said" – with a perceptible hesitation – "she had a headache and went up to her room immediately after dinner."

The inspector made an entry in his notebook.

"And Mr. Courtenay?"

Lady Medchester wrinkled her eyebrows as if trying to remember.

"I don't remember seeing much of him. He was playing bridge for some little time. But not, I think, all the time you mention. Probably he was in the billiard-room."

"In the billiard-room, I thank you," Stoddart said politely. He waited a minute, then he dived into his pocket and produced the crystal beads. "Have you ever seen this before, Lady Medchester?"

She leaned forward and looked at it, hiding her eyes.

"I don't think so," she said slowly, her mouth setting in a hard line. "I am not sure, though. It seems somehow familiar. But, then, so many people wear this sort of thing nowadays."

"It is not yours?"

"Certainly not!" Lady Medchester smiled with regained composure. "It is not at all valuable," she added with a certain contempt in her tone.

"So I imagined." The inspector dropped the beads in his pocket. "Thank you, and I shall be obliged if you will say nothing about the beads. That is all for this morning. I should like a few words with Miss Courtenay."

Lady Medchester got up. "I will send her to you. She is expecting the summons. Lord Medchester told us both you wanted us. But Miss Courtenay will not have much time to spare," she added as the inspector opened the door. "Her grandfather, whom you may have heard of, had a stroke, and the doctors do not give us much hope. He is not so well this morning."

"I am sorry to hear that," the inspector said politely. He waited until she had got out of hearing. "Rather a daisy, isn't she? I don't know that I envy Lord Medchester his wife."

"I don't, anyway," Harbord said bluntly. "I don't envy anybody his wife. Mostly a damned nuisance, it seems to me."

The inspector looked at him.

"What! Turning misanthrope? This business is enough to make one of any man. Some damn fool of a woman is always at the bottom of it."

Anne Courtenay did not keep them waiting. She looked a curious contrast to Lady Medchester in her plain, black frock, which just left her pretty, rounded throat bare. Yet a curious look came into Stoddart's eyes as he set a chair for her so that her face was well in the light, while he himself remained in the shadow nearer the fireplace.

"I am very sorry to trouble you in the circumstances, Miss Courtenay," the inspector began. "But I am sure you will understand that I have no choice in the matter. I will keep you only a few minutes."

Anne bent her head.

"It is no matter," she said quietly. "The nurses are with my grandfather. I am only allowed to see him for a few minutes at a time."

"Then I will begin at once by asking you to tell me how much you knew of Mr. Saunderson."

"Very little," Anne returned, raising her eyes to the inspector's face. "He was kind to my brother and they were very friendly, but I am very little in town and naturally did not see much of him."

"He never visited the General?" Stoddart hazarded.

Anne shook her head. "My grandfather receives very few visitors, only quite old friends."

"I take it that you and Mr. Saunderson were strangers when you met at the house-party here for the Doncaster races?"

"No, not quite that. I believe" – Anne hesitated a minute – "that I first met Mr. Saunderson when I was staying with Lady Medchester last spring, but I saw very little of him."

"And at the house-party here?"

"Well, naturally I saw more of him then." She paused and then went on more quickly. "I may as well say at once that it was as little as I could help, for I did not like Mr. Saunderson at all, though he was a friend of my brother's, and though perhaps I ought not to say so now he is dead."

"Oh, I quite understand," the inspector said sympathetically. "Mr. Saunderson does not seem to have been a general favourite. I suppose you did not expect to see him again when the party for the St. Leger broke up?"

"I hoped I should not," Anne said candidly. "I did not think Mr. Saunderson's influence did my brother any good."

"Will you tell me just what you were doing after dinner last Thursday night?" As he spoke the inspector produced his notebook and laid it on the table.

Anne considered a moment.

"I had a headache," she said slowly, "and it was hot downstairs, and all the talking at dinnertime made it worse. So I went up to my room and lay down."

"Did you stay upstairs all the evening?" the inspector asked quickly.

A subtle change in Anne's expression did not escape him. For one moment her eyes wavered, then the girl said quietly:

"I came down for a few minutes. My head seemed to be worse and I thought the air would do me good. I went out by the side door and walked on the terrace."

"How long were you there?" The inspector's tone was sharper now.

"Oh, not long. There were too many people about."

"Too many people," the inspector repeated. "Miss Courtenay, did you meet Robert Saunderson?"

Suddenly Anne shivered from head to foot, but her voice was steady enough as she answered:

"Certainly not. In fact, I do not think I went out until after the time at which he – died."

The inspector apparently consulted his notebook again. Harbord, watching, saw that his fingers were merely making meaningless strokes, and wondered.

Anne waited too, her brown eyes looking scared.

The inspector drew out the crystal beads and held them up. "Have you ever seen these before?"

"Why!" Anne uttered an exclamation of astonishment as she leaned forward and took them in her hand. "They are just like some beads I have that I am rather fond of. Where did you get them from?"

The inspector countered her question by another: "Is this your chain, Miss Courtenay?"

"Certainly not," Anne said decidedly. "I saw mine in my dressing-case only a few minutes ago."

The inspector dropped his on the table.

"Would you allow me to see your chain, Miss Courtenay?"

"Of course I will." Anne got up. "I will fetch it at once."

The inspector opened the door for her and waited while she went across the hall and ran lightly up the stairs.

At the top, in the wide corridor that led to the principal rooms, she paused and her breath came quickly. She pressed her handkerchief to her lips and when she brought it away there were two little spots of blood upon it.

"What does it mean?" she whispered to herself. "What can it mean?"

Stoddart and Harbord did not speak. Their eyes met significantly as she came back, dangling in her hand the crystal beads.

She laid them beside those the inspector had thrown down.

"You see they are really awfully alike. There is rather more chain between each bead in mine, and the stones are cut differently – and there is a bead missing in yours, look at the gap – but you have to look very closely to see the difference."

"You do, indeed," said the inspector, holding up the two chains together. "Does your chain break easily, Miss Courtenay?"

Anne's pale lips smiled.

"I don't know. I have never broken it, but I should think it wouldn't be difficult to do so. Why do you ask?"

"I asked," the inspector said slowly, "because, as you see, this one is broken, and three of the beads from this chain" – tapping it – "were found in the pocket of Robert Saunderson's overcoat."

CHAPTER VII

"Saunderson's flat is on the ground floor," the inspector said as he and Harbord paused before the Polchester Mansions – a new palatial block in the immediate neighbourhood of Piccadilly. "It has been locked up and the old housekeeper sent away, and Venables has been on guard ever since last Friday, when we were summoned to Holford. I fancy we shall find the clue to the mystery here."

"If there is one," Harbord interposed.

Stoddart raised his eyebrows.

"Certainly there is one. It is scarcely like you to be so pessimistic, Alfred."

"I ought to have said if there is one that can be found," Harbord corrected. "We are up against a criminal who knows how to hide his traces. And really Saunderson might have been trying his best to help him."

"Or her," the inspector interjected.

"Or her," Harbord acknowledged the correction. "I can't help feeling, sir, that the clue, if there is one, is connected with those crystal beads."

"Well, you may be right or you may be wrong," the inspector said judicially as he led the way into the hall.

The porter touched his hat and the lift-boy stood in readiness. The inspector passed them and turned up a couple of steps to a door at the side. A man stood before it, easily recognizable as a policeman in plain clothes. He saluted as the inspector took a key from his pocket.

"Anything to report, Venables?"

"No, sir. Nobody has been here but the postman. And he has only been twice. Of course the housekeeper came just now. She said you told her to be here to-day."

"I did," the inspector assented. "But of course she could not get in. What has become of her?"

"She has gone down to the caretaker's, sir. I expect they are having a good old gossip. I was to tell her when you wanted her."

"Well, I think we will have a look round first," the inspector said as he opened the door and glanced about him curiously.

The hall was luxuriously carpeted. The inspector raised his eyebrows as he felt the softly padded divans at each side, and then glanced into the two good-sized rooms, one on each side of the door. Both were well furnished, one as a sitting-room, the other as a bedroom. Behind were a small room evidently used for smoking, a bathroom, and a kitchen which was scrupulously neat and tidy.

"Did himself well, Saunderson, I should say," the inspector remarked. "No servants but the old housekeeper, apparently; but in these service flats they do not want much waiting on."

"Servants might have been in the way sometimes," Harbord grinned. "It might have been tolerably easy to manage the housekeeper."

"Quite! Now I wonder where we had better begin. I think this looks as if it had been the most used," turning into the smoking-room.

A big, padded arm-chair, leather-covered, stood near the electric fireplace; a square, solid-looking table beside it held an open box of cigars and a jar of tobacco. There was an array of pipes in a rack on the wall on the other side. On another table against the wall was a tantalus, a couple of glasses, and a siphon of seltzer water.

"Looks as if he expected to come back all right, poor chap," Harbord commented.

The inspector did not answer; his keen eyes were searching every detail of the room and the furniture. At last he walked over to the table against the wall and took up a small morocco leather box that stood behind the tantalus.

"Locked, of course!"

He shook it, then he set it back on the table and took a curious-looking little steel implement from his pocket and applied himself to the task of forcing the lock. In a very few minutes it was done and the box lay open before them.

The inspector pounced at once upon a small, thick book about the size of a pass-book, labelled outside "Memorandum".

"Just what I was hoping for."

Then, while he was bending his brows over it, Harbord glanced over the other contents of the box. They were a heterogeneous collection: a bundle of old letters tied together, a cheque-book, a couple of miniatures – a fine-looking man, a girl with a sweet wistful face – then more letters; lastly a long envelope containing an application for income-tax.

The inspector uttered a sharp exclamation.

"This memorandum-book tells a curious story. Listen, Alfred. 'Six hundred from Lady F. paid in to Usher & Snell. Two fifty Colonel O'Brady – Usher & Snell.' And so it goes on. Different sums paid in to Usher & Snell, varied occasionally by 'Paid in to account in Imperial and Overseas.' What do you make of it?"

"Blackmail," Harbord said laconically.

"Quite!" the inspector agreed. "So much the different initials make certain. But it is Usher & Snell that I am thinking of."

"Usher & Snell!" Harbord repeated thoughtfully. "Money-lenders, aren't they? I have heard of them, but –"

"Money-lenders and sharks," the inspector said emphatically. "What I am asking myself now is, what was Saunderson's connexion with them? Was he in their power or was he a member of the firm, or connected with it? More probably the latter, I imagine, though –"

"If he had borrowed from them as a young man and let the debt accumulate, he would have found it a pretty hard job to get out of their clutches," Harbord remarked.

"Yes, he would," Stoddart assented. "But from what I have heard of Saunderson I should suspect he was the spider, not the fly. However, we must pay Messrs. Usher & Snell a visit, then we shall know more than we do now. At any rate, there can be no doubt from this book that a great part of his income was derived from blackmail. I'll just have a squint at the cheque-book now."

Harbord took up the memorandum-book while Stoddart turned the counterfoils over rapidly.

"Business cheques these, all of 'em. One or two biggish ones to Owler & Vigors, the jewellers in Bond Street. Some of Saunderson's lady friends doing him in the eye, I suppose."

"Several cheques paid in lately are from T," Harbord remarked. "Paid in to Usher & Snell, I mean. I wonder who T is? There is one from C. C might stand for Courtenay."

"Also for Cox and Carter and a few others," the inspector remarked sarcastically. "No use, Alfred. Things can't be fitted in like that. That book is simply a record of blackmailing transactions, and it probably supplies a motive for the crime. The person blackmailed may have turned, like the proverbial worm, and shot the blackmailer instead of paying up. I think we will take a look at the bedroom now. There may be letters there." He led the way across the hall. Harbord followed.

"Saunderson kept no man, you say, sir?"

"No. Just the one old housekeeper to look after things and see to his breakfast. These are service flats, so he would manage all right. I wish he had had a man, but we must see what the housekeeper can tell us."

There was nothing of the Spartan about Saunderson evidently. His bedroom, like the rest of the flat, was extremely well furnished. The floor was softly carpeted, a big easy-chair stood by the electric radiator, and the satin down quilt on the bed was almost as thick as a French one.

The inspector went straight over to a small inlaid table near the window.

"A blotter, by Jove! Just the thing I was looking for."

He took it up. There were no loose papers inside, but the blotting-paper had the appearance of having been fairly well used. He held a sheet up to the light. At first sight it was not easy to read anything – it was written over and criss-crossed and blotted; but at last he made out a few words – "And unless I receive it before Monday –"

The rest was just a jumble of incoherencies. The inspector took up the next sheet. "Not with you. You must –"

The other two sheets yielded even less.

"Yours sincerely, Robert Saunderson ... yours faithfully, Robert Saunderson ... If Battledore ..." That was all that could be made out. And, though, such as it was, it went to confirm the inspector's previous opinion, in itself it proved nothing.

"Not much good going on here," the inspector remarked. "We will just go through to the sitting-room. And then perhaps we might have a word with the people in the restaurant. They must have known Saunderson fairly well."

The sitting-room was expensively furnished, but it seemed to hold even less in the way of a clue to the mystery than the other rooms. It had the appearance of a room rarely used; a bowl of faded flowers stood on the table, a comfortable chesterfield in the middle of the room appeared to have been little sat upon. There was a low book-case under one of the windows, containing a number of doubtful-looking French novels in garish covers. On the top of the case stood a couple of Oriental vases, and the photograph in a frame of beaten copper of a dark, handsome woman with unshingled hair, in the fashion of a few years previously. The inspector looked at it, then took it out of the frame and glanced at the back.

"Taken at Southampton, and some time ago by the look of it," he said as he set it down. "Well, she is not one of the ladies at Holford Hall. So much is certain."

Harbord held out a letter.

"I found this in one of the dressing-table drawers."

The inspector drew his brows together as he got a whiff of the patchouli which emanated from the paper.

"Beastly stuff! I wonder why women must put this stink on their letters. It is a woman's writing, and I think I have seen it before," glancing at the big square envelope. "Yes! Why, the postmark is Holford!" He drew out the enclosure and read it aloud. It was not dated and began abruptly. "He will be out from Friday to Monday. Come by the rosery entrance and up to the side door and I will let you in. Yours, M."

"M – Minnie, Lady Medchester," said the inspector. "Well, it looks as if what London has been saying for some time – that the gossip about Saunderson and Lady Medchester had a solid substratum of fact." He glanced again at the postmark. "This Friday that she speaks of is ten days before the murder. This makes one think. I wonder whether Saunderson went. Anyhow, he can't tell us and I am sure Lady Medchester won't. We shall have to make inquiries. But I don't much like the look of things. It doesn't seem probable that the man had two ladyloves at Holford; therefore, presumably he went there on the day of his death to meet Lady Medchester."

"He may have had half a dozen – and the motive of the crime may have been jealousy," Harbord hazarded.

The inspector drew in his lips. "Only one person was likely to be jealous. Lady Medchester's meretricious charms are scarcely likely to rouse any strong feeling nowadays, whatever they may have been in her youth."

"I see what you mean," Harbord said rather slowly, frowning as he spoke. "But isn't there rather a snag there, sir? You see, this note asks Saunderson to come down on the Friday because 'he' will be out. Would she have asked him to come again on the evening of the murder when presumably 'he' would be certain to be at home as they had people coming to dinner as well as others staying in the house?"

"It doesn't seem likely on the face of it," the inspector agreed. "But we don't know what had happened. Something may have turned up that made a second meeting imperative. I think – I rather think we shall have to ask Lady Medchester for an explanation of this letter."

"She will probably swear it isn't hers at all."

"I think the internal evidence shows plainly enough that it is. But still" – the inspector regarded Harbord with an indulgent smile – "I have no intention of going to her bald-headed with it just at present. But now we will have a word with the housekeeper."

The housekeeper, Mrs. Draper, came to them in the hall. She was a tall, angular-looking woman, if, with big, dark eyes that had a scared look in them as she glanced at the detectives.

"You sent for me?"

"Yes. I wanted to ask you a few questions." The inspector moved a chair forward for her. "I shall keep you only a few minutes, Mrs. Draper. I understand you have been some time with Mr. Saunderson?"

Mrs. Draper passed her apron over the chair before she sat down.

"Yes, a matter of three years and a half. And I am sorry you gentlemen should come in to find the place all in a muddle and the London dust over everything, getting in through every chink. But if the flat being locked up directly I heard of poor Mr. Saunderson's death I couldn't help it."

"I'm sure you couldn't," the inspector assented heartily. "And I know what work is. I can see the place has been well looked after. Now, Mrs. Draper, can you tell us what took Mr. Saunderson to Holford?"

The housekeeper threw up her hands.

"Not a bit of it, I couldn't. I knew he was to be away the night, for he said to me joking, like, when he went out – 'You won't see me till tomorrow morning, Mrs. Draper.' He never was one to stay out all night without telling me, wasn't Mr. Saunderson. But, as to where he went, that was another matter. You might have knocked me down with a feather when I heard he had been killed at Holford."

"Do you know of anyone that had a grudge against him?" the inspector asked.

"Eh, no! That I don't." Mrs. Draper stared at him. "He was always a pleasant, joking sort of man."

"You know of no quarrel of any kind? Now please do think well, Mrs. Draper," the inspector said sternly as the woman stopped and hesitated. "We must be quite sure about this."

"Well, there was a bit of unpleasantness between him and a young gentleman a week or two ago," the housekeeper said unwillingly. "But I am sure it meant nothing, and anyway it is all over now."

The inspector produced his notebook.

"This young man's name, please."

"A very nice young gentleman he is," Mrs. Draper said with emphasis. "Well, then" – as the inspector moved impatiently –

"it was Mr. Harold Courtenay. He was a friend of the master's, too, except for that little quarrel, and that didn't last, for I heard them part the best of friends last Monday. I heard Mr. Courtenay call out 'So long, old chap!' as he went off."

"H'm!" The inspector produced the photograph he had found in the sitting-room. "Mr. Saunderson was rather a man for the ladies, wasn't he?"

"Well, I never saw anything of it if he was," Mrs. Draper said, pleating up the edge of her coat. "He didn't have ladies coming here after him, or anything of that."

"Not even this lady?" said the inspector, holding up the photograph.

Mrs. Draper's change of colour did not escape him.

"Yes, I have seen that one," she said slowly. "I let her in once. And I know she was here once more, anyhow. I heard her talking. She had that loud kind of voice, you couldn't mistake it."

"Did you hear her name?"

"Well, I did hear it, but not to remember it," Mrs. Draper said doubtfully. "Something beginning with D it was. Miss De something or other. I took the lady for an actress – or a music-hall person."

"I see. Well, we must look that up," said the inspector, placing the photograph in his pocket and producing the three beads found in Saunderson's pocket. "Was the lady wearing anything if like this when you let her in?"

Mrs. Draper hesitated. "I couldn't say, sir. She had a lot of dangling things on – I know that; but I didn't look particular. I couldn't say more than that."

The inspector looked disappointed as he replaced them in the little box.

"Well, Mrs. Draper, I must take your address, and you must notify me of any change. I shall probably want to see you again before long."

CHAPTER VIII

"I shall never marry. I have changed my mind."

Anne Courtenay's tone was dull and lifeless. She was standing in the little drawing-room of the cottage that had been General Courtenay's home for years and stood on a corner of the estate that had once been the Courtenays'. The cottage and the land surrounding it was their last remaining possession. Anne was in mourning – just a simple black frock that suited her fair skin to perfection. That very morning General Courtenay had been laid to his rest, and his old sister, saddened and broken, had returned to her home in London. Anne was feeling lonely and frightened. Her eyes were glancing round the room now as if she feared something that might lurk amid the gathering shadows.

Opposite to her stood Michael Burford. The famous trainer was a strong-looking man – strong-looking in both senses of the word. He was not tall; he hardly reached middle height, but on his lithe, muscular frame there was not one ounce of superfluous fat. His lean, dark face was tanned nearly mahogany colour; against it his steel-blue eyes had a startling, vivid effect. Meeting their glance fully, it was easy to realize that here was a man of indomitable determination, a man who would always conquer in a contest of wills, whether of man or beast. In his training career Michael Burford had been singularly successful. No horse of his ever became sour. Burford's colts were never led on the course blinkered or muzzled. Very early in their training they found they had met their master, and the sooner they realized it and submitted the better for them.

He was looking at Anne now, and as he watched her face and heard her constantly reiterated words – "I shall never marry now" – there was no anger in his eyes, only a great pity.

"Why have you changed your mind, Anne?" he questioned gently. "Don't you think you owe it to me to give me some explanation?"

"I can't!" Anne raised her hands, then let them fall helplessly to her sides. "It is just that I do not mean to marry anyone. That I must be alone – always alone – as long as I live."

"Why?" The steel-blue eyes kept their watch on the set white face. "I shall not release you, Anne," Michael Burford went on quietly. "You have promised to marry me. I shall keep you to your promise."

"You can't."

Anne's voice sounded as if she were tired – very, very tired. Her eyes, swollen and dark-circled, looked as though they had wept until they could weep no more. Her slim, young figure was bent as if she had no strength in it. The pity in Burford's eyes deepened.

"Is your love for me dead, then, Anne?"

The girl nodded, tried to speak, but the lie refused to come. Her throat twitched convulsively; with a gesture of utter despair she flung her hands before her eyes.

Burford watched her silently for a minute. Then he moved nearer.

"Anne –"

With a moan she put out her hands as though to push him away.

"Please – go. Don't you see that I can't –"

Very deliberately, in spite of her best efforts to avoid him, Burford took one of the outstretched hands. It lay in his like a lump of ice.

"Tell me why you have changed your mind, Anne."

"I – I can't," the girl said miserably. "It is just that I have changed, that is all. People do, you know," steadying her voice with a supreme effort.

Michael Burford laughed aloud.

"They do, I know. But you haven't, Anne." He had captured both hands now. "You belong to me, you are mine. I will never let you go. I am going to marry you at once and carry you right away home to East Molton. Is that what you are afraid of, dear? Of Anne Courtenay becoming Michael Burford the trainer's wife?" Anne tried to free her hands from his.

"No! A thousand times no!" she cried passionately. "I must go right away – away from every one I know – where no one ever sees me." As she spoke she wrenched her hands from Burford's grasp and clasped them in front of her.

"Always in my dreams I see them, staring, watching every movement. Never, never can I get away. Oh, the world is all eyes – everywhere there are eyes!"

"I will take you away from them." Michael Burford spoke very gravely. "You shall never be lonely or frightened again, Anne. It is very safe at East Molton. No one will worry you there. Just we two in the house and the horses and men outside. We will go for long gallops over the moors, the winds that come down clean and fresh from the north shall blow the cobwebs from our brains, and you shall be strong and brave again."

Some of the terror faded from Anne's eyes. Only she, and Heaven, knew how she longed for the home, the peace thus pictured. She had dreamt of other careers before she was engaged – sometimes she had thought of the stage; she had been well spoken of as an amateur actress; but now – now she dared not face an audience, not knowing how much people guessed, how much they knew. East Molton looked like a paradise of peace and rest to her. Yet, she asked herself, would she really be safe there? Would she really be safe anywhere?

Burford saw the softening in her eyes and his face brightened.

"You will come, Anne? You will let me take you away now, at once?"

Suddenly the frozen calm of Anne's face broke up, big tears welled up in her eyes.

"I – I can't. I daren't."

"Daren't!" Burford repeated. "That is not a word for your father's daughter, Anne."

"Ah!" In spite of her tears Anne held up her head now. "It is because of him that I am afraid. You do not know –"

"No." Burford's tone was very grave now. "I do not know perhaps, but suppose I guess. Harold –"

"No, no!" Anne backed against the wall. "You shall not guess. It was not Harold. It was I –"

There was a dawning comprehension now in Burford's eyes.

"Anne, I think I do know. Saunderson –"

"No, no!" With a hoarse cry the girl shrank from him. She pushed herself back, her hands held out to keep him off. "You shall not," she panted. "I tell you, you shall not guess!"

"No, I will not guess," Burford said very quietly. "Because you are going to tell me yourself, Anne. Because I know – I have known all along that you were out the night that Saunderson died."

"What!" Anne's eyes were full of terror. She seemed to shrivel up literally beneath his gaze. "How – how could you know?" she stammered.

"I saw you coming in," he said gravely. "I went over to Holford on some business with Lord Medchester, and then Captain Williamson, who has a colt with me, came there after me. We were in the library and the window was wide open, for it was a hot night, and I saw you."

"And Captain Williamson?" Anne questioned breathlessly.

"He didn't see you. He was looking the other way. And he would not have known you. I could see only a tall figure in black, but you could not deceive me, Anne."

"Then – then – if you saw that," Anne spoke with difficulty, "you know – you know why –"

"I know why – what?"

"Why I cannot marry you – why I cannot marry anyone?" Very haltingly the words came now.

A sudden flame leapt into the blue eyes watching her.

"I see why you should marry me," Burford said steadily. "I mean to take care of you, Anne. You can trust me."

"Yes, yes!" the stammering voice said brokenly. "But I can bring you shame – disgrace –"

"I can stand them if I have you, Anne, beside me." There was no hesitation in his tone. "But why didn't you come to me before, Anne? Why didn't you let me help you instead?"

"No, no!" Anne broke in with sudden passion. "I did not – I did not – you do believe me, Michael?"

"I believe in you as I do in God Himself," Burford returned. Eyes and voice were as steady as ever. "Saunderson deserved his fate, Anne, though you had no part in it. But – Harold –?"

"I don't know – I don't know!" Anne moaned. "But I am frightened – so frightened, Michael."

There was a tender look in Burford's eyes as he watched her. "But now you must not be frightened any more. I am going to take care of you –"

But with a cry Anne shrank from him.

"You can't, you can't! Nobody can. He – we must just go on to the end. And then – oh, God help us then!"

"Anne!" With a quick forward movement Burford captured her hands. "What do you mean? Do you think that Harold –?"

Anne interrupted him with a cry.

"I don't think – I daren't think. Only I am afraid – afraid of everything."

"You will not be afraid with me at East Molton," Burford said with a certainty that was in itself reassuring. "And by and by when you are strong enough to tell me all, I think we shall be able to help Harold. I have faith in your brother, Anne."

"You don't know – everything," the girl said with difficulty. "I did not think – I never believed – that Harold would do what he has done. But now – now, I just don't know. I don't feel – sure of anybody – not even myself."

Michael Burford smiled. "I do. Of you both. And I am going to prove it to the world by marrying you, Anne. We will never rest till the truth about Saunderson's death is known. And then – and then I won't even say I told you so."

"You – you can't!" Anne said brokenly. "Nobody can help!"

"We will get help," Burford returned positively. "Truth will out. And now – when will you marry me, Anne?"

"I haven't said I will marry you at all."

"Oh, yes, you have. And you are going to." Burford gave the hands he held a little shake. "As soon as I can get the licence, Anne. Say yes!"

"It – it doesn't seem any use saying no," the girl said quaveringly.

"It isn't," Burford agreed as he drew her to him. "Not one bit of good, my dear."

CHAPTER IX

"Well, I have ascertained one thing for certain," Stoddart exclaimed as the train steamed out of St. Pancras. He had just arrived on the platform at the last minute and managed to spring into the compartment where Harbord was impatiently awaiting him. "How did you manage to get the carriage to yourself, Alfred?"

"Tipped the guard pretty extensively," Harbord answered laconically. "I knew it would be money well laid out."

Stoddart nodded.

"May save time when we get to Derby. I have interviewed Messrs. Usher & Snell. I had some difficulty in getting what I wanted from them. Began to sympathize with the dentists before I had finished. But at last they caved in and I became fulsomely anxious to give me all the information I wanted. Saunderson was a partner in the firm, though his name did not appear. In fact, he seems to have been more than a partner. I fancy he was the leading spirit in the whole affair. Practically he *was* Usher & Snell. But of his blackmailing Messrs. Usher & Snell professed entire ignorance. The sums of money which his pass-book shows makes it evident he was constantly paying in to their account were used mainly in the transactions of the firm, which of course required a large amount of capital. Saunderson also held quantities of shares in many foreign undertakings in the name of Usher & Snell. So, you see, the motive for the murder may have been supplied in as many different quarters as that interesting firm had clients, to say nothing of his blackmailing transactions. Of course the knowledge he acquired as the head of Usher & Snell as well as anything he picked up as a man about town was used to put the screw on the unfortunate beggars. Oh, there is no doubt that Saunderson was one of the biggest scoundrels unhung, and whoever potted him did the world a damned good turn. It goes to my heart to try to track the poor beggar down."

"Still, it wouldn't do to allow people to take the law into their own hands," Harbord argued. "Even a money-lender has his rights."

"And a blackmailer!" the inspector assented. "Well said, Harbord. Always remember you stand for British justice."

Harbord did not reply. For a minute or two he watched the flying landscape with unseeing eyes. At last he said:

"If it was one of Usher & Snell's clients that did Saunderson in, I shall never understand why they should have followed him down to Holford."

Stoddart looked at him.

"As I have said before, I don't agree with you. Unless one is tempted off the beaten track, London is the safest place in the world. Besides, there are wheels within wheels. Saunderson had a decent colt or two in training at Oxley. They are expected to do well as three-year-olds. One of them, Mayfair, runs for next year's Derby. It may have been to some one's interest to get rid of Saunderson and render Mayfair's nomination void. Certainly it doesn't seem much of a motive, but then half the murders that are committed are for such very slight motives that one marvels how any sane man or woman could risk his or her neck for such trivialities."

"I suppose they always think they will not be found out," Harbord observed meditatively. "But if the criminal is a man in this case where do the crystal beads come in? The chain must have broken and the links must have fallen into Saunderson's pocket when those letters were thrown out, and when, it seems to me, that some paper was searched for and presumably found and taken away. Now who could have gone through the pockets but the murderer?"

"Several people," the inspector said sharply.

"The men who found the body, for instance, or quite possibly an earlier visitor. Though that wouldn't explain them, if one accepts Superintendent Mayer's statement that the beads were not in the pocket when he first arrived on the scene."

"I don't accept it," Harbord said bluntly.

"How should the beads get there afterwards?"

"There was the interval when the superintendent went to the barn," the inspector went on, "but only of a few minutes. If it was done then there must have been somebody on the watch

– which doesn't seem likely. Also, whoever might have been watching would have known Mayer had searched the pockets and removed any papers."

Harbord shook his head doubtfully.

"And here is another question for you," the inspector went on. "If your theory is correct, and the three beads dropped into Saunderson's pocket when his assailant was getting out the letter or the paper the possession of which was the motive for the murder, what did the woman do with the rest of the chain?"

"It must have been broken when the beads caught in the lining of the pocket, and I suppose the other piece fell off."

"Well, it didn't fall where it was found, in the middle of the rhododendrons at the side of the Dutch garden," the inspector returned. "The murderess assuredly did not attempt to push her way through that hedge. No, the chain was thrown there. That is a certainty."

"But who could have thrown it?" Harbord speculated. "The woman who wore it, whoever she was, would not have thrown her chain away; even the silliest of 'em would have realized that it would certainly be found, and might be a clue that would lead to her discovery."

"Spoken like a book," the inspector commented. "No, certainly the woman who wore that chain did not throw it away in the bushes. And I do not agree with you that Saunderson was shot by a woman. I fancy we shall find that the motive was either jealousy or the getting out of Saunderson's blackmailing clutches. And I am strongly of opinion that Superintendent Mayer was right and that there were no beads in the pocket when it was searched. But how they got there any more than the rest of the chain got among the rhododendrons I am not prepared to say. It's a nasty case, simple as it looks, and there'll be wigs on the green before we have cleared it up. But I have got something – in fact, two things – here that may interest you, though at the same time they do not appear to have any particular bearing on the case."

He took up a paper that he had thrown upon the seat beside him and turned it over. Harbord watched him curiously.

"Here it is," Stoddart said at last. "In the society news. It is headed 'Romance of the Racing World.' 'Mr. Michael Burford, second son of the late Sir William Burford, of Burleet, and Miss Anne Frances Courtenay, only daughter of the late Captain Harold William Courtenay, V.C., and granddaughter of the late General Courtenay, were married, very quietly on account of the bride's mourning, at St. John's, Downmouth, last Saturday. Mr. Michael Burford has made himself a name as a trainer, and Miss Courtenay belongs to a well-known racing family. The bride was given away by her brother, Mr. Harold Courtenay, and directly after the ceremony the newly-married couple left for North Cornwall where the honeymoon will be spent.'"

"Miss Courtenay!" Harbord said doubtfully. "I thought she was rather pat with her crystal chain. She knows or suspects something, I am certain."

"Well, maybe," the inspector assented. "Possibly she saw Lady Medchester go out and come in that night. You remember they both had headaches and were prowling about apparently. But" – he paused and looked out of the window silently for a minute – "one point in favour of the people at Holford is this. Not one of the people I have questioned has a satisfactory alibi. An alibi is the easiest thing in the world to fake, and the least satisfactory of defences. When I find a suspect with a nice watertight alibi I generally devote a little special attention in that direction. But you have not seen my second paragraph." He turned to another page of his paper. "Here it is. 'Fatal Accident to the Hon. James Courtenay. Sudden Death of Lord Gorth. The Hon. James Courtenay, only son of the fifth Lord

Gorth, met with a fatal accident while riding in the Home Park at Gorth yesterday; his horse put its foot in a rabbit-hole and pitched forward. Mr. Courtenay was thrown on his head, and his neck was broken. Death must have been instantaneous. He was unmarried. When the sad news was conveyed to Lord Gorth, who had been in a delicate state of health since the death of his wife last year, he collapsed and passed away of heart failure in a couple of hours. The new peer is Mr. Harold Courtenay, grandson of General Courtenay, of Afghan fame, who died on the 14th of last month, and who was the first cousin of the fifth lord. The father of the new Lord Gorth was the late Captain Harold William Courtenay, V.C., who was killed at Ypres. The new Lord Gorth is twenty-three years of age and, like his cousin, is unmarried. His only sister is the Miss Anne Frances Courtenay whose marriage to Mr. Michael Burford, the well-known trainer, is reported in another column.' There!" said the detective, slapping down the paper. "That's that."

"It's very interesting," Harbord said dryly. "But it doesn't affect our case much, does it, sir?"

"I don't know," the inspector said slowly. "I really don't know, but I fancy it will all work in. At any rate, neither the new Lord Gorth nor his sister likes being questioned with regard to the tragedy. I am afraid, too, that I shall have to intrude upon the honeymoon to interview Mr. Michael Burford."

When the train drew up at Medchester and the detectives stepped out, the first person they saw on the platform was Superintendent Mayer. His broad, red face was shining with excitement as he made his way to them.

"I'm glad you'm coom back, inspector," he said, his Loamshire accent growing broader as he spoke. "I ha' got something for you this time."

"What is it?" questioned the inspector. "Or who is it?" with a quick glance at the superintendent's perspiring face.

"Well" – the superintendent cast a quick glance round – "it is one of those poaching fellows, an' he – But maybe it will be best for you to hear what he has to say for yourself. He came to me at the police station an hour ago."

"You are holding him?"

The superintendent nodded. "I am that, till you've heard what he has to say."

"We'll get off at once," the inspector said, beckoning to Harbord.

It was but a step to the police station. Stoddart was a quick walker and the stout superintendent had much ado to keep up with him.

A constable stood at the door. The superintendent led the way to his office.

"I heard this chap, Garwood by name, had been talking in the village," he said as he opened the door, "so I sent for him. But you shall question him for yourself."

Garwood sat on the edge of a chair set as close to the door as possible. He lurched heavily to his feet as the detectives entered. At first sight there was nothing prepossessing about the gentleman. He was a short, thin man with a narrow face, none too clean, and adorned with several days' growth of stubbly beard; his small, dark eyes were set under heavy, overhanging brows, and the eyes themselves were cunning-looking and had a trick of glancing obliquely at anybody or anything in their line of vision. They were so glancing at the inspector now as Mr. Garwood twisted a greasy fur cap about in his hands uneasily.

"Now, Bill Garwood," the superintendent said briskly, "I want you to tell these gentlemen what you told me."

Garwood cleared his throat noisily and drew the back of his hand across his mouth.

"Taint much as I can tell," he said hoarsely. "An' – an' if it gets me into trouble I looks to you gents to see me out."

"We will look after you," the inspector said reassuringly. "Come, my man, tell us your tale, and then, superintendent, I dare say that man of yours would step across to the 'Arms' and get us a tankard of ale."

Garwood's eyes began to shine as he glanced from one to the other.

"There won't be any need for that," the superintendent broke in, whereat Garwood's face fell. "I ha' a good tap in the house; since these 'ere confounded temperance folks got the upper hand, 'tis the only thing to be done, to keep a barrel on the premises."

"Ay, it is that," Garwood growled. "Wring all their blasted teetotallers' necks, I would."

Stoddart laughed. "I'm afraid there are a good many others of your way of thinking, Mr. Garwood. But now will you tell us what you know of that night when Mr. Saunderson was shot?"

"There ain't much as I do know," the man said sulkily, shuffling his feet about. "And afore I begin, I must tell you gents as I'm a pore man, a pore man I ha' always been with a sickly wife an' a heap of chillen allus with open mouths cryin' out for somethin' to fill 'em. It's hard lines on a father when he sees the things running about wild as would save his chillen's lives, an' him not allowed to touch 'em."

"It must be," the inspector agreed sympathetically. "I think I see now, Mr. Garwood. You were trying to pick up one or two of those same wild things?"

"I were," Mr. Garwood assented, his shifty eyes turning about from the inspector's eyes to the superintendent's. "Just a rabbit or two, you understand. The missis, she weren't not to say well, nor one o' the kids, and there were no work going."

"I – I quite see," the inspector murmured.

Moistening his lips, Garwood proceeded:

"I were in the paddock just looking round. I ha' often picked up a fat rabbit there, an' I see a man come along in a car. He stops it – parks it, as they calls it – on that there bit o' waste ground by the west lodge, like. Well, then he come out and goes in the blue doors and across the bit o' the park to the rosery. I began to think as there might be money in it, for there's been a deal of talk goin' about her ladyship in the village, so I went after him, keeping my distance, you see. An' he jumped the railings an' went on, not into the rosery, but into the bit o' waste ground beyond. I went after him an' then found I was not the only one. It had been raining, but now the moon were shining out like, an' I could see the gentleman I come after quite plain; right across the grounds he went, as if he knowed his way, but there were some one else as I couldn't get proper, right among the bushes. I could hear a kind of rustling, as if somebody was trying to walk quietly in among the rhododendrons, side o' the flower garden. I waited where I was, an' –"

"If anyone wanted to follow Mr. Saunderson they would have done much better to keep out of the bushes and walk along the grass," the inspector interrupted.

"Well, I don't know," Garwood said slowly. "The moon were fairly bright just then an' him as they was after would ha' bin safe to see anyone as walked on the grass. I didn't dare go any nearer myself. An' I went on, keepin' on the walk at the bottom of the clearin' that brings you out through another of them little gates on to the pine grove, and then if you turn to the right you come to the old quarry where the pheasants are. I didn't mean to do nothin' to them – 'tain't likely. But I thought as I might come across a rabbit – one o' those white ones his lordship sets such store by maybe – an' it 'ud make a bit o' stew for the chillen. But I found 'tweren't such an easy job as I thought. There was a party on at the hall, an' there was footmen and such-like strollin' about in the pinetum, so I turned back; as I passes the clearing again I looks up, but there weren't no one about and nothin' to be seen. But it were drizzlin' o' rain an' the moon had gone in, an' I stopped a minute agin the rosery gate. While I was standin' there in the shadow some one come runnin' out o' the clearin' fast as she could go like as some bogle was after her."

Garwood stopped.

"Go on." The inspector drew a deep breath. "Who was it? Man or woman?"

"I could do with a drop o' that there beer now, guv'nor. 'Tis dry work goin' on like this on your lone. I dunno how t' parsons does it, but maybe they keeps a drop i' th' vestry."

The superintendent opened the door and beckoned to a subordinate, who presently appeared with a foaming jug of beer and a couple of glasses. The superintendent pushed them towards Garwood.

"Help yourself."

The man's eyes shone. "That's the stuff," he said greedily.

"Well, get a move on," the inspector said impatiently. "Who was this other person, man or woman?"

Garwood took a mighty draught. "I feel a bit better now, mister. About this 'ere person. I understands there might be money in it."

"There might be jail in it if you don't speak out quick, Bill Garwood," the superintendent said sharply.

"You needn't be so down on a chap," Garwood grumbled. "I see who it was plain enough, for the moon were trying to shine again. 'Twere her ladyship plain enough, cuttin' along she were, too, an' cryin'. I see her plain when she pulled the gate open."

"Did you see any more of the man who went in before you?"

"No-a. I did not; he'd disappeared like." He took another drink of beer. "I wor a-wonderin' how I should do the best for myself out o' what I'd seen."

"Did you see anyone else?" the inspector asked.

Mr. Garwood scratched his head.

"No-a, I dunner think as 'ow I did. Only 'er ladyship – I'd swear to 'er all right, but I couldn't tell you any more not if you kep' me 'ere all day, gents.'

"I am sure you have told us a great deal, Mr. Garwood," the inspector said politely. "And, now, I am sure you will understand that there must be no talking or gossiping about what you saw that night. You will be wanted later."

"I unnerstand." The man got on his feet and stood turning his cap about. "Ain't there no reward given for me tellin' you all this what happened that there night?"

"There is no reward offered at present," the inspector answered, glancing at his case-book.

"Then I calls it a shame," Garwood said truculently. "I'd ha' kep' my mouth shut if I'd ha' known – 'er ladyship might ha' paid me to do that. A man's got his wife and chillen to think of. I've allus heard there was reward given for them as helped to find out who done things."

"For them as helped to find out who done things –" the inspector repeated. "I don't think you have quite done that, my man. But, as you say, there are rewards – sometimes. There are also punishments if a man is mistaken, or people think he is. I fancy Lord Medchester might remember that."

CHAPTER X

The stable at East Molton was well known in the racing world. It had been bought from a famous North Country trainer by Sir William Burford for his younger son. A farm-house in the immediate vicinity which had served as a residence for his predecessor had been altered and improved by Michael Burford, for his bride, almost beyond recognition.

A big semicircle of lawn in front big enough for croquet or tennis had a drive running round to the door, which was flanked on each side by big stone vases filled with different flowers in their season. At the back of the house ran a low terrace with a stone balustrade. What had been the farmyard in the old days was now a wide, flagged court; on the other side of it were the loose boxes and the stables that housed Burford's precious charges. On the west side of the house and stables was the paddock and the loose rails where much of Burford's work was done. Beyond that again stretched the moor where the morning gallops were taken. The grooms and stable-boys were housed near the stables.

It seemed a very harbour of refuge to Anne Burford as she stood on the steps at the front door. Though she had only been at East Molton a week, already her eyes had lost much of their frightened look. Her nerves, too, were steadier; no longer did she start and glance round nervously at the faintest sound. Surely, she said to herself, she would be safe here, safe and forgotten – no sign of any other house was in sight. And, though every now and then some sound from the busy life of the stable reached her ears, it was all pleasant and familiar and home-like. As she stood there, rejoicing in the peace of her surroundings, there came to her no premonition of how short-lived it was to be – no faintest suspicion that even now it was at an end.

The white gate at the end of the drive banged noisily. Anne looked up. Some one – a woman – was coming towards her. As the new-comer drew nearer, she saw that it was a tall girl, well, even fashionably, dressed. As Anne glimpsed the red hair, peeping out from the small pull-on hat in curls over each ear, noted the small white face, looking almost too small for the big blue eyes, she had a sense of familiarity, a certainty that somewhere she had encountered that distinctly hostile gaze before.

Anne felt an odd desire to run away, to refuse to see this girl whose lips were smiling, though her eyes looked hard and defiant.

But Anne's desire was hardly definite enough to have become an intention, and it was frustrated. Her visitor did not trouble to go round by the walk, but came straight across the lawn to her.

"I expect you don't remember me, Mrs. Burford. And yet I know your brother so well that I don't feel like a stranger to you," she said in a slow, drawling voice that roused some faint memory in Anne. "I thought you wouldn't remember me," the drawling voice went on. "But I am going over to East Molton to see, I said to Minnie Medchester. I am spending a few days at Holford, you know. I am Sybil Stainer, Maurice Stainer's sister. You will have heard Harold speak of me."

"Yes, I have heard Harold speak of you," Anne found herself repeating mechanically. An icy fear gripped her heart, paralysed her. Certain memories were coming back to her: the red-haired girl who had been with Harold in the paddock looking at the St. Leger horses; the voice, Saunderson's voice – what had he said? – "The Stainers are bad companions for Harold. The man is a spend-thrift, a rotter, and the girl – well, the less said about her the better." And now this same girl stood before her smiling impudently in her face.

"Well, I suppose you are going to ask me in?" Miss Stainer proceeded with a laugh and a slight forward movement.

Instinctively Anne stepped aside.

The other apparently accepted this as an invitation to enter. She walked in and gazed round the wide, low hall with interest. The quiet austerity of it, the dark-panelled walls, the old oak chest and settle appealed to her as little as did the polished floor and the faded colours of the prayer rug in the centre.

"Your house looks pretty highbrow considering all things," she remarked. "I shouldn't have thought this would be the style of thing Mike Burford would go in for."

Anne was not inclined to be effusive with her unwelcome visitor, but she did not want Sybil Stainer there in the hall when any minute Michael might appear, with some of the men who were continually coming to see him on business.

She opened the door of the drawing-room, the prettiest room in the house in her eyes. Like most of the house it was panelled. The big windows and the glass door on to the lawn occupied most of one side of the room; a piece of tapestry hung at the end opposite the fireplace. There was a big modern chesterfield and a couple of capacious armchairs and an old spinet stood near the fireplace. For the rest the chairs and tables were plain and solid, and the short curtains were of blue casement cloth. There were no knick-knacks or pictures, but a great pink chrysanthemum stood in one corner and a log fire burned cheerily on the well hearth.

"Now, this is something like!" Miss Stainer remarked, going up to the fire and holding out her hands to the blaze. "There's a tidy breeze coming across the moor, and I hadn't got my fur coat on. I found it pretty cold walking up."

"Why did you walk up?" Mrs. Burford's tone was not encouraging.

"Because I wanted to see you. I've told you so, and I thought on the whole it would be as well we should have our first interview without any third person," Miss Stainer returned with a loud laugh. "At least that was why I came to that little one-eyed station of yours. As for walking up – well, there weren't exactly any taxi-cabs about. I got an old motor-bus that set me down at a deserted hole they called the Four Corners. I rather hurried off, for I knew if she had any idea where I was coming Minnie Medchester would have insisted on sending me over in the car, and perhaps have come over with me, and that might have been a little awkward, don't you think so?" She drew one of the big easy chairs up to the fire as she spoke and dropped into it. "You see, I am making myself at home, Mrs. Burford."

Anne herself did not sit down, did not move nearer that cheerful blaze on the hearth. She looked with unsmiling, sombre eyes at the insolently defiant face opposite.

"Why did you come at all?" she asked, her hands clasped together before her, gripping one another tightly as she waited for the answer.

Miss Stainer's lips, red with lipstick, smiled on still, but the menace in the blue eyes grew more definite.

"It isn't very friendly of you to ask that, Mrs. Burford." The hard voice was growing softer now, a silkier note was creeping into it that somehow made Anne shiver more than the hardness.

"I came because I wanted to tell you a certain bit of news myself. Harold would have written, but I said, 'No, better let me go, woman to woman – we shall understand one another better,' I said. Don't you agree with me?"

"I don't know," Anne said dully. The icy fear that had gripped her heart a few minutes ago had her in its clutches now body and soul together.

"Oh, I think we shall," Miss Stainer said confidently, in that new purring voice of hers. "We really must, you know, because" – her eyelids flickered – "I am engaged to Harold. We shall be sisters, you and I." She looked down with an affectation of coyness.

"Never!" The words burst from Anne's white I lips. "You shall not!" she cried. "I will stop it. I –"

"How?" questioned Miss Stainer softly, yet with the ring of steel beneath the softness. Somehow the fact that she was sitting down while Anne stood, instead of placing her at a disadvantage, seemed to put her in a position of authority.

"How will you stop our marriage?" she inquired again. "Harold has always been fond of me. He is a friend of my brother's. Formerly he had no money to marry on, no position, but now everything is altered. Isn't it natural that he should stick to his old love?"

"He shall not marry you," Anne reiterated.

Miss Stainer's eyes narrowed like those of a cat about to strike. "I think he will. I fancy you will not be able to prevent it. No, the only thing for you to do now is to bow to the inevitable. You are going to tell people you are delighted with the engagement. You are going to ask me to stay with you so that you may become better acquainted with your future sister-in-law."

"What!" Anne laughed scornfully. "Certainly you are not going to stay here. What do you suppose my husband would say if I suggested such a thing?"

Miss Stainer shrugged her shoulders.

"I have not the slightest idea. Wouldn't he think it the most natural thing in the world that you should ask your brother's fiancée to pay you a visit?"

"It would depend on the fiancée," Anne said with brutal frankness. "In this case you must remember that my husband knows you."

"Ah! So he does – poor Mike Burford!" Stainer said with a slightly contemptuous accent that brought the blood hotly scarlet to Anne's cheeks, a flush that ebbed as swiftly as it came as the cruel voice went on: "Then perhaps – why not? – it will be best to tell him the truth." The amusement in the cold blue eyes grew and strengthened. "Who was it said the truth is always the safest?" the mocking voice went on. "Shall we try it? Will you tell him? What do you say?"

"Say?" Anne cried with sudden passion. "Say I would die first."

"Ah, die!" Miss Stainer said softly in that slow, drawling voice. "We all say we should like to die when everything does not turn out just as we have planned it should. But there are different ways of dying. Have you ever thought of them, Mrs. Burford?" She put up her hands and clasped her firm white throat. "One way is to have something tight put round here – to choke and choke and never get one's breath. It must be pretty bad that. And they do hang a lot of people nowadays. And a man wouldn't like to have his brother-in-law hanged."

"Stop!" Anne raised her clasped hands above her head, then brought them down heavily.

For a second the girl before her quailed; then in a moment she recovered herself.

"So I think he might wish you to welcome your sister-in-law, Mrs. Burford."

Anne pulled herself together. After all, she told herself, this girl must be talking at random. It was – it must be – the merest guess-work.

"I cannot prevent my brother doing what he likes," she said quietly, "but I can at least choose my own friends."

"Your own friends!" Miss Stainer laughed; aloud. "I don't want your friendship," she said scornfully. "I should probably be bored to extinction. But I don't mean to marry a man and have his family look down on me. So you had better make up your mind to accept me as Harold's wife without any more bother. You will have to do it in the end whether you like it or not."

Anne did not speak. One look she gave the sneering face before her – a look that spoke of contempt unutterable. Then her eyes dropped. She turned towards the door.

Miss Stainer's face went faintly red beneath its powder. She stood up. For a moment she looked as if she were going to pass Anne, to go out of the house. Then she stopped, she gazed straight into the white, haughty face before her and said in a voice that shook with anger:

"It's an ill wind that blows nobody good. Saunderson's death was a godsend – to somebody! Wasn't it, Mrs. Burford?"

CHAPTER XI

"'Pon my soul, Minnie, I can't understand you." Lord Medchester stared at his wife I and then rubbed his domed forehead with his hands, forgetful of the fact that he had no hair. His baldness was a continual marvel to Lord Medchester.

Lady Medchester sighed. It was obvious in spite of her make-up that she had grown considerably paler of late. She was thinner, too, and her eyes had a haunted, terrified look as she gazed round.

"How much longer is this girl Stainer going to stay here?" Lord Medchester pursued.

Lady Medchester did not look at him; she turned her head away.

"Oh, not long. She is going on to Anne very soon."

"I wonder whether Burford will stand her," his lordship commented.

"Well, she is going to marry Harold," Lady Medchester said gravely.

Her husband shrugged his shoulders.

"Because Harold is going to make a fool of himself is no reason for the rest of the world to put up with her. I should have thought you, and Anne too, would have been moving heaven and earth to prevent such a disastrous marriage. The girl's a rotter if ever I saw one."

Still Lady Medchester did not look at him. Her eyes, gazing straight through the window, watched the tall rhododendrons at the side of the Dutch garden; the group of pines beyond that stood round the summer-house where Robert Saunderson was murdered.

"You are not fair to her," she said in a muffled tone. "She is not a bad sort, Sybil."

"Isn't she?" his lordship scoffed unbelievingly. "Then I don't know a bad one when I see her. That's all there is to that. Who's paying for all these clothes she's buying?"

Lady Medchester gave an affected little laugh.

"How funny you are, Medchester. How should I know? Her brother, I should imagine."

"Well, I shouldn't, then," his lordship retorted bluntly. "Stainer's pretty well down on his uppers, I can tell you that. The girl couldn't squeeze a penny out of him."

"Well, perhaps the tradespeople are giving her credit as she is going to marry a rich man. I don't know."

"Well, I do," Lord Medchester returned.

"Rich man, indeed! Let me tell you that Harold will be a lucky fellow if he manages to turn himself round this next year. These damned death-duties take every penny you have. It's bad enough when the estates pass from father to son. But when it's a matter of cousins about six times removed such as Harold and old Lord Gorth, why it is a case of skinning the eel. But I can't believe Harold will make such a fool of himself as to marry Sybil Stainer yet."

"I am sure he means to," Lady Medchester said positively. "He is going to get a special licence and the wedding will be very soon. I should like to have it here."

"What!" His lordship stuck a pair of eye-glasses on the bridge of his Roman nose. "Well, then, I can tell you I won't have it. Married here, indeed! I think I see myself marching up the aisle with that Stainer girl hanging on my arm! and the choir singing the 'Voice that breathed o'er Eden,' or whatever it is they do sing. It's no go, Minnie. And you can tell her I say so. Or I will myself, if you like."

"Ah, no!" The interjection was so loud and decided that it sounded almost like a shriek. "You must not, indeed you must not! I won't have her feelings hurt."

"Sybil's feelings! She ain't got any," scoffed his lordship. "Rhinoceros hide, I should think, or she'd have been out of here before now. Hello! What's this chap after? Seems in a deuce of a hurry!"

Lady Medchester turned her head. Her husband was looking through the end window, which gave a view of the drive.

Superintendent Mayer had just come into sight, swinging along at a trot which made his red face and rotund figure look ludicrous.

"Bless my life! I wonder what he wants. I think I'll go and see. Getting a bit fat for trotting, I shall tell him."

Lady Medchester stared at him.

"Why do you suppose he is hurrying like that?"

"Lord! How can I tell?" her husband responded. "Looks as if he were a bit balmy. Anyway, I will toddle down and meet him. He may have found something that will show who did Saunderson in."

"I wonder –" Lady Medchester drew a deep breath as she strained her eyes on the hurrying figure. "I – I don't see how he could, do you?"

"Don't see who could what?" his lordship responded vaguely. "Oh, I see. Mayer couldn't find out who did Saunderson in, you mean? I wouldn't be so sure of that. Mayer ain't such a fool as he looks, not by any means."

He dashed out of the room as he spoke, banging the door to behind him.

Lady Medchester's eyes widened and darkened as she stared after him. She drew her handkerchief across her lips, rubbing off the scarlet lipstick. "Has he found out anything? Merciful heavens, what has he found out?"

Meanwhile, downstairs, his lordship strolled out at the hall door just in time to meet Superintendent Mayer.

"Hello, Mayer," he began genially. "Doin' the double fox-trot, aren't you? A bit warm, I should say?"

"Well, yes, my lord." The superintendent mopped his perspiring face. "A warmish day it is, too, for the time of the year. I'm in a bit of a hurry, my lord."

"The devil you are! Must say I thought you looked like it," responded his lordship. "What's up, Mayer? Spotted the blighter that did Saunderson in?"

The superintendent went on mopping himself for a minute or two without speaking. At last he said slowly:

"No-a! I can't say I ha' done that, my lord. Not exactly, that is to say. But I ha' foun' out that as may help to find it out."

"I'm damned glad to hear it," said his lordship heartily. "What is it, Mayer?"

The superintendent eyed him doubtfully.

"I don't know as I ought to say, my lord, not just now like. It mayn't mean anything. Then I again it may. But, my lord –"

"Oh, please yourself!" his lordship said somewhat huffily. "Don't you let the beggar slip, that's all."

"I was a-going to say as your lordship said I might use the phone." Superintendent Mayer's eyes were glancing sharply at the other's face.

"An' I were a deal nearer here than to the police station, so I thought I would just come on here an' see if I could get a trunk call through. It would save time, and time is money, as your lordship knows."

"I should like to catch the blighter that said so," his lordship ejaculated wrathfully. "I have always had plenty of the one and precious little of the other. I have never found I could change 'em."

"Well, it is just a saying, my lord," the superintendent agreed politely. "There's a lot o' such, an' I don't know as there's much sense in 'em. But about the telephone, my lord?"

"Oh, you are welcome to use the phone as much as you like," his lordship said graciously. "Here's the darned thing," leading the way to the inner hall and pointing to the telephone standing on a small table by the open window. "You may be some time getting on, but there's a chair at hand. Sit down and take it easy after your exertions, and when you've finished there will be a glass of beer for you in the justice-room." His lordship went across to the justice-room as he spoke.

Superintendent Mayer got his trunk call through more quickly than he anticipated. He lowered his voice considerably, but certain words could have been heard distinctly if anyone had been listening.

"Room 5 ... That Inspector Stoddart?; Mayer speaking ... Yes, important – very –, best clue we've got yet ... Can you come down at once? ... Could you come down to-night? ... Yes. I've got a line. Sure thing – motive? Good and plenty ... Yes, the five o'clock. I'll be at the station to meet you. That's all."

The superintendent rang off, and then remembering Lord Medchester's alluring invitation to the justice-room turned his steps there. Lord Medchester was standing with his back to him, apparently staring with absorbed interest at a map of the county hanging on the wall near the fireplace. He turned as he heard the superintendent's ponderous movements.

"Come along, Mayer. You will be glad of something to drink. You are a bit long in the tooth to go trotting about like a two-year-old after murderers or what not. We are none of us getting younger, you know. Sit down and rest yourself." He rang the bell. "Sit down, man. The drink will be here in a moment. Did you get on to the inspector chap?"

"Ay, my lord, I did."

He waited a minute, while a footman deposited on the table a tray with glasses and a foaming jug of beer.

Lord Medchester poured out a bumping glass and pushed it across. "Well, what did he say?"

The inspector, my lord? He's coming down by the next train."

Lord Medchester raised his eyebrows.

"He thinks your news important, then?"

"He doesn't know what it is yet – not rightly, that is to say," the superintendent said slowly. "But he's aware that I shouldn't send for him if it wasn't important."

"I suppose not," Lord Medchester agreed. "I'm just about consumed by curiosity, Mayer. When shall you let us into the secret? Her ladyship will give me no peace till she knows it."

A slow smile overspread the superintendent's features.

"Ay, my lord, I know what it is myself. I expect the womenkind be pretty much alike whether they are ladies or not."

"The Colonel's lady and Judy O'Grady," Lord Medchester muttered. "Well, you would be safe in trusting me, Mayer."

The superintendent hesitated. He realized that beneath his jesting manner Lord Medchester was distinctly anxious to know the nature of his latest discovery. A Holford man born and bred, some of the old feudal feeling still existed in him; he felt more than half inclined to gratify his lordship. He opened his mouth to speak, then the recollection of Inspector Stoddart's warnings as to absolute silence regarding the case to all the inhabitants of Holford Hall recurred to him. With a snap he shut his mouth again.

"I'll do my best to let you know about it, my lord, when I ha' spoke to the inspector," he promised.

His lordship smiled pleasantly.

"Well, so long, Mayer. I shall look for a visit from you and Stoddart soon after he gets here."

The superintendent hurried off down the drive. Lord Medchester watched him for a minute or two, then he too went out, and crossing towards the Dutch garden immediately caught sight of a figure coming towards him. He frowned as he recognized Sybil Stainer's brother, Maurice. He disliked seeing them hanging about as though the place belonged to them.

Lord Medchester shook hands in a perfunctory fashion.

Maurice Stainer was not much like his sister. His hair, instead of being red like hers, was sleek and dark, his eyes, too, were dark and set rather close together under overhanging brows.

"I am on my way to Newcastle and was just making plans with Sybil," Stainer explained.

"Lady Medchester was kind enough to ask me to stay a day or two here on the road, but I am sorry I can't. Great disappointment," he murmured. He seemed oddly ill at ease under Lord Medchester's scrutiny. "But I hear there's a chance of picking up a bit on the Pitman's Derby. They say Blue Button is a cert, and as he owes me a tidy pocketful it's a chance of getting a bit of my own back. I came here to-day because Lady Medchester and my sister spoke of putting a pony or two on, and I thought it might be as well for me to do it on the course. There's a chance the S.P. may go out, for there's a pot of money on Tailleur, and he was tightening last night at the Beaufort."

"Well, sounds a tidy sort of proposition if Blue Button is as good as he's reckoned to be," said his lordship. "I think I must have a bit on myself. Eh, what?" he added in an effort to make the best of it – though what the devil Minnie was up to in encouraging these Stainers was past his comprehension.

CHAPTER XII

"If you please, my lord, Inspector Stoddart would like to speak to your lordship."

Lord Medchester was idly knocking the balls about in the billiard-room by himself. He looked up with an air of relief.

"Show him in! Hello, inspector!" as Stoddart appeared.

"Good evening, Lord Medchester." The inspector hesitated a moment. "I asked to see you," he went on at last, "because I understand that Superintendent Mayer had a long interview with you this morning."

Lord Medchester frowned. "Shouldn't call it a long interview myself. He wanted to use my phone – as a matter of fact, it was to send a trunk call through to you, I believe. And he seemed a bit excited and beside himself, don't you know. He'd got an idea he'd found a clue to Robert Saunderson's murderer. But he was in a desperate hurry to tell you, inspector. Do you mean that you haven't seen him?"

"I haven't, Lord Medchester. And, what is more, he can't be found."

"Can't be found!" His lordship rubbed his forehead and stared. "What are you getting at, inspector? Mayer isn't exactly the sort of little chap to get mislaid and lost, you know – what?"

The inspector permitted himself a slight smile. "He is not. I suppose he has gone to see some one at a distance. But he didn't go home to dinner or tea. And though, as you say, he seemed very anxious to see me he was not at the station when I arrived, and I have had no message from him."

"That seems a bit queer. For he said he was in a great hurry. He went away from here at a tremendous pace. Must have been after something special. But I wonder he was not back to meet you. He rang you up from here, you know, and he told me you were coming down by the five o'clock from Euston."

"Did he tell you why he wanted me to come down?"

Lord Medchester pulled his chin thoughtfully.

"Seemed to think he'd got a line on Saunderson's murderer. But I don't know any more."

The inspector looked puzzled.

"I suppose he didn't tell you what his new evidence was?"

"Devil a bit of it!" his lordship responded. "Just asked if he could use the phone to save him going back to the police station. But he was tremendously bucked, don't you know."

"So I gathered," Stoddart assented. "You have no idea in which direction he would be likely to be going?"

His lordship shook his head. "No more than you have yourself. Stay a minute, though – he did say something about the Empton bus, and went off trotting down the drive like a two-year-old."

"And yet the lodgekeeper says she feels sure he didn't go out that way. It seems she let him in and he promised to see her on his way back. Said he was going to Empton and she wanted him to take a message or something. They are old friends."

"Well, he seemed to be making for the lodge as hard as he could go the last I saw of him," his lordship remarked. "Still, he might have headed off and gone along the footpath to the Home Farm. I have seen him talking to Tom Purling sometimes. I fancy they were by way of being cronies. He may have gone in to ask Tom's advice."

"No. I met Purling on my way up. He hadn't seen anything of the superintendent. Was rather surprised he hadn't, for that matter. I wonder if you would just allow me to ring them up at the station and see if they have heard anything since I left?"

"Ring 'em up at once," his lordship said graciously. "I expect you will find he is there all right."

But he did not turn out to be a true prophet. Inspector Stoddart's call was answered by Mrs. Mayer, voluble and incoherent. No, nothing had been heard of the superintendent since early morning. Mrs. Mayer could not understand it at all. Her husband had never been a man to stay out like that. No, he had had no letters that morning but official ones, and he had not appeared interested or excited in any way. He had not expressed any intention of going up to the Hall. It was his day for Empton, a neighbouring village. Nothing had been said of any change in his plans.

Nothing more was to be obtained from Mrs. Mayer, and the inspector's face was grave as he rang off.

"That's what it is," Lord Medchester said with an air of relief. "You may depend upon it that's what it is. He came up here first and that made him late for Empton and he has been detained there."

"No, it isn't that," dissented the inspector. "Jones told me when I went up to the police station that it was the superintendent's day for Empton and I rang them up from there. They had been expecting him there all day and he had not put in an appearance then. That would be round about six o'clock."

"That's a queer story," his lordship said, beginning to look concerned. "I told the old chap he wasn't exactly the figure for fox-trotting. And he'd made himself pretty hot racing about here. He may have brought on an attack of some kind and be lying ill on the way to Empton, or have been taken in somewhere."

The inspector shook his head.

"No, Lord Medchester, it isn't that, either. The superintendent meant to go by the motor-bus that goes through Empton on its way to Loamford. He would catch the one that passes Huglin Corner at twelve o'clock, generally had a bite of lunch before he started and got home by another bus about 4.30 for tea. He was a man of regular habits, was the superintendent."

Lord Medchester looked at him sharply.

"Why do you say 'was' instead of 'is', inspector?"

Inspector Stoddart looked surprised.

"I don't know. I suppose I did it without thinking. Well, I hardly know what to do next. I think I will institute a house-to-house visitation in the village and see if anyone has seen anything of him since he left here. If we don't find him in the village I am afraid we shall have to go through the park and gardens to see if we can find any trace of him about here."

"Go through the house if you like. I'm sure you're welcome," returned his lordship accommodatingly. "The poor old chap may have tumbled down in a fit somewhere. When a fat man takes to galloping about as he was doing this morning one doesn't know what may happen."

The inspector walked sharply down the drive. It was growing dark; just outside the gate he encountered Harbord.

"Any news?" he questioned.

Harbord shook his head. "We have been to all the likely places we can think of – Constable Jones and I – but nobody has seen the superintendent since early morning. Mrs. Mayer is in hysterics."

"Poor soul!" said the inspector sympathetically.

Harbord looked at him.

"What do you think of it, sir? I fancy somehow we are making mountains out of molehills and that the superintendent will walk in presently and have the laugh of us all."

"I don't," the inspector said, staring straight in front of him with a puzzled look. "I can't get the hang of it; but Mayer wasn't the sort of man to play tricks of this kind, and he was very anxious we should come down by the earliest possible train. If some news of him doesn't come along within the next hour, I shall get the gamekeepers to help me, and search the park and gardens."

"Why?" Harbord asked in a bewildered tone. "Do you think he –"

"I think nothing," Stoddart interrupted. "Except that he undeniably was at the Hall this morning and that nobody has seen him since – not even the lodgekeeper upon whom he promised to call."

"A pity it was practically dark when we got here," observed Harbord.

"I don't think it matters much," Stoddart said gloomily. "Anyway, there will be a moon later on and we shall be able to see our way about unless it rains all the time, as it generally seems to in this benighted part of the world."

But it was not raining when the two detectives with Constable Jones and another man from Empton left the police station for the Hall. Not one word of Superintendent Mayer had reached them.

The most stringent inquiries both in Holford and Empton had failed to find the smallest trace of the missing man. From the moment that Superintendent Mayer left Lord Medchester and started off down the drive he had apparently disappeared off the face of the earth. The lodgekeeper, repeatedly interrogated, was positive that he had not left by her gate – she had been watching for him, she said, as he had promised to deliver a little parcel for her in Empton. There remained, of course, the possibility that the missing man had left the Hall by some other way, but in that case what had become of him and where had he gone?

The further lodge and the rosery side of the grounds were both fairly accessible, but both were a considerable distance from the corner, where the Empton bus picked up the Holford passengers, and the superintendent had had little time to spare when he left the Hall. Why should he turn back from the drive down which he was last seen hurrying, and which was on the direct route to the stopping-place of the Empton bus, to leave the Hall grounds by some other way? It was a curious problem, and the more the inspector thought of it the less he liked the look of it. At the lodge they found the head gamekeeper and another man awaiting them. The lodgekeeper stood outside talking to them. As Stoddart approached she turned to him.

"He never left the park, didn't the superintendent," she said in an agitated voice. "Him and me have always been good friends, and he never passed without stopping to pass the time of day. This morning I wanted to send a little parcel to my girl that's married and lives at Empton and I was going to walk down to the corner and give it to the bus conductor. But the superintendent he said no, he was going right past the house and he would leave it for me. 'You have it all ready against I come back, Mrs. Yates,' he said, 'for I may run it a bit fine.' He couldn't ha' gone by and forgotten it, with me looking out for him all the time. No. You may take my word for it he never left the park – not by this gate, anyway, dead or alive."

"Did he seem excited when you saw him?" the inspector inquired.

"Well, yes, he did seem a bit fresh like," Mrs. Yates answered, twisting her apron about. "The thought come to me that he had maybe had a glass. But 'twas early in the morning for that, and he explained himself – 'I'm in for promotion, Mrs. Yates,' he said. ''Im as finds out who murdered Mr. Saunderson he's sure to get it. An' I ha' pretty well done that,' he says."

"Did he tell you what he had found out, or who it was that had shot Mr. Saunderson?"

"No, sir. Not if it was my last word he didn't. I put the question to him. But he only laughed. 'Ay, Mrs. Yates, but that would be tellin',' he says. He was always a man for his joke, was the superintendent. I – I'm hoping there's no harm come to him, like there did to that other poor gentleman."

"Oh, you mustn't think of that," the inspector said, assuming a cheerfulness he was far from feeling.

They all tramped in through the gate. Although the moon was up, the trees in the drive made it dark. The gamekeeper looked at Stoddart.

"Where shall we begin, sir?"

Stoddart waited a minute.

"The last place he was seen in was the turn just before you come to that old bridge over the hollow."

"Ah, that's where there used to be a pool years ago," the gamekeeper said thoughtfully. "I mind when I was a boy there used to be talk of an old mine shaft at one end of it. My father used to say there was more of 'em about than folks knew about, the tops just covered over with wood, and then earth and then grass growing. Time would come, he said, when the boards would rot and give way and folks would fall in. I wonder – I suppose – there isn't anything of that happened to the superintendent?"

The inspector wrinkled his brows.

"Doesn't seem likely. Why should he walk off the road when he was in a special hurry and fall down an old coal mine that everybody has forgotten?"

The gamekeeper scratched his head.

"Well, he hadn't any enemies as would have thrown him down – the superintendent hadn't. We have brought lanterns, but it seems they won't be wanted, for the moon's that bright."

"I dare say they will come in later," the inspector said, staring round and vaguely noticing the dappled shadows on the grass cast by the trees in the drive. Right round the park, masking the high wall that stood next the high road, ran a belt of trees and shrubs. They extended from the left side of the Dutch garden to the front lodge. The inspector pointed to it.

"I think we will begin there."

"Shall we begin right by the lodge, inspector?" the keeper said, beckoning to his man.

"Please." Stoddart nodded. "And I think we shall want your lanterns now. The undergrowth is pretty thick and the trees make it dark. We must see what we are doing."

They walked along by the side of the park, under the trees, throwing the light of their lanterns as they passed along.

"Don't look as if there had been any disturbance here," the gamekeeper remarked when they had gone a hundred yards or so.

The words had hardly left his mouth when the inspector uttered a sharp exclamation. Near to them stood an overhanging copper beech; close to it the bracken had been crushed and broken, and near the trunk a man was lying a little on one side. At first sight he looked as if he might be asleep. The inspector hurried forward. The gamekeeper flashed his lantern on the quiet figure. "It's him, sure enough!"

"Ay, sure enough!" the others echoed as they saw the broad face, pale enough now, and the burly form of Superintendent Mayer.

"Eh, poor chap, he must ha' fell here and died," said Constable Jones, blowing his nose noisily.

The inspector knelt down and put his hand inside the superintendent's coat.

" I am not sure that he is dead," he said, looking up. "I fancy I can detect a faint movement of the heart. We must get Dr. Middleton here at once. Constable Jones – No, Harbord, you will be the quickest. Send the doctor here and go on for the ambulance."

"I wonder now if he had a fit, like?" Constable Jones hazarded.

The inspector was busy unfastening the superintendent's rather tight collar. He did not answer for a minute, then he beckoned to the constable.

"Look here!"

Constable Jones was not a slim man. He moved forward slowly and ponderously and got down on his knees beside the inspector.

Stoddart turned back the superintendent's coat and waistcoat. On the shirt beneath was a dull red stain extending right across. Nearly in the middle was a small round hole.

Constable Jones stared at it, his eyes growing rounder.

"It looks as if he'd bin shot."

"It does that," the inspector agreed.

The constable's mouth dropped.

"But there's nobody in Holford would go out of their way to shoot Superintendent Mayer."

"Do you think so? What about the person who shot Robert Saunderson?" the inspector inquired grimly.

CHAPTER XIII

"Good Lord! The devil must be about the place!" Lord Medchester ejaculated.

He was staring at Inspector Stoddart with an expression of utter bewilderment.

They were facing one another in the study, so-called. Lord Medchester had been fetched away from his dinner to hear the inspector's account of the discovery of Superintendent Mayer.

"It is unbelievable – inconceivable!" he went on, rubbing his bald forehead. "Another man shot close to my house. It – it's damnable! What's the meaning of it all, inspector?"

"I would give a good deal to know, Lord Medchester. We can only hope that Superintendent Mayer may be able to tell us –"

"Well, of course," his lordship assented. "But while we are waiting for the superintendent to tell us the devil who shot him may have got clean away."

"I don't think so," the inspector said with an odd smile. "We shall comb out the village, and we have drawn a cordon round the park."

"That's a nice, jolly sort of thing, to have a lot of damned policemen stuck round your house. I beg your pardon, inspector, but you know what I mean."

"I think I do. But on the whole the police round the house may be better than the murderer going undiscovered."

"The very devil is in it, I should say," Lord Medchester continued profanely. "And it seems to me – it really does seem to me – that when you were trying to find the murderer of Robert Saunderson, if you didn't do that you might at least have prevented another man being shot."

The inspector coughed. "It is not so easy as it sounds; short of making the police go about in couples it is not so easy to accomplish. If we could only get the smallest idea of Superintendent Mayer's discovery, which he thought had given him the clue to Robert Saunderson's murderer, we should be in a very different position. You cannot recollect anything that can give us the faintest indication – put us in any way on the right track, Lord Medchester?"

"Not the very least!" Lord Medchester pulled thoughtfully at his upper lip. "I did my best to get him to tell me," he added candidly. "But it was no use: he was as close as wax. Shouldn't have believed it of the man myself. When he gets better he will tell you –"

"Ah, when?" the inspector echoed. "The doctor has not been very definite yet, but I'm afraid it's a bad case – a very bad case. There is internal haemorrhage."

"Oh! I hardly understood. Tell Middleton to get any bigwig he likes down from town. I will stand the racket. We must have Mayer well again. Now I think of it, I will motor you down to the Cottage Hospital and see what Middleton has to say."

"I shall be glad if you will, Lord Medchester. Two heads are better than one."

As they bowled down the drive in Lord Medchester's runabout, they did not speak at first. The inspector's brain was hard at work. It was only a few hours before that the superintendent, full of health and strength, had come down exactly the same way. What had happened before he reached the lodge? How had he been lured across the grass to the spot where he was found? These questions rang the changes in Stoddart's mind, together with another couple. What was – what could be – the discovery that the superintendent had made? And was it this discovery that had led to his death?

When they reached the bridge over the ravine; Lord Medchester stopped the car.

"There! It was here that I lost sight of him, just on the road. Hurrying along he was, too, as if he hadn't a moment to spare. There's a short cut through the shrubbery from here to the garden, but possibly he didn't know it, and came the longest way round. Why he didn't go straight on to the gate I can't imagine."

"No; it is but a step from here to the gate." The inspector looked round meditatively. "And yet in this short distance a murderer must have been lurking, waiting for him."

His lordship stared round apprehensively. "I wonder where the blighter is now? Nice, cheerful thought that is of yours, inspector."

Stoddart cast a strange and searching glance at his companion. "I fancy you will be quite safe, Lord Medchester."

"I don't know that I shall, by Jove," his lordship said, shrugging his shoulders. "As I look at it, it was because he had found out who shot Saunderson that Mayer was done in. Now they know the superintendent was with me the last thing, I suppose they think he gave the whole show away to me. I shall be the next one they will go for."

In the bright moonlight his face looked white and drawn. The inspector smiled slightly.

"In that case I fancy you would not be here now."

"Oh, I don't know. I have been sticking pretty closely to the house so far. Her ladyship isn't well, been going into hysterics ever since she heard Mayer was missing. What she will be like when she knows what has happened I can't imagine. Women are like that, scare themselves into fits. Not that there hasn't been enough to scare anybody about here lately. She won't be well until she has been away. I'd have taken her abroad, but she wouldn't come. Said she wouldn't go away until Saunderson's murderer was found. I had begun to think I should have to take her by main force. But now there will be other things to do. We shall have to find out who shot Mayer. You can't go away and leave the place to itself when a man has been shot just outside your front door, can you?"

"No, not very well," the inspector said slowly.

"I quite agree with you. I think it would be wise for both you and Lady Medchester to remain at Holford for some time at least."

His lordship looked keenly at the inspector's impassive face as he stroked his chin thoughtfully.

"I felt sure you would see matters in that light," he said.

The inspector made no rejoinder; his eyes were glancing here, there, and everywhere; his right hand was thrust into his hip pocket.

As they neared the belt of trees in which the superintendent had been found, his fingers closed more tightly round a small, cold object; every muscle in his hand and arm was taut and ready. Lord Medchester was looking from side to side, starting at every slightest sound.

In silence they drove through the lodge gates, where a policeman stood on duty, and turned up the hill to the Cottage Hospital. This was a recent erection. The land had been given by Lord Medchester and there had been a public subscription to build the hospital itself. Constable Jones was outside to-day walking up and down the veranda, which faced south, and where in the daytime convalescent patients might be seen taking a sun-bath.

Constable Jones saluted. The inspector jumped out of the car.

"Any news?"

"No, sir. Dr. Middleton is there now."

At that moment there came a burst of sobs and cries from the hospital.

"Mrs. Mayer, sir," Constable Jones explained.

"She has been going on like that all the time – ever since she saw Dr. Middleton."

"Poor soul!" the inspector said sympathetically. "You will want to see the doctor, I expect, Lord Medchester?"

"Yes. I must hear what he has to say. I must speak to poor Mrs. Mayer too."

He got out of the car, the inspector following. Mrs. Mayer was huddled up in a chair in the wide hall, weeping bitterly, a white-capped nurse was trying to calm her. She looked up as Lord Medchester came in and made a momentary effort to rise.

Lord Medchester laid his hand on her shoulder. "I am so sorry for you, my poor woman. But you must not give up hope like this, Mrs. Mayer."

Mrs. Mayer raised her head. Ordinarily a comely, middle-aged woman, to-day she was shaking from head to foot and her pale face was tired and drawn and tear-stained.

"There isn't any hope to give up, my lord," she sobbed. "Dr. Middleton, he said he couldn't give me any. And him the best husband and father that ever lived. Just put out of life by that cruel, murdering brute! Who could have killed him, my lord? If I could get at him!" The tears momentarily forgotten, she clenched her fists and shook them in the air.

"When we find him we will take care he gets his deserts," Lord Medchester promised. "And don't you be down-hearted, Mrs. Mayer. While there's life there's hope is a good saying. And don't you worry about ways and means. I'll look after you until Mayer is about again. And now I'm going to tell Dr. Middleton he is to spare no expense, and to get down another doctor from town, the best he can think of for the case, and special nurses that can help the recovery. Oh, we will have the superintendent saved for you, Mrs. Mayer."

A ray of hope lit up the poor woman's face. "Your lordship is very kind. I always said there was no one like you and her ladyship for looking after the folks in your own village."

"Oh, I don't know about that, but we will do our best for you now, Mrs. Mayer. But there's the doctor; I will see you again when I hear what he has to say."

Dr. Middleton had come quietly down the stairs; he held open a door at the back of the hall, and as soon as Lord Medchester and the inspector were inside closed it behind them. When he turned his face was grave. Lord Medchester began at once:

"Well, doctor, can you save him?"

The doctor shook his head. "No, from the first there was no real chance. But now the internal haemorrhage is increasing and the heart is weakening. It is only a question of a very short time."

Lord Medchester took a few steps up and down the room.

"It's the most damnable thing I've heard of. But I won't give up hope, doctor. Get a second opinion at once!"

"Glover is here now – from Empton, you know. His opinion coincides with mine."

"Oh, Glover," his lordship said contemptuously. "Wire for some one from town. The very best you can think of in this line."

"There wouldn't be time to get him here. As a matter of fact, I know of no one anywhere to beat Amos Treherne, of Leeds. But I doubt if there is time –"

"Send for him at once! Tell him it is a matter of life and death, and that he is to take the very fastest car and driver he can get. Deuce take the regulations. I'll pay the fine if he gets one."

"I will send for him, but I must warn you that there is very small prospect of its being the slightest use. The end may come at any moment."

"Is there any chance that he will recover consciousness and be able to tell us what devil shot him?" Medchester asked.

Dr. Middleton pursed up his lips. "There may be a conscious interval before the end. It is a possibility, that is all I can say. It is out of the question to be definite one way or the other."

He hurried off to the telephone. Medchester turned to the door.

"Well, I suppose there is nothing more to be done, inspector. I must get back to the house and her ladyship. Where are you off to?"

"Nowhere, at present. I shall wait on the chance of the conscious interval Dr. Middleton thinks a possibility. It is above all things important to find out whether the superintendent recognized his assailant. Any word he lets drop may give us the clue."

"Ah, well, I'm no good at that sort of thing. I'll toddle off now and send down to see how the poor chap gets on last thing. Come in if you are passing, inspector, and let me know how you get on."

"Certainly I will."

The inspector watched the other across the hall; then he went over to the small ward on the ground floor in which the superintendent had been placed. The door was open, a screen had been placed round the bed. The sister came to him.

"Will you tell the doctor that there are signs of returning consciousness?"

The inspector turned, but the doctor was close behind him and they went in together. Mrs. Mayer was sitting by the bedside now, her eyes fixed anxiously on her husband's face. The superintendent was rolling his head from side to side and moving his hands restlessly. At a sign from the doctor the nurse came forward with a glass of some restorative, but the difficulty of getting Mayer to swallow even a drop was great, and at last they had to desist. But his eyes were open now and there was the light of reason in them.

He looked at Stoddart; tried to speak, but no coherent words came.

Dr. Middleton glanced at the inspector and then took the dying man's hand in his.

"Can you tell us who shot you, Mayer?" he asked, his fingers on the weakening pulse.

The listeners held their breath as the superintendent tried to answer.

"Shot? Was that it?" he whispered faintly. "Some one called me – and then – my heart –"

The doctor glanced sharply at Stoddart. "You had better be quick!"

The inspector bent nearer. "You sent for me, superintendent. You wanted to tell me something. Can you remember what it was?"

The pallor of death was settling over the superintendent's face. "Tell – tell –" he repeated, the poor, gasping breath coming in painful sobs, "my lord."

"My lord," the inspector repeated. "Was my lord there when you were taken ill?"

They waited, every eye fixed upon the dying face, but no answer came.

Mrs. Mayer laid her head on the pillow close to her husband's. "Who was it that hurt thee, Jack? Tell us, lad!"

The familiar voice penetrated the dying ears. The fast-glazing eyes sought the familiar face.

"Eh, Polly, lass. You and the kids – no father."

"Eh, lad, don't thee give up. Tell us who it was as made thee ill."

But the momentary accession of strength was passing.

"Tell us, Jack," Mrs. Mayer urged. "Who was it?"

"It's hid – safe – tell my lord – you'll find –"

As the last word left the white lips the head slipped sideways, the mouth opened wide with a moan. There was a dead silence. Mrs. Mayer knelt by the bed with her face on her husband's arm. At last the doctor laid down the hand he still held and took out his watch.

"It is all over now. He is at rest, poor fellow. And you see now, inspector, that he could tell you little more than you knew already."

The inspector dissented. "I don't know about that. I really do not know about that. What is it that's hid – and where?"

CHAPTER XIV

"Well, that's that," said the inspector.

"And so another chapter in the Holford mystery is finished."

He and Harbord were sitting in their room at the "Medchester Arms." The inspector had his case-book open upon the table before him and was going over his notes.

"This last affair is most unaccountable," Harbord rejoined. "Its taking place in the park is so puzzling."

"Robert Saunderson was not far from the park when he was shot," the inspector said significantly.

Harbord looked at him. "The superintendent found out something that solved the mystery of Robert Saunderson's death. Why shouldn't we do the same? We have the same data to go upon."

The inspector took up a silver cigarette-case with a laudatory inscription upon it. He toyed with it for a minute, then took a cigarette from it, lighted it, and in leisurely fashion asked:

"Are you quite sure that we have?"

Harbord got up and walked to the fireplace. "You don't think the superintendent kept anything back?"

"The superintendent – and other people, possibly," Stoddart assented.

Harbord drummed his fingers upon the wooden mantelpiece.

"It is a thousand pities Mayer did not take Lord Medchester into his confidence. What did he mean when he said something was 'hid'?"

"A thousand pities he did not ring us up from the police station instead of going to the Hall at all," the inspector agreed dryly.

When Harbord spoke next it was hesitatingly and without looking at the inspector:

"At any rate, somebody must have known well enough what the superintendent had discovered." The inspector knocked the ashes from his cigarette.

"You mean Who?"

"His murderer."

The inspector nodded. "That seems likely. The superintendent might have been shot to prevent him stumbling on the truth as his assailant thought."

"I see! But the two things are pretty much the same, aren't they, sir?"

"Well, I have gone through Mayer's movements yesterday morning pretty thoroughly. First thing after he had had his letters he had to make arrangements for an inquest at Twistleton – old chap who had tumbled down dead in the street, presumably of heart disease. After that he had to go through a report from Sergeant Thompson of Bastow. Then he appears to have looked over his accounts, which took him some time, he having had, as his wife said, no head for figures. Followed an interview with Constable Jones, in which he appears to have given no faintest hint of any discovery in connexion with Saunderson's murder. As a conclusion he went his usual round, which seems to have taken him pretty nearly all over the village. He posted some letters, but I can't make out that he stopped to speak to anybody. Several folks, with that desire to be in the know which distinguishes so large a portion of the British public, say that he passed the time of day with them, but nothing more seems to have been said until he reached his old crony, Mrs. Yates, at the lodge. Then he was, as we have heard, excited, and throwing out hints as to his discovery which would lead to the solving of the mystery of Robert Saunderson's death and his own consequent promotion. Therefore, as far as we can judge, the discovery must have been made between his leaving the police station and reaching the front lodge, though it seems impossible to find out at present when or how it was made."

"Is it certain there was nothing in his letters?" The inspector shrugged his shoulders. "Nothing is certain, but Constable Jones swears only five letters arrived, and all those five are on his desk in the office. Purely official, all of them."

"It seems pretty much of a deadlock," Harbord said thoughtfully. "But –"

The inspector looked at him. "Speak out, Alfred."

"Well, as far as we have got," Harbord went on diffidently, "only three people had conversations of any length with the superintendent. One of those three, it seems to me, must know more than they have said."

"Those three being?" the inspector interrogated.

Harbord looked away, right through the open window, to where, through the trees, it was possible to catch a glimpse of Holford Hall.

"Well, there's Constable Jones and Mrs. Yates at the lodge and – Lord Medchester. If all these three would speak out I think from one of them we should get a hint of the truth."

The inspector raised his eyebrows. "Especially the last, eh, Alfred?"

"And the first," Harbord said slowly. "We have only his account of his interview with the superintendent, you know, sir. And he was pretty much on the spot when Saunderson died."

"He was," the inspector assented. "Oh, I have had my eye on Constable Jones, but I have gone through him pretty well with a tooth-comb and I don't think he had anything to do with shooting Saunderson. Besides, where's his motive? There were plenty of men, and women too, with first-class motives for doing Saunderson in, but Constable Jones wasn't one of them. As for Mrs. Yates, I haven't quite made up my mind about her. Remains the last of your three – Lord Medchester. What he knows he won't say, and how much he knows it isn't easy to find out – and he may know nothing. As you remarked about Constable Jones just now, we have only his account of what took place yesterday morning between Superintendent Mayer and himself. The same thing applies to Mrs. Yates and Lord Medchester. But one thing is clear: whatever the superintendent discovered was after he left the police station, or he would have rung me up instead of coming to the Hall."

"Yes, one sees that," Harbord agreed. "But he doesn't seem to have done anything but his usual trot round, and if there was nothing in his letters how the dickens did he find out anything about Saunderson's murder? Mrs. Mayer says he gave her not the slightest hint of any discovery before he went out."

"No; whatever he found out, he found out after that, I am convinced." The inspector glanced curiously at Harbord. "Didn't it strike you – but I am sure it did – that there was something rather significant about the superintendent's last words? – 'Someone called me.' Who called him?"

Harbord met the inspector's eye. "It makes one think, sir. We know who Mayer had just left, but –"

"Exactly! But if he was called back with some ulterior motive by the person to whom he had been talking – and we know who that was – the question that presents itself to my mind is, why was he allowed to leave that person at all? And we can verify that person's alibi through Mr. Maurice Stainer."

Harbord looked right away from his superior now. "As I see matters, it might have been done to establish a sort of alibi, to show that Mayer had got out of the Hall and off the immediate premises before he was shot."

The inspector considered a minute. "It might have been so, but I think the odds are against it. It was a pretty dangerous thing to do anyhow, and he'd have had to be pretty nippy about it. And whatever Mayer had found out about Saunderson's murderer it must have been fairly conclusive, or a second murder wouldn't have been risked."

"'Called me,' the poor old chap said," Harbord went on, taking up an ornament from the mantelpiece and twisting it about as he spoke. "Has it struck you, sir, that the distance from the bridge where he was last seen by Lord Medchester to the spot where Mayer was found isn't great?"

"H'm, yes!" The inspector nodded. "But Lord Medchester says he watched him from the house, and the bridge is a long way from the house."

"Nobody came through the lodge gate after the superintendent went up, according to Mrs. Yates," Harbord said thoughtfully, "so that the murderer must have been in the park or in the gardens."

The inspector shrugged his shoulders. "Not necessarily; the park is quite accessible in several places. I shouldn't imagine that the murderer would walk up to the front entrance and ring the bell; he could come in across the Home Farm, go round by the small gate on the edge of the wood, and up the rosery way, as Saunderson did on the night he was murdered. Or he might have come by the gamekeeper's cottage, through the old quarry, and across the pinewood to the park."

"I wonder," Harbord said thoughtfully. "I wonder; the trainer Burford was up here yesterday you see, sir."

"Michael Burford, h'm!" The inspector wrinkled his brow. "I have made a few tentative inquiries and I can't make out any harm about him. I will have him looked up, though. I was certain at the time of Saunderson's death that Mrs. Burford knew more than she said, and her brother – Lord Gorth, as he is now – was a young rotter, if ever I saw one. I shouldn't think he had the pluck to commit one murder, let alone two. Still, he was in with Saunderson, and a bully like Saunderson goes too far sometimes, and even a weakling like Gorth can turn."

"The proverbial worm," Harbord assented.

"But I think myself –"

Just as the last word left his lips there was a tap at the door, and the landlady put her head in.

"There's a lady to see you, sir."

"A lady!" The inspector looked at her.

"Who is it, Mrs. Marlow; anybody you know?" Mrs. Marlow shook her head. "No. She's a stranger to these parts, I should say, sir. But she tells me her name is Saunderson – Mrs. Robert Saunderson." The landlady lowered her voice as she spoke the name.

"Mrs. Robert Saunderson!" the inspector repeated. "Show her up at once, please, Mrs. Marlow."

When the landlady had departed he looked across at Harbord. "This is an unexpected development, Alfred. And yet I don't know that I am altogether surprised. Robert Saunderson was the kind of man who might have had a dozen Mrs. Saundersons hanging round. I wonder where this one has sprung from?"

They had not long to wait. The landlady reappeared, ushering in a tall, showily-dressed woman, quite evidently not in her first youth. She looked from one to the other of the two detectives with a smile that showed two rows of expensive teeth.

"Which of you two gentlemen is in charge of the Saunderson case?"

Harbord drew back. Stoddart moved forward and pulled out a chair for her.

"I am. Mr. Harbord here is my most trusted assistant. Mrs. Robert Saunderson, is it? Not related to –?"

"The Robert Saunderson that was murdered in the park here," the lady finished. "Only his wife, and wives don't count for much nowadays – never did in Saunderson's eyes."

"But," the inspector hesitated, "we have so far had no knowledge that Mr. Robert Saunderson was married."

"I dare say not," the lady returned. "He knew he had a better time if he passed as a bachelor – a rich bachelor. But we were married right enough in the Register Office up at Marylebone, a good five and twenty years ago and more. We had a nice home in Bayswater for a bit, then the dibs grew scarce and Bob ran off to the Argentine, and I went back to the stage."

"The stage! Why, of course!" the inspector resumed. "You are –"

"Tottie Delauney of the Frivolity," the lady finished for him. "I dare say you have seen me, inspector."

"I have that, Mrs. Saunderson," Stoddart rejoined, "and enjoyed your performance too. I little thought I should ever meet you and sit chatting here like this."

Mrs. Saunderson bridled. Quite evidently this was the style of conversation to which she was accustomed.

"He was away some time, Bob was," she went on. "And when he came back I didn't see why he should hang up his hat in my hall, seeing he hadn't attempted to keep me while he was away, I'd made a name on the stage then and I liked my work, and I stuck to it. Bob, he set up as a money-lender; he'd always done a bit of that in a small way, but now he began to make it pay. He went out to the War for a time, but he didn't stick that long – too fond of his own skin. After he came back he picked up a pretty good income by his wits. But I didn't come here to talk about that, inspector. Bob Saunderson had his faults, but, after all, he was my husband, and his murderer has got to be punished."

"He will be, if we can catch him," the inspector assured her quickly.

"And if that doesn't happen to be a 'him' at all?" Mrs. Saunderson questioned.

"The punishment will be about the same," the inspector returned. "Women have their rights, you know."

"I know. And some of them they've lost, I guess," Mrs. Saunderson said sharply. "I can tell you who shot him, inspector."

"Can you?" Stoddart allowed no touch of surprise to appear in his voice. "I need not say that we shall be grateful for any help you can give us."

"Oh, I can help you right enough," Mrs. Saunderson said with a nod. "The woman who shot Robert Saunderson was Anne Courtenay – Mrs. Michael Burford she is now."

"Mrs. Michael Burford?" the inspector repeated. "You have some proof of this assertion, I suppose?"

"Proof? Bless you, I know what I'm talking about!" the lady retorted sharply. "I saw Saunderson on the Tuesday before he was shot. I had seen a lot about him in the papers – there was his name in the society news every day pretty nearly. I saw he had race-horses in training, and you can't do that on nothing. So I thought it was his duty to do something for me. After all, it is supposed to be a man's duty to keep his wife, though it's precious few of 'em that do it nowadays, if you come to that. I didn't want Bob to keep me, but I thought he ought to do his bit. So I went over to his flat. He was nearly scared out of his skin when he saw me; pretended he thought I was dead. And then after beating about the bush for a bit, and looking mighty ashamed of himself, he told me that he had deceived me and that the registrar who married us was a friend of his and that we weren't really married at all. It was a lie, and I knew it, but it suited my book to pretend to believe him. So I said that if he would make me an allowance while I was resting he could wash his past out as far as I was concerned. Then when it was all settled he told me that there I was a girl, a lady, he had taken a fancy to, and he meant to marry her. She was engaged to some one else, he said, but he had got the means of breaking it off, and he was going to do it."

The inspector looked inquiringly at her. "How did you know he meant Miss Courtenay?"

"I went to his flat to find out," Mrs. Saunderson said, a note of fear creeping into her voice. "When he saw I was quite friendly like and not going to interfere with his doings, he began to talk quite freely. And when I suggested a night-club to finish up with he came with me like a lamb. We had cocktails and what not, and by and by I ferreted out of him what I wanted to know. He wouldn't tell me her name, but he said he'd got hold of her through her brother, who was in his power. She would have to marry him, he said, or he would send her brother to gaol. It would all be in the papers, for she was going to give him his answer that week. I didn't know about the murder just at first. I don't read the papers much, bar the theatrical news and the divorces. When I did, I didn't realize what it meant until I saw a paragraph about the new Lord Gorth, and it said that he and his sister, Mrs. Michael Burford, the wife of the famous trainer, had been included in the house-party at Holford Hall, when his friend, Mr. Robert Saunderson, had been murdered. Then I saw plainly enough how it must have been. It was Anne Courtenay he went to meet, and it was Anne Courtenay who shot him."

"That doesn't quite follow," the inspector said. "But we will have Mrs. Burford's movements carefully looked into; and Lord Gorth's while we are about it."

Mrs. Saunderson got up. "Well, with what I have told you it ought not to be a difficult matter to bring it home to Anne Courtenay – Anne Burford, I should say. But if you want me again I shall be staying here a day or two. You know where to find me, I shall be up at the Frivolity next week."

"I will make a note of that at once," the inspector said, producing his notebook. "And your address in Holford, please, Mrs. Saunderson? We might want to communicate with you at any moment."

For a moment Mrs. Saunderson looked embarrassed; she stared from one detective to the other. "Well, I don't know why you shouldn't know; I am not ashamed of it. I am staying at the lodge, and I am not ashamed of it."

"The lodge!" the inspector echoed. "What lodge?"

"Holford Hall lodge," Mrs. Saunderson returned, a shade of defiance creeping into her voice, "and I am not ashamed of it, I tell you. Mrs. Yates is my mother – I am not ashamed of that, either. Miranda Yates, that's my name – was, before I was married to Bob Saunderson leastways. I'm not ashamed of having got up in the world."

"Ashamed!" the inspector repeated. "I should think not – I can see nothing but a cause of pride in that."

"Oh, well, I don't know about that!" Mrs. Saunderson said as she got up and turned to the door. "But if there's anything you want me for there I am."

When the door had closed behind her Stoddart looked at Harbord.

"Well, this is an unexpected development. Apparently it complicates matters considerably, though we've only got her word for it."

"I suppose so, and I wouldn't believe her on her oath without confirmatory evidence!" Harbord assented. "Nice sort of lady, wasn't she, sir?

"She was that," the inspector agreed. "I can't help sympathizing with Saunderson. If I had been fool enough to marry Tottie Delauney I should have done my best to get rid of her."

Harbord laughed. "You mightn't have found it so easy, sir. What do you think of her story?"

"I think it will bear a good deal of investigation, and it will have it," Stoddart said grimly.

"It was she who was at the lodge yesterday, then."

"You didn't question her about that?

"No. That will come when we have inquired a little more into her story. In the meantime –" The inspector paused, and there was a far-away look in his eyes.

"Yes, sir?" Harbord queried.

"I think we will go over to East Molton and interview Mrs. Michael Burford," the inspector finished.

CHAPTER XV

The inquest on the body of Superintendent Mayer was held in the club-room at the back of the "Medchester Arms." A great crowd had gathered round the door long before the hour fixed for the opening. Holford folks were there in strength, for the late superintendent was a Holford man born and bred, and all his acquaintances were there as a matter of course. People had come by train from York and Liverpool, and even the London papers had sent representatives. The fact that it was the second inquest to be held at the "Medchester Arms" within a month was much commented upon. The connexion between the two murders was discussed, and all sorts of theories were put forward. The general idea seemed to be that some maniac haunted Holford Hall and gardens. A local paper created a sensation by appearing with, "A Modern Jack the Ripper" in big head-lines across the front page.

Lord Medchester, accompanied by Lord Gorth and Michael Burford, was among the first to enter. All three were accommodated with seats near the coroner. The jury, nine men and three women, were sworn in, and then departed to view the body in the mortuary, escorted by a couple of policemen from Loamford, who had been imported to fill the vacant places at Holford. They returned shortly, looking very white and shaken, and took their places.

Stoddart and Harbord sat just behind the lawyers engaged in the case, quite near the witness-box, flanked by a bevy of reporters.

The coroner glanced curiously at them as the proceedings began. The fact had leaked out that the great London detectives who had been at Holford to inquire into the murder of Robert Saunderson had come down again, and had indeed been with the Holford men who found Superintendent Mayer dying.

A solicitor from Empton, Mr. Robert Willet, appeared for Mrs. Mayer and the family of the deceased, and Mr. Belton Carter watched the case, for Lord Medchester.

The medical evidence was taken first. Dr. Middleton told them that the wound could not have been self-inflicted, and said that the superintendent had been shot by some one standing in front of him and at tolerably close quarters. He and Dr. Glover, who conducted the post mortem, gave the result of their investigation, and told how certain organs had been taken from the body and sent up to London to the Home Office pathologist for further examination. The result, he said, might be expected in about a fortnight.

At the end of Dr. Middleton's evidence, Lord Medchester was called, and in answer to the coroner's deferential questions told his story of the superintendent's visit to the Hall on the morning of his death. He gave due importance to the fact that some news had reached the superintendent which he thought might give a clue to the assassin of Robert Saunderson, and described how he allowed Mayer to use the telephone to summon Inspector Stoddart. The last he saw of the superintendent the deceased was hurrying down the drive for all he was worth, and had just reached the bridge over the ravine. No one was more astonished than he was when he heard from Inspector Stoddart the same evening that the superintendent was missing. He could scarcely imagine it possible that any harm could have happened to Mayer between the point at which he lost sight of him and the lodge – although there was a good step between them. Asked if he knew what could have induced the superintendent to leave the drive and go across to the belt of trees, he shrugged his shoulders and said he had no idea. The superintendent appeared to be in a hurry to get off to Empton, and he, Lord Medchester, watched him start almost running down the drive.

There was a distance of three-quarters of a mile between the house and lodge, unless you went by the short cut. He himself had gone out into the garden, where he found Mr. Stainer and talked to him for ten minutes or so on racing prospects.

There was nothing more to be got out of Lord Medchester, and he stepped back to his seat near the coroner.

Mrs. Yates from the lodge was the next witness. The old woman was shaking, and apparently on the verge of tears, as she took her place in the box and repeated the oath. In reply to the coroner's questions she repeated what she had told Inspector Stoddart. Then there was a pause. The coroner glanced at his notes. Presently he looked up.

"Was there any third person present when you had this conversation with the superintendent, Mrs. Yates?"

Mrs. Yates's ruddy cheeks turned curiously white. She fumbled with the edge of her long cloak.

"I don't understand, your worship!"

The coroner leaned forward.

"Were you alone with the superintendent when you talked with him? Was anyone else there?"

"I – I came out, when I saw the superintendent, to open the lodge gate," she faltered.

"I quite understand that," the coroner said patiently. "But when the superintendent was telling you of the discovery he had made was there anyone else there?"

Mrs. Yates burst into tears. "There – there was my girl, sir – Mary Ann – Mirandy, she likes to call herself; she just came out to pass the time of day with the superintendent for the sake of old times."

"Did this daughter of yours hear all the superintendent said?"

Mrs. Yates produced a voluminous handkerchief, and wept copiously into it.

"She might ha' done," she sobbed. "She wasn't there at first but she came running down the steps when she saw the superintendent, she having known him from a child, like."

"Why haven't you told us about this daughter before?" the coroner inquired severely.

After one glance at his face Mrs. Yates's sobs redoubled.

"I didn't know as it mattered, sir. Mary Ann, she just thought she'd like to have a word with the superintendent. There – there wasn't any harm in it."

"No harm at all," the coroner assented. "The curious thing about it is that you have not thought fit to mention the fact that your daughter was at the lodge to anyone."

Mrs. Yates chokingly reiterated that she didn't know it mattered to anybody, and the spectators, scenting a mystery, leaned forward to get a look at her.

"Was this the daughter that had lived at Empton?" the coroner asked.

"No, sir. That's my youngest."

Mrs. Yates rolled her handkerchief into a damp little ball and rubbed her eyes. "Mary Ann is my eldest, and a good girl she has been to me in the way of sending me money."

"Well, when you and your daughter had had this conversation with the superintendent, what did you do?" pursued the coroner.

"I went on with my jobs about the house, sir, keeping my eye on the gate all the time to see the superintendent when he came back."

"And your daughter, was she helping you with your work?"

"No, sir; she don't know much about house-work, don't Mary Ann," Mary Ann's mother went on with misplaced pride. "She was always one for the theayter. She was tired, too, that morning and she went and lay down."

"What time did she get up?" the coroner inquired sharply.

"Oh, she came down to dinner about one o'clock." Mrs. Yates put away her handkerchief with an air of resolution and waited.

Inspector Stoddart sent up a small folded note to the coroner, who read it and then consulted his notes again. At last he said to the usher:

"Call Mary Ann Yates."

There was quite a sensation in the court as in answer to the usher's call Tottie Delauney made her way to the witness-box. She had evidently got herself up for the occasion. Her pink and white skin, her scarlet lips, and her pencilled eyebrows, making of her face something like a mask, were quite unlike anything Holford was accustomed to. Even her ladyship and the visitors at the Hall did not go as far as this.

Miss Delauney's garments were all black. Her heavy coat of cloth with wide collar and cuffs of black fur was opened to display what seemed like a black satin shift, so short and skimpy was it. Her plump neck was encircled by two rows of pearls, and her fat legs were encased in black silk stockings.

The coroner stared at her. She was indeed an astonishing vision, considered as the daughter of old Mrs. Yates.

"Your name is Mary Ann Yates?" he said at last.

"It used to be," Miss Delauney replied with what was meant to be a bewitching smile. "But now I generally answer to 'Tottie Delauney'."

"Tottie – what?" asked the coroner who was no frequenter of theatres or music-halls, and to whom the name meant nothing.

"Tottie Delauney," the witness replied, raising her voice under the impression that the coroner must be deaf. "Of the Frivolity," she added in explanation.

"Oh, an actress! Mrs. or Miss Delauney?" The coroner paused.

The witness looked embarrassed. "Well – Miss – we're all supposed to be single on the stage." There was a faint titter from the spectators, instantly suppressed by the ushers. "But, as a matter of fact, I married years ago."

The coroner was getting tired of the lady. "Your real name, please?" he rapped out.

"Well, it is Mary Ann Saunderson," witness replied, her eyes dropping before the coroner's.

As the last word left her lips there was a sensation in court; even the officials turned and stared at her. Only the coroner and Inspector Stoddart remained unmoved.

"Any connexion of the Mr. Saunderson who was shot in Holford gardens a month ago?" the coroner inquired.

"His wife," the witness assented. "Leastways his widow, I should say now."

"Why didn't you come forward at the time of his death?"

Mrs. Saunderson did not look quite comfortable.

"Well, I was laid up just then with flu, and I'm not one for reading the papers at the best of times, and when I did hear – well, I hadn't known much of Bob Saunderson for years, and the papers said they had a clue and the murderer would be arrested in no time, so I didn't think it was my business."

The coroner looked at her. "What made you change your mind?"

Mrs. Saunderson fidgeted beneath his scrutiny. "Well, if you must know, I suspected that Bob had left a lot of money and, if there wasn't any Will, I should come in for some of it. So I thought I'd better see about things."

"When did you come to your mother's?"

"Three days ago. Last Sunday morning," Mrs. Saunderson went on glibly. "I was resting, you understand. There'll be a new revue on soon at the Frivolity and I am taking the principal part. We shall start rehearsing next week, but I had nothing on for a day or two. And, after all, he had his faults, had Bob Saunderson, but he was my husband, and I don't see why he should be done in and nobody punished."

A faint inclination to applaud this sentiment was instantly quelled by the coroner.

"Well, you came down to your mother's and, you were there last Monday –"

The coroner paused and, after a short conference with Inspector Stoddart, continued:

"Did you see the superintendent go in through the lodge gates?"

Mrs. Saunderson nodded sullenly. "Mother called me out to speak to him. I didn't want to particularly. I used to know Bill Mayer when I was a kid and lived next door to the Mayers. But I hadn't seen him for years and I wasn't anxious. But Mother, she would have me down."

"You heard the superintendent say he was going up to the Hall?"

"Yes, he said he wanted to phone and that it would be quicker than going back to the police station."

"You gathered his errand had to do with Saunderson's murder?"

"He said it had," Mrs. Saunderson admitted. "He said he should get promotion over it."

"Did he know you were Saunderson's wife?"

"No; of course he didn't!" Mrs. Saunderson said with a sudden accession of energy. "There was nobody at Holford knew, not even my mother."

"And you didn't tell him?"

"Not much!" Mrs. Saunderson shook her head vigorously. "I believe in keeping a still tongue, anyhow until I see how the land lies."

"What was the last you saw of the superintendent?"

"The last I saw of him that morning he was going up the drive towards the Hall. I watched him round the corner where the shrubs stick out in a point and you can't see the road any further. He said he would call in again on his way back – as Mother told you."

"And what did you do then?"

"I went back into the house and went upstairs and lay down. You've got to use your legs in this world whether you like it or not, so give 'em a bit of a rest when you can. That's what I say. Mother was in the house all the time. I could hear her messing about round the rooms."

"And you saw no more of Superintendent Mayer?" the coroner asked.

"Never a glimpse! But if you want my opinion as to who murdered Bob Saunderson –" she began.

"I do not," the coroner intervened sharply, "and if you take my advice you'll hold your tongue. There's such a thing as the law of libel!" And he ordered the witness to stand down.

CHAPTER XVI

After a brief interrogation of Inspector Stoddart with regard to Mayer's final halting words at the hospital, the inquest had been adjourned pending further inquiries. The most important point to be solved seemed to be what was the nature of the evidence that had come to the superintendent's knowledge between the police station and his arrival at Holford lodge and, equally important, through what sort of channel did he receive it? What connexion had it with his murder which so speedily followed?

That there was some connexion between the two murders seemed pretty obvious; so Stoddart and his subordinate decided over a supper of cold beef and ale at the "Medchester Arms."

"Same hand did both, in my opinion," the inspector remarked. "If we find the one we find the other. Considering all the circumstances, it's difficult to leave Lord Medchester out of it entirely; he was on the spot when Mayer, poor chap, sent his telephone message, and heard him mention he'd got an important clue of some sort. And yet he was talking to Stainer when the murder was taking place – that's true enough, for I've verified it all right. Then, again, the arguments I used with regard to Lady Medchester hold good with him; Mayer would never have been so pleased with the line he'd got if it implicated either Lord or Lady Medchester. He'd have been embarrassed, if you know what I mean. It's a puzzling case, Harbord, so many 'might-bes' and 'couldn't-have-beens'." The inspector took a final pull at his tankard and rose. "First thing to-morrow morning I am going to pay a visit to Mrs. Michael Burford, and you can come with me. I have an idea she may know more than she lets on, though Miss Tottie Delauney – heavens above, what a woman! – is probably overshooting the mark. Mrs. Burford doesn't strike me as the type that would do anything desperate. But it wants looking into."

Anne Burford was sitting down to answer her morning's letters when the sound of well-drilled footsteps on the gravel outside drew her eyes to the open window.

Her brother Harold had dined with her and her husband at East Molton overnight, and related at some length, subject to the corrections of his brother-in-law, what had passed at the inquest on the previous day. His story was rather confused – a faculty for piecing together a concise relation of events was apparently not his, but as the evidence had led to nowhere in the coroner's court it was not to be expected that it would lead to anywhere in particular in Lord Gorth's less practised hands.

The only noticeable point about it had been that never once during the whole story did Harold meet his sister's eyes.

Both of them had changed. From Anne's delicate, finely-drawn features something of the joy of life, the sparkle of youth had faded; but in its place there was a great peace and a tranquillity very different from the unrest, the anxious, troubled expression that had haunted the depths of her eyes since Saunderson had been found dead in the summer-house. Michael Burford, although to discover the solution of the mystery might well be beyond him, had proved a tower of strength to lean upon in trouble.

Her brother had more definitely altered, suddenly transformed from boy to man. His features, set in firmer, sterner lines, might almost have reassured Anne's doubting heart as to a lesson learned that would last him his life had it not been for this culminating act of folly in his projected marriage with Sybil Stainer, whom his sister abhorred with her whole heart. How much and how little did Sybil Stainer know? What was it that seemed to have placed them all in the hollow of her hand?

At dinner the previous evening, whenever Anne had mentioned his engagement to Miss Stainer, Harold had shied away from the subject, glancing at her with miserable eyes. It puzzled her. If this marriage was as distasteful to him as she believed it to be, why did he go through with it? In this unexpected heritage of his surely lay salvation? With the chief actor removed he had only to meet the bill, forged though the signature on it might be; without the principal witness it would be difficult to prove the name a forgery even if the question were raised.

There was an alternative explanation, but she turned from that with a shudder, resolutely shutting out the shadow that had mouthed at her ever since that terrible evening when

Saunderson, with all Harold's future in the hollow of his hand, had been found dead in the summer-house.

"You've married the right man, Anne," her brother said to her that evening as she stood on the doorstep watching him start off into the night.

"Funny though – how Fate turns things upside-down sometimes. You can count on me – all the way." With which enigmatical remark he shot away into the darkness.

Anne was on her guard when the well-drilled footsteps resolved themselves into the sturdy figures of Stoddart and his companion, though her heart sank at the prospect of a further and perhaps more rigid interrogation. She instantly made up her mind that no pressure on their part should make her swerve from her original statement. It was not the danger to herself that lay behind what Stoddart subsequently described as her obstinate attitude. Least said soonest mended is never more apposite than when attempting to fence with Scotland Yard.

"You are certain," the inspector urged with the steely glint in his eyes that had struck terror into more than one guilty soul, "that you neither saw nor heard anything that night in the garden that might throw any light on the crime?"

"Nothing," Anne rejoined firmly, though shrinking instinctively from meeting his eyes. "I took a turn in the garden and went back to my bedroom."

After all, that was true enough as far as it went, and not all the ingenuity of the inspector could succeed in pushing it farther.

"And what about your brother – Lord Gorth that is?" Stoddart questioned, keeping his eyes fixed on her face.

"How do you mean? I don't understand," she replied uneasily.

"What was he doing that evening – while you were out in the garden?"

Anne's eyes dropped a little more perceptibly.

"How should I know?" she said steadily. "Playing billiards or bridge or something in the house, I suppose. I thought you found out what he was doing when the first investigation took place."

"Do you know anything of his relations with Saunderson?" the inspector pressed. "Had he business dealings with him?"

Anne shook her head. "I don't think he liked him very much, but then I don't think anybody did. They had a mutual interest in racing. But wouldn't it be better to ask Lord Gorth himself?" she added distantly. "He can tell you a great deal more about it than I can."

The inspector, ignoring the rejoinder, paused in his interrogation and glanced at a page in his case-book. Then he said suddenly, looking Anne full in the face:

"Did you know Robert Saunderson was a married man, Mrs. Burford?"

The shaft drawn at a venture told. Anne flushed and caught her breath.

"I didn't know it – till last night," she replied haltingly, "when my brother told me. It came out at the inquest, he said." Then, pulling herself together, "I had never been sufficiently interested in Mr. Saunderson to ask if he were married or not."

"H'm! that may be," her interrogator remarked doubtfully; then as Anne's eyes met his he added more kindly, "Believe me, Mrs. Burford, there is nothing like frankness on these occasions. The police are here not only to find the guilty but to help the innocent, and they can't do that unless the latter make a clean breast of it. Otherwise the sheep and the goats are liable to be rounded up together."

But Anne shook her head. "I can tell you nothing more," she said stubbornly.

With a shrug of his shoulders the inspector turned away. There was nothing to be gained by divulging Miss Delauney's accusation till they had something more substantial to go on than her bare word.

"What's up, Anne?" Michael Burford asked when he came in to luncheon later on. "Anyone been bullying you again? I won't have it." He slipped an arm round her and drew her to the window overlooking a square-paved garden on one side of the house.

"The inspector has been here – questioning me again," she said wearily.

"Damn him!" was the frank rejoinder. "Send him to me next time, Anne."

"But he knows that you – I mean, he thinks that I – Oh," she wailed, "he tries to trap me into saying something about Harold –" Fearful of saying too much, even to the man who still held her close to him, she stopped in confusion, and as the bell summoned them to luncheon said no more.

At Holford Hall the midday meal was also in progress, and Lord Medchester, perceptibly chafing under conditions that were as unwelcome as they were inexplicable, was answering in curt monosyllables Sybil Stainer's lively efforts at conversation.

From his point of view the situation was becoming unbearable. The Stainer woman, as he called her behind her back – referring to her in his own mind in even less complimentary terms – was getting on his nerves; it seemed they were never to be rid of her! Her brother, undesirable as he might be, had sufficient decency not to appear at the Hall unless specially invited to do so by Lord Medchester himself on such occasions as made an invitation inevitable. But his sister had planted herself on them for days, showed no signs of going away, and was making herself at home in a fashion that made her unwilling host wonder how on earth his wife could stand it.

He had complained to her only that morning. "I found her in the library alone. She'd had the cheek to ring the bell – ring the bell, if you please! – and tell George when he answered it to bring her a cocktail. I don't mind my guests having cocktails, but I object to a woman like that ringing the bell as if the place belonged to her and ordering the servants about. I turned my back on her and went out of the room – damn it all! – you can't be rude to anyone under your own roof, and in another minute I should have said something I should have been sorry for."

"Well, she'll be married soon and that'll be the end of it," Lady Medchester had answered, "and in the meantime I can't have her feelings hurt."

"Feelings!" was the contemptuous retort. "Feelings be blowed! That sort has got no more feelings than –" His stock of similes failing to stand the strain of the sudden call upon it, he stopped and began again. "I can't understand you, Minnie. I may not always have seen eye to eye with you as regards your friends, but when it comes to a rank outsider like Sybil Stainer it's a bit too thick!"

"She is going to be your cousin by marriage, so you'd better make the best of her." Lady Medchester sighed.

"I don't believe it. Harold isn't such a fool – got into some entanglement with the woman and now is too much of a gentleman to sheer off. I'll see to it – a word in season and soon. Something's got to be done."

Lady Medchester, on the point of leaving the room, looked back quickly.

"You'll do nothing of the sort, Dick. How can you put your oar into other people's business in that fashion! Harold is his own master – and I have told Sybil she can be married from here in a couple of months' time. I don't ask you to give her away; you can go up to London and be out of it all if you want to, but I'm not going back on my promise. If the thing has got to be why not make the best of it?"

"But why the devil should it be? That's what I want to know!" Lord Medchester asked.

But his wife had already left the room and closed the door behind her.

So when a few hours later they and the unwanted guest met at the luncheon-table he was not in the best of humours. He was not accustomed to being flouted in his own house, and he rather resented – would not have stood it had life been running a normal course. Easy-going up to a point, hail-fellow-well-met with all and sundry as he might be, he had his reservations, and he was inclined to draw the line at the Stainers.

And here was Lady Medchester encouraging the woman as though to see her the wife of his cousin, the new Lord Gorth, was all that could be desired.

Eating the food placed before him almost automatically while he ruminated over the crisscrossness of life – and life had hitherto run in even and undisturbing lines – he suddenly became aware of the fact that his wife and Sybil Stainer were discussing the arrangements for the latter's wedding from his house as though that event were a settled proposition.

"Two months is quite long enough to wait," Sybil remarked complacently. "A long engagement is always a mistake, and Harold and I have known one another for quite a long time now. So if that will suit you, Minnie, we can get on with it."

Lord Medchester looked across the table at his wife, who avoided his eyes.

"Get on with what?" he asked sharply.

"Sybil means the arrangements for her wedding," Lady Medchester replied. "I am sure you will agree with her. I have often heard you say there is no sense in long engagements."

"Miss Stainer's affairs are no concern of mine," he replied formally, as the butler poured out his customary glass of port before leaving the dining-room. "I was speaking on general principles."

"But Minnie is making my affairs your concern, Lord Medchester," Sybil said with an arch smile. "It can hardly be otherwise when I am to be married from under your own roof."

There was an awkward pause. Lady Medchester flushed violently and kept her eyes on her plate. Lord Medchester glared from one to the other, evidently trying to keep himself in hand. Miss Stainer was the only one of the trio who appeared entirely unconcerned and mistress of the situation.

Her host finished his port and pushed his chair back.

"'Pon my soul, Minnie," he said at last, red in the face, "it's too bad to have made these arrangements without consulting me, and, what's more, with all due respect to Miss Stainer, who is a guest in my house, I won't have it. I don't like weddings; 'pon my soul I don't – tomfool affairs at the best – and Harold's too young; doesn't know his own mind; hasn't got accustomed to being a man of affairs." He moved towards the door, still keeping his eyes fixed on Lady Medchester, whose nervous fingers were drawing patterns with a fork on the table-cloth. "Also," he went on, a hand on the door-handle, "until this business is cleared up there aren't going to be any festivities at Holford. See what I mean? Rotten bad taste. First a man murdered in the garden, then poor old Mayer – known him ever so long – shot within a few yards of my own drive! And you talk of wedding marches, eating and drinking and what not on the place. I won't have it, 'pon my soul I won't, and that's that!" He opened the door, turned on the threshold and repeated emphatically, "Jolly well that, and don't you forget it!" And, having finished what for him was a very long speech, he passed out and shut the door behind him.

Lady Medchester turned a pair of distressed eyes to her guest. "He means it, Sybil. I always know when it's no use saying any more. He seems easy-going, but once he has really made up his mind he sticks to it – like a mule," she added after a moment's consideration.

"He will have to alter it this time," Miss Stainer rejoined calmly. "I intend to be married from here. Maurice can give me away if you like; after all, perhaps it will look better as he's my brother. I don't object to that. But I intend the future Lady Gorth to make a good start on her married career and" – she looked at the other with a meaning smile – "you, my dear Minnie, are going to do your best towards that desirable end," and, rising, she too left the room.

Lady Medchester watched her go with miserable eyes.

"What am I to do?" she muttered. "I can't go on with it, I can't!" Her eyes filled slowly with tears. "I didn't know there could be such hell upon earth!" She stared unseeingly across the deserted table. "If it goes on much longer I shall – shall face the music and make a clean breast of it. If I only knew how much she knows!"

CHAPTER XVII

It was a fine, bright morning after a wet night. The sun was forcing its way audaciously through the lattice-windows of the lodge, touching with gold everything within its reach, and Miss Tottie Delauney, responding to the call of nature, was inclined to be loquacious. Breakfast was in progress.

"It isn't so much what they say, mother," she began, spreading a piece of fresh bread left by the baker in the early hours with butter, "it's how they say it. Asks one all sorts of questions about little things that don't matter, and when one has got something to say worth listening to shuts one up with, 'If you take my advice, you'll hold your tongue. There's such a thing as the law of libel!' Sickenin' I call it. What do they want?"

"Well," Mrs. Yates replied slowly from behind a heavy electro-plate teapot that was the pride of her life, and only used on occasions such as this – a visit from the daughter who had done so well for herself – "maybe they know as much as you do, and don't want it talked about till they're ready. The police know more than they let on sometimes."

"They didn't know I was Bob Saunderson's lawful wife, anyway."

"You are not quite sure about it yourself, are you?" her mother asked anxiously.

Miss Delauney tossed her head.

"Bob was lying when he said we weren't married. I am pretty well sure of it, and anyway I am going to pay a visit to that Register Office –"

"Which the police is likely to have done already," Mrs. Yates interpolated.

"And make sure," her daughter finished, ignoring the interruption. "As long as Bob gave me an allowance and did the right thing by me 'twas as much to my advantage as his to be single, and I didn't care. But I bet he's left a tidy bit, and, if he'd died without a Will, who has so much right to it as his lawful wife? And anyway," she added, "I'm not sure I'd have let him marry this Anne Courtenay – 'twould have been a shame on any girl." A furtive slyness crept into her eyes as she added hastily, "Though if I'd known she was going to murder him she could have taken her chance. He was my own husband when all's said and done."

Mrs. Yates looked round nervously.

"I wish you wouldn't talk like that, Mirandy," she urged. "You never know who's listening, and with the police here, there and everywhere it isn't safe, I tell you."

"Who cares? I'm not ashamed of being Bob Saunderson's wife."

"That wasn't what I was thinking about – though there's something to be said about that too. But if you go talking about Miss Anne Courtenay that was – Mrs. Burford that is – having done the murder, you'll find yourself in trouble. A little delicate thing like her! Besides –"

"Well?"

"The police say whoever it was killed Mr. Saunderson did poor Bill Mayer in too, and if you knew Mrs. Burford as well as I do you'd know she couldn't ha' done one murder much less two. An' it's only guess-work you're goin' on at that. You better be careful, my girl."

Mrs. Yates finished her tea and, pushing her chair back, reached for a tray propped against the wall behind her and began to clear away the breakfast things. Her daughter looked on, making no attempt to help her mother, and lit a cigarette.

She then rose, strolled to the window and looked out, indifferent to the fact that the sunshine was playing havoc with shingled hair that was in debt rather to art than nature for its sheen, and a complexion that had seen better days. It was early for the visits of neighbours, and a mother was hardly worth "doing up" for.

"Bill Mayer's death upset my plans more than a bit," she remarked without turning round, "and if it hadn't been for you I shouldn't have spoken out so soon about being at the lodge. I meant to lie low till I found out how the land lay – about me being Bob Saunderson's wife, I mean. It was you brought me into it by calling me out when there was no need for it to speak to Bill Mayer. I didn't want to come, for all you told the jury I did. I could have been here on the Q.T. and let things take their course till the right moment arrived for me to step forward. Who knows what it was Bill Mayer had found out?" She paused thoughtfully, then added with a slight irritation, "You forced my hand, mother."

Mrs. Yates, one folded corner of the blue check table-cloth between her teeth while she doubled the rest of it carefully along the crease, was necessarily speechless for the moment, and her daughter went on:

"I grant you to have that coroner man shooting questions at you and the jury waiting with their mouths open for the answers is a bit rattling – more especially with that Mrs. Carthorn from Empton with legs like a pair of tongs sitting among 'em."

"I don't see what that has to do with it. The jury don't listen to the evidence with their legs, Mary Ann," her mother remonstrated without any idea of being funny. "And why shouldn't I ha' called you out to speak to a man you'd known all your life and hadn't seen for a month o' Sundays?"

"Well, anyway you did it; and when it came out afterwards that Bill Mayer had got himself shot not more than a few hundred yards from this house I wasn't fool enough not to speak up. They'd have found out sooner or later I was here – you'd never have been able to keep it to yourself, mother, when question-time began – so I went to the police and told 'em myself; and, what's more, I told 'em Mrs. Michael Burford killed Bob Saunderson."

Mrs. Yates turned round from the dresser drawer in which she was carefully bestowing the folded cloth, dismay on her face.

"You never told the police that! – then you're a fool, Mary Ann! I wondered when the coroner asked me how they'd got to know about you bein' here. Do you suppose Mrs. Burford's 'usband is going to sit down and let you talk like that? His lordship's cousin too! You'd ha' been a sight wiser to ha' held your tongue and let the police find out things for themselves!"

Her daughter turned on her fiercely.

"They'd never have found out what I knew – and that's a motive for the crime. That's what they look for first – the motive – and I got that out of Bob when I'd got a drop of drink into him. There was a girl who would have to marry him or he could send her brother to gaol. That was why he wanted to make out he wasn't married to me. I know how to put two and two together, I do. Miss Tottie Delauney wasn't born yesterday, I can tell you. There's motive there right enough – and the police can get on with their business."

She paused, arms on hips, chin tilted, and as Mrs. Yates stared at her dumbly added sourly:

"His lordship's cousin indeed! That'll not save her. Bob Saunderson was my husband, and I'll see she gets her deserts."

Her mother, removing her gaze from the angry face confronting her, glanced anxiously through the window beyond.

"Hush, Mary Ann!" she urged, terror driving the colour from her face. "Don't talk like that, somebody may be listening. If it's motive they want – what about yourself? How can you prove you didn't know he hadn't made a Will – and who but his wife would benefit by his death? There's motive there all right, and," she added tearfully, "the police know already you heard Bill Mayer say he had got a clue to who killed Mr. Saunderson. There's motive enough, Mary Ann! There's motive enough for the two murders – and you're a fool to talk so free!"

Mrs. Yates would not have been reassured had she known that in their room at the "Medchester Arms" the two detectives had just arrived at the same conclusion.

"That Delauney woman's story wants looking into, in my opinion," Harbord remarked as, having lit a cigarette, he wandered restlessly about the room.

"There's more than her story that wants looking into," his superior agreed, "and one of the queer things about this case is the absence of alibis. I've established one or two myself, but no one seems anxious to do it on their own account. There's Miss Courtenay, that was, for one" – he ticked them off on his fingers as he spoke – "and Lady Medchester, with what one might say worse than none, the two of them by their own admission absenting themselves from the rest of the party that night, but with no witnesses forthcoming to prove they were doing what they said they were, and one of them, again by her own admission, strolling about in the garden. In the light of Miss Delauney's statement that wants a bit more looking into – and it'll get it."

Stoddart leaned back in an arm-chair, covered in well-worn American cloth and slippery from the friction of more than one generation, and stared at the faded design of unbelievably impossible roses presented by the carpet.

"Young Courtenay's record – Lord Gorth as he is now – is nothing to boast about. He says he was either in the billiard-room or playing bridge. He gave the names of three people he was with that evening, and I've seen them all – Lady Frinton, Captain Maddock and Sir James Wilson. But they can none of them vouch for his having been there all the time, and the question is, how long an interval may there not have been when nobody saw him? Time enough possibly to get to the summer-house and back."

"And if Saunderson had his claw on him the motive was there – same as his sister, if the Delauney story is true," Harbord supplemented, Stoddart nodded, his eyes still glued to the carpet.

"Then there's Lady Medchester. I've got my own ideas about that. There's no doubt she was there – out in the garden – for all she said she was in her room with headache. That man Garwood will swear to that. Now what was she doing out there at that time of night – with guests in the house, and then saying she wasn't?" Harbord ceased his uneasy movements and came to a halt on the hearth-rug.

"What would she have wanted to kill the man for?"

Stoddart shrugged his shoulders. "How should I know? Jealousy perhaps. Rumour says she and Saunderson had been pretty thick, and you can never tell what a jealous woman will do – or man, either. But I don't believe she did it. Not, mind you," he added quickly, "that she doesn't know something she doesn't want to let out, and Lord Medchester too, for that matter, but neither of them, in my opinion, murdered Robert Saunderson."

He paused to light a cigarette, and the other waited expectantly.

"You remember Lord Medchester's account of that last interview he had with the superintendent? Mayer had got hold of something important – we don't know how or what as yet – and, although he said it might lead to nothing, he had already declared in conversation with Mrs. Yates at the lodge that his promotion on the strength of it was pretty well assured. According to her, he was in fine spirits – 'fresh' she called it – so much so that if it hadn't been so early in the day she might have thought he had been having a drop!"

Harbord nodded, but said nothing.

"Mayer was a Holford man," Stoddart went on, "that's to say born and bred at Holford, although he'd been at Medchester for some time. You know how it is in the country – the place looking on the squire as a little tin god. Lord Medchester owns half the countryside round here, and was a magistrate on the Bench. Do you think" – he paused impressively – "that if the evidence he had got hold of implicated Lady Medchester he'd have gone bald-headed to the Hall – to use the phone or for any other reason? You bet not! The man would have been beside himself with not knowing what to do – torn between his duty and disinclination. He'd have gone back to the police station rather than face Lord Medchester in the first flush of such information. He'd want to think it over."

Harbord nodded slowly. "I see what you mean, and he was on the point of telling Lord Medchester, according to the latter's account, what it was he had found out – would have, in fact, if he hadn't thought better of it, and was in good spirits about it too. No" – he shook his head – "whatever it was that had come to his knowledge it wasn't that Lady Medchester had shot Robert Saunderson. I grant you that."

They were both silent. Then Harbord added: "Funny to think that what's written on a chap's brain is no use to anybody else."

Stoddart smiled. "When he's dead, you mean? Exasperating too. Half a dozen words either to Lord Medchester or Mrs. Yates might have saved us weeks of hard work and brought a criminal to justice. But there it is. Must have been something he heard, or there would surely have been some record of it. But whom did he hear it from?"

"He got it, whatever it was, before he met with Miss Delauney, or it might have been connected with her."

Stoddart shook his head. "No, he got it, whatever it was, before he ran up against her." He paused. "There's another reason why we can rule Lady Medchester out. Whoever it was shot Saunderson, shot Mayer – all the evidence points that way. The poor chap had got something that would have given us a line on the crime, and the murderer knew it. Well, at the time Mayer was shot Lady Medchester was in her room, putting on her hat to go out for the day. I got it from the lady's maid without her knowing what I was after. A perfectly good alibi this time all right." He rose and laid a hand on the ancient bell-pull hanging beside the fireplace. "Talking's thirsty work, Alfred. What do you say to a mug of Mrs. Marlow's ale?"

"I've known worse," the other assented heartily. "I wish it would put something into our heads that would give us a line on this tangle."

He waited till an old-fashioned toby jug, crowned with bubbling foam, and a couple of pewter tankards stood on the table between them and then he resumed.

"If – remember I say *if* – Miss Delauney's story is true – it savours a bit too much of the film to please me – then one question that's been worrying us might find an answer. That is, what brought Robert Saunderson back to Holford when, his visit having come to an end, he had ostensibly left it for good?"

The other nodded. "Yes; that struck me too. If Saunderson was mixed up, so to speak, with Harold Courtenay and his sister, he could have arranged a meeting with either or both in the summer-house on the Q.T. From what we have discovered about Saunderson he might well want to keep the business as secret as possible – and if it was meeting a lady he'd hardly expect her to travel up to London to meet him."

"I wonder how much Burford knows?" Stoddart took a pull at the tankard and wiped his lips before speaking.

"I've wondered that before now. He married Miss Courtenay in the middle of it all, which looks as if he thought her innocent, anyway."

"I wasn't thinking of her so much as I was of him. His alibi is all right the night Saunderson was shot; but if Miss Delauney's story is correct he may have got a line on what Mayer knew that might implicate his wife. His movements on the day Mayer was shot are open to question. He says he was away on the downs that morning, and one of the stablemen testifies to having taken his horse from him when he came in. But the man can't swear to where he'd been to, and no one else either – so far as I can make out. So long as there appeared to be nothing to bring him into this business, I only looked into his movements on general principles, as one might say. But if this story is true, and Saunderson was using his hold over young Courtenay as a lever for forcing his sister into marrying him? He didn't do it himself perhaps, but Michael Burford comes into it good and plenty!"

"Gives him a motive, don't you see? Miss Anne Courtenay was engaged to marry Mr. Michael Burford, and if the latter had got an inkling of how the land lay – well, any man might see red and even things up. His alibi may be sound, but the motive's there all right."

Harbord looked doubtful.

"When a line of inquiry is more or less perfunctory," Stoddart continued, "one may accept a plausible alibi at its face value. But if – we must still say if – in Mr. Burford's case, motive can be proved, weak spots in an alibi become apparent and a more rigid investigation becomes necessary. For instance, on pushing the matter further, if it should transpire the evidence of the helper is based only on the fact that Mr. Burford said he had only been on the downs it means nothing; it's easy for him to have been to Holford in the time."

"Miss Delauney's story has got to be proved," Harbord objected. "We've only got her word for what Saunderson is supposed to have told her at the night-club, and even if that part's true we don't know for certain that he was talking about the Courtenays."

Stoddart rose. "Right you are," he said with a sigh, "it's a baffling case. So many in it – or seems so – and all of them slippery as eels. But there's one thing, Alfred," he said, turning to the other, who had also risen, "you remember those beads? I didn't let anything about them come out at the inquest, and Mrs. Burford isn't likely to have talked."

"Well, what about them?" Harbord asked, his eyes brightening with interest.

"I've got a notion about those beads," Stoddart said thoughtfully. "Can't tell you why, but I have an idea somebody knows more about them than she lets on."

"Who?" Harbord shot the question at him.

"Lady Medchester," was the answer, "and I am going to make it my business to find out. Presumably in her room with a headache, and the same lady seen by Garwood near the summer-house that evening, are two different propositions."

CHAPTER XVIII

Anne Burford sat with her hands before her, staring into the empty grate.

Life that had seemed so full of promise, of which in Michael Burford's love she thought she had plucked its fairest blossom, was withering into Dead Sea fruit in her mouth. She rose every morning with a dead weight of misery to be faced; went to bed at night thankful another day was safely past.

It had nothing to do with Michael. He was all she had pictured him, a kind, thoughtful, loving husband. Busy all day – and she hated an idle man – in the stables, superintending the morning gallops over the smooth, green uplands crowned with heather and stretching away to the west, often occupied in the office with the business side of his calling, or interviewing applicants that had to be dealt with personally, she had no wish to intrude her own worries and anxieties. Indeed, she felt it would not be of much use if she did, for unless she made a clean breast of it, telling him everything – *everything* – he would not be really in a position to help her.

He knew something. He believed Harold had not committed the murder. But how could she tell him to what extent her brother had been involved in the events of that evening without betraying the fact that he had been willing to sacrifice his sister's lifelong happiness for his own salvation? How could she tell him that?

The more immediate worry was her prospective sister-in-law, Sybil Stainer.

How much did she know about the affair of that night – and how little? The latter point was of almost as much importance as the first, for Anne had a suspicion that half Miss Stainer's insinuations were pure bluff; and bluff when applied to a guilty conscience may go far.

Whatever it was she had found out it was something that mattered, something that had put Minnie Medchester, Harold, herself, and who knew how many more, in her power. As far as she herself was concerned, she knew well enough what she feared. If she only had the courage to demand an explanation, or to defy her openly, it might prove that Sybil Stainer was banking on some slight negligible trifle, enough to give her an inkling of more lying behind, but not enough to justify putting on the screw in the way she was doing, and apparently doing so successfully. If Anne had had nothing to hide – and, oh, how bitterly she wished she had not – she might possibly have been in a position to burst Sybil Stainer's bubble by a few well-directed questions.

She was not afraid for Harold, as circumstances were at the moment. The future Lady Gorth would have no wish to bring discredit in any form on the man whom she proposed to marry, and through whom she would be able to satisfy her dearest ambitions. Harold now could give her both wealth and position. And yet there must be some screw she could turn even in regard to Harold, some lever that could force him to fall in with her designs. For Anne had no doubt in her mind that this marriage was as distasteful to her brother as it was to the rest of the family, and she thanked God that her grandfather, with his pride and fine traditions, was at peace in a world to which it was to be hoped no Sybil Stainers were likely to gain admittance.

But, if for some reason the marriage were to fall through, or Harold refuse to go through with it, what then? If the prospective satisfaction of personal ambition were to be changed into a desire for revenge, what would be the woman's attitude? What was it she knew that could be turned into an effective weapon to be directed against Anne herself or her brother? Sitting there with miserable eyes staring in front of her, Anne knew well there was enough and to spare that she might know – the point was, what did she know?

But to that there was no answer. The police, who should be regarded as friends by the innocent, had been transformed by circumstances into potential enemies. Once the events that had led to that assignation in the summer-house were known, and the relations between herself, her brother, and Robert Saunderson made clear, the police would see motive enough to hang a man twice over. He might have agreed to his sister's sacrifice in the first dismay at his own position, but what more natural than that when actually faced with its accomplishment he should have taken any desperate means of frustrating it?

She might herself believe – and did – in his innocence unswervingly, but it would be a different matter to get the police to see it in the same light. Also, if investigation were to be pushed to its limits, how was she going to exonerate herself?

The sound of a motor-horn and the throb of a car outside, followed by a ring of the door-bell, brought her back to realities.

The next moment Lady Medchester and Miss Stainer were announced. Anne felt thankful she was not called upon to face the latter alone.

"For a newly married wife you don't look over-happy, Anne," Minnie Medchester remarked, with an attempt to give a free-and-easy tone to the conversation. "I hope it doesn't portend a little rift in the matrimonial lute? I've brought Sybil over to see you. She's got a message for you or something of the kind. First time I've been here since you were settled. Quite pretty" – she looked round appraisingly and sank into an armchair – "though a bit too bare of furniture for my taste. The last time I came you had hardly got the furniture arranged."

"I am very happy, thank you," Anne rejoined, successfully avoiding an attempt on Sybil's part to implant a kiss on her cheek.

"Your looks belie it then," Miss Stainer sneered. "But we didn't come, Minnie and I, to inquire after your health. I have brought a message from Harold."

Anne raised her eyebrows.

I should have thought my brother might have been his own messenger," she said coldly.

"That's a nice thing to say to his future wife! the girl he is going to be married to in two months time. It would serve you right if –"

"Now, Sybil," Lady Medchester interrupted,

"Anne doesn't mean to be disagreeable. It's quite natural for a sister to be a bit jealous when her brother – her only brother – is going to be married."

"Do *you* approve of this marriage, Cousin Minnie?" Anne asked, looking directly at her guest.

The colour rushed into Lady Medchester's face and ebbed again.

"Why insist on the 'Cousin,' Anne?" she said evasively. "You are a married woman now, and there are not so many years between us when all's said and done. It makes me feel as if I had come out of the Ark."

"As 'this marriage,' as you call it, is going to take place from Holford Hall, you may take Minnie's approval for granted," Sybil said aggressively. "As Lady Gorth I shall have to live in this neighbourhood, and I intend to be treated decently by Harold's relations. Let me tell you, Anne Burford," her voice rising with her temper, "as Lady Gorth's sister-in-law you may consider yourself to a certain degree safe from – you know what as well as I do. But, if anything should interfere with my marriage to your brother, I should have no more consideration for you or your family than that!" and she snapped her fingers as an inelegant indication of contempt.

"Now, Sybil," Lady Medchester remonstrated, "what's the use of getting excited about it? Anne will be all right when the time comes. You can't expect Harold's relations to be overjoyed about his marriage to – to –" She broke off awkwardly, finding herself getting into deep water. "Well, as Lord Gorth he might have married an American heiress and brought a bit of money into the family. He'll want it before he's paid off the death duties."

"It's always the way – when a girl does well for herself, everybody's down upon her. What's Lord Gorth or his precious sister either, I should like to know, that they should turn up their noses at me? The Stainers are as good as they are any day. When I'm Lady Gorth they'll all be ready enough to eat out of my hand! I know them!"

Anne winced at the blatant vulgarity, and even Lady Medchester put up a restraining hand.

"Come, Sybil, don't talk such stuff. Goodness knows I'm doing the best I can for you – the wedding to be from Holford, and your brother to stay for the night and give you away. What more do you want?"

"And Lord Medchester swearing he will have business in town that day and won't appear at the wedding – and he head of the family!" Sybil replied angrily.

"Nonsense! Harold's head of his own family now, and you will have nothing to complain of." She rose. "Give Anne your message, and let's get back. It's getting late."

Miss Stainer, who was already regretting a loss of temper out of harmony with her claim to have the whip-hand, pulled herself together.

"It will be much wiser of you to be friends, Anne." The girl she addressed winced at the use of her Christian name. "I am not one to bear malice – but I mean to have my rights."

"Give the message, Sybil, and come along," Lady Medchester urged.

"Harold says it will be better if you and he don't meet at present," Sybil said with slow satisfaction. "The fact is, he doesn't like your attitude with regard to his marriage – and me. He thinks the less you see of one another the more likely you are to keep the peace. Harold doesn't mean to stand any nonsense about his future wife, I can tell you!" And with a curt nod she followed Lady Medchester to the waiting car.

Hardly had the sound of it died away in the distance before the door-bell rang again, and Anne, with a gesture of impatience and an effort to resume her ordinary demeanour after the trying interview with her late visitors, found herself confronted by Inspector Stoddart, this time alone. She felt unprepared, and at the appeal in her eyes even the stem eyes of the law appreciably softened.

Stoddart paused on the threshold, taking stock of the slender lines of Anne's girlish figure, the small, piquant features, the little hands, fingers entwining themselves nervously with one another as he stepped into the room and closed the door behind him. With a natural habit of appraising character and weighing the value of evidence, a vision of Miss Delauney rose in his mind, powdered, bedizened, all agog for the enforcement of her rights. If evidence were to be produced wholly dependent on the statement of either of these two women, whose word would he most readily take?

He had no doubt of the answer in his own mind. Moreover, he flattered himself that after vast experience he knew a criminal type when he met it. There would have to be considerably more evidence forthcoming before he believed Anne Burford to be a murderess on the word of the so-called Tottie Delauney.

But inquiry along the line her accusation suggested might yield fruit. In spite of the number of possible suspects, he and Harbord did not seem to be getting any nearer the solution. It might almost be said they couldn't see the wood for the trees. There would be trouble with headquarters if they did not get on a line of some sort soon, and there would be no harm in pressing Anne for a more detailed account of her relations with Saunderson. That in turn might yield something suggestive with regard to Lord Gorth, whose account of himself on the fatal evening left much to be desired – with his acknowledged proximity to the scene of action and an alibi whose armour was full of joints.

At Anne's invitation the inspector sat down.

"There is nothing to be alarmed about, Mrs. Burford," he began. "I have really come to ask you to do me a slight service. But first as a mere matter of form I should like to know where you were on the afternoon of Superintendent Mayer's death. Between eleven and twelve o'clock in the morning?"

Anne's fingers relaxed their nervous grip and she raised her eyes frankly.

"I was here, inspector, here in my own house. I remember it, because my husband brought me the news of the police superintendent's murder just before dinner that evening; he heard it from one of the stable-men, and I hadn't been out of the house all day. If you want corroboration," she added, smiling wanly – here at all events she was on safe ground – "I had a friend with me and she didn't leave until nearly half-past twelve. If you want her name and address –"

But the inspector put up his hand.

"Time enough for that," he smiled, mentally adding another mark in Anne's favour; he felt so sure one and the same hand had been guilty of both murders, and if Anne could establish this alibi she was at all events not guilty of Mayer's. "Am I right in thinking Mr. Robert Saunderson was not a favourite of yours?"

"You are quite right," was the emphatic answer.

"Why – particularly?"

"Not particularly at all, I just didn't like him." The blood rushed to Anne's face as she felt herself again on thin ice. "I don't like – that sort of man."

"Nothing against him personally?"

Anne gulped down her scruples and shook her head. Frankness would involve her brother; she lied bravely.

"And you are sure you neither heard nor saw anything suspicious while you were taking that walk in the garden?" Then, going off apparently at a tangent, "Were you wearing your crystal beads that night?"

Anne looked puzzled.

"No," she said slowly. "I thought you knew –"

"I knew the broken string found on the scene of the murder didn't belong to you, but you might have been wearing your own."

"I wasn't," she replied, still wondering what the question had to do with the matter, "and I have never worn them since. I hate the sight of them: they remind me – of all I want to forget."

"I can quite understand that," the inspector agreed in his matter-of-fact voice. "But I am going to ask you to wear them again. This is what I want you to do." And drawing his chair closer to Anne's he dropped his voice.

For a quarter of an hour or more the murmur of voices might have been heard in that pleasant room looking out on the emerald downs, across which Anne's husband at that moment was walking briskly towards the house.

He entered the house a few minutes after Inspector Stoddart had left and opened the door of the room where Anne was still standing, staring thoughtfully through the window in an effort to follow the inner working of the inspector's brain.

"That police chap has been here again, hasn't he? I saw him crossing the hill towards Medchester. Hasn't been bullying you, has he? What did he want?" her husband asked.

"What a lot of questions! I can't answer them all at once. He certainly hasn't been bullying me," she replied, making light of the visit. "He only wanted to know where I was the morning the police superintendent – Mayer his name was, wasn't it? – was shot; said he had to ask everybody as a matter of form."

"And where were you?"

"I was here – Rosie Meekins motored over, but wouldn't stay to lunch, so I had my alibi pat. To find oneself in such a horrible world of suspicion! It takes all the joy out of everything." She flung herself into a chair and hid her face in her hands.

Michael Burford dropped on to the arm of it and drew her to him.

"Don't worry, darling," he comforted. "Harold will come through all right. The police can't take him upon suspicion alone. So far as we know, nothing has been definitely proved against him yet. The only thing that worries me," he added, as Anne, yielding to the sense of security the touch of the man she loved gave her, dried her tears, "is, why Harold is going to marry that awful woman. It almost looks as if –" he hesitated – "as if she knew something he didn't want other people to know."

"Blackmail," Anne said tersely.

Burford nodded gloomily.

"Well, as long as she hopes to marry him, she'll keep it to herself," his wife rejoined, and finished sadly, "poor old Harold! Do you know," she went on, sitting up and leaning her head on the shoulder so near her own, "whatever it is, I believe Cousin Minnie must be in it too. Minnie has her faults – lots of them, and she hates *me* for some reason, and always has – but she wouldn't put up with a woman like Sybil Stainer unless she was obliged to!"

Two days later in their comfortable sitting-room at the "Medchester Arms" Inspector Stoddart and Harbord were coming to the same conclusion. They were quite conscious that a woman of Miss Stainer's type would not have been tolerated unless some very good reason lay behind.

"Since Garwood told his story we know Lady Medchester has something to hide. When she said she had not been outside that evening she lied, and people don't lie unless they have something to lie about, and Miss Stainer may have tumbled to what it is. I'm not quite ready to face Lady Medchester with Garwood's statement yet, but I have found out something and it was no more than I expected."

Harbord looked at him inquiringly. "What was it? Got a line on Mayer's source of information?"

The other shook his head. "No; I wish I had. But I got an idea Lady Medchester knew more about those crystal beads than she let on, and I laid a trap for her. It turned out I was right – and I was wrong."

"That doesn't seem to get us on much," Harbord said with a laugh, as he lighted up. "May one ask, sir, exactly what you mean?"

"What I found out was that she doesn't know as much about those beads as she thought she did. And, as you say, it doesn't seem to help us on overmuch. What I did was this," he went on as the other looked at him expectantly. "I asked for another interview with Lady Medchester, having first enlisted Mrs. Burford's help to carry out my notion. It was arranged for this afternoon in the library at Holford. I put a few questions to her more to mark time than for any result I hoped to get from them, and I confess I was a bit tempted to spring Garwood's tale on her and see how she took it."

"Why didn't you?"

"Because so far it's a case of hard swearing between the two of them. Garwood says she was out in the garden, she says she wasn't, and there you are. I believe his story all right, but we've got to get a bit more to go on."

"Well, what was the idea?"

"I had stationed Mrs. Burford outside the library door, and at a given signal – a loud cough from me – she was to walk into the room as if by accident, which she did – with her own string of crystal beads hanging conspicuously round her neck." He laughed reminiscently and lit a cigarette. "Mrs. Burford stood in the doorway as if taken aback at finding her cousin engaged; did it to the life, and I never took my eyes off Lady Medchester's face.

"When she saw Mrs. Burford standing there, the beads gleaming on her neck, she went white as a sheet, caught her breath, and stared till I thought her eyes would have dropped out. 'Why, Anne,' she cried, pointed a hand at the necklace and dropped it at her side, 'where did that – Why, I thought –' and stopped short, fearful no doubt of saying too much. 'Why, Cousin Minnie, what's the matter?' Mrs. Burford asked, genuinely astonished, for I hadn't told her just what I was after.

"Lady Medchester pulled herself together. 'The matter,' she repeated angrily and evasively, 'when you come into the room like a Jack-in-the-box! It's enough to startle anybody!' 'Whom do those beads belong to, Lady Medchester?' I asked sternly. 'And why were you taken aback at the sight of them?'

"She looked from them to me as if she could have killed me. 'I haven't the least idea!' she stammered, then realizing she was giving herself away, added, 'At least, I suppose they belong to Mrs. Burford, as she is wearing them round her neck!'

"But my little trap had succeeded. I had found out what I wanted to know."

"What was that?" Harbord asked curiously.

"Lady Medchester had imagined the beads found after the murder belonged to Anne Courtenay," Stoddart replied slowly, "and when she saw that string hanging round Mrs. Burford's neck she got the surprise of her life. What I should like to know is this – why did Lady Medchester get the shock of her life when she realized the beads found in Saunderson's pocket did not belong to Anne Courtenay?"

CHAPTER XIX

Mrs. Mayer was taking her trouble hardly. As she had passed out of the depressing, whitened walls of the Cottage Hospital where her husband had just gasped out the last words he would ever speak in this world, she felt the light had gone out of her life. Like other women of a certain type, she was inclined to give way to her feelings as long as there was some hope left; but, that once swept away, the calmness of a great despair had enveloped her, and she had arrived at her home feeling as though the bottom had fallen out of the world.

She and Bill Mayer had led such a happy life together. In that lay her one drop of comfort. She might be suffering at the moment more than many other wives bereft like herself, but whoever may be the presiding genius in charge of life's scales sees to it that the balance is kept pretty even, and at least there was no touch of remorse in her grief.

She could look back over the years without any of the gnawing regret so many wives experience in the first flush of realizing the time has gone irrevocably for undoing any regrettable act in the past.

She and her husband had had the usual tiffs of married life, and had made them up; no one could nurse resentment long in face of her Bill's good-humoured smile, backed as often as not by the remark that they wouldn't be entering for the flitch of bacon that year. But she had been a good wife to him, borne him children, and made his home a comfortable haven to come back to after a day's work. She had nothing to blame herself about in that way, and many a time he had looked at her, a twinkle in his eyes, and congratulated himself on knowing how to appreciate a good thing when he'd got it.

As a husband and father no one could have asked for better. Rising steadily in his profession step by step, he had reached the position of superintendent by a stolid devotion to duty and intelligence, not always apparent in country districts where experience is necessarily more limited than in large cities. He had won the respect of his superiors, and Stoddart had spoken no more than the truth when he said, "Those little pig's eyes of his see more than you think."

Mrs. Mayer was suffering from the greatest loss it is possible for a woman to suffer in this world – that of a good husband.

Betty Morgan, her daughter, married to a baker and living on the edge of the town, had been waiting for her mother when she returned from that sad visit to the hospital. She had been hastily summoned from her own home, and read all she needed to know in the stony despair of her mother's eyes.

"He's gone," Mrs. Mayer said, dropping into a sleepless night, and insisted on doing her share towards getting the breakfast and putting the house straight.

Betty Morgan, having a husband and children to see to, caught the eleven o'clock bus from Medchester town hall, next door to the police station, leaving her mother with a promise to return early in the afternoon. Both her sisters were in service, and her brother, following in his father's footsteps, had become a policeman; being stationed in a far-away Devonshire town, he could only hope for leave to come home in time for his father's funeral. She felt therefore that the care of her mother devolved for the moment entirely upon herself, Mrs. Mayer shrinking from seeing any kindly-intentioned neighbours in the first flush of her grief.

By three o'clock Betty Morgan was back at the police station.

She found her mother sitting in the kitchen, hat and coat on, and concluded with slight surprise she had been to the only decent draper's shop the town could boast to see about mourning.

But Mrs. Mayer fiercely repudiated any such suggestion.

"Not me!" she said, adding with a curious note of defiance, "I've been to see the place where your poor father was killed. That's where I've been."

"Whatever made you do that, mother?" Betty raised her eyebrows.

"Why shouldn't I? It's natural enough; and I had a feelin' somehow" – she hesitated and pulled off her hat – "I don't know why, but I just wanted to go and see it before every sightseer in the place went treadin' about there. It's sacred ground to me – can't you understand?"

"Yes, perhaps I can," the other said gently. "Not far from the lodge, wasn't it?"

"Not more than a few hundred yards. I found the spot easy enough by the description, leastways thereabouts. I knew I was right because –"

"Because why?" her daughter asked, hanging her coat and hat on a peg in a corner.

But Mrs. Mayer shut her mouth with a snap and left the sentence unfinished.

"Susan Yates called to me as I came back through the lodge gates," she went on, glancing furtively at Betty, "wants to come and see me. Very kind she was."

Betty nodded.

"But I asked her to wait a day or so," Mrs. Mayer continued. "I don't feel up to it. She had somebody staying in the house with her; I don't know who it was, but somebody pulled a blind down in one of the bedrooms while we were talkin'."

At the inquest two days later Mrs. Mayer learnt the visitor at
the lodge had been "that there Mary Ann Yates, or Saunderson,
or Delauney, or whatever she calls herself." Her own evidence,
being practically nil, she was quickly through. After informing
the court that the superintendent had left her in the morning
as usual for Empton, and had never returned, that was all she
had to tell, and when given she had been allowed to leave the
court and go home.

Then had come a visit from the inspector. That was two
days after the inquest, and the day before the funeral.

"I've come to tell you, Mrs. Mayer," Stoddart said, removing
his hat as she opened the door to him and following her into
the little parlour, "that there isn't a man in the Force who is not
sympathizing with you in your trouble. It's a bad job, that it is."

Mrs. Mayer's face hardened. She was too sore and her
wound too fresh to be able to look at things dispassionately,
and in some unreasonable fashion she was inclined to hold
Scotland Yard responsible for her husband's death. What was
the good of the police if they let honest members of their own
force be murdered in broad daylight?

So she nodded her head and remained silent. Inspector
Stoddart coughed and blew his nose; not because it required it,
but merely to give him time. He was not sure of what to say on
occasions such as this.

"I was thinking, Mrs. Mayer," he began again, "now the
inquest is over, and perhaps you may be settling down a bit,
there might be some little thing you might remember – all
you've had to go through is enough to upset anybody's memory
– that maybe might give us a line on what it was that came to
the superintendent's knowledge between his leaving you in the
morning and his meeting with Mrs. Yates at the Holford lodge
gates. A lot hangs on that; and you'll be wanting to track the
villain that murdered him as much or more than we do at the

Yard. Was he to your knowledge expecting to hear of anything?"

Mrs. Mayer shook her head. Her eyes travelled uneasily round the room, and something in her manner urged him to press the point.

"No," she said shortly, "there wasn't anything; not that I knew of. But Bill kep' his business affairs, as he called them, to himself sometimes. Not that he didn't trust me," she added fiercely, "but he liked to get away from them – forget he was a policeman, he used to say."

"I can quite understand that, and I'm sure you would have no wish to hide anything from the Yard, Mrs. Mayer."

The hearty assent expected by the inspector was not forthcoming. Mrs. Mayer dropped her eyes.

"Surely," he went on, slightly puzzled by her manner, "you would keep nothing back that would help us to trace the criminal?"

This time the reply came eagerly enough; a look of relief lightened Mrs. Mayer's pale blue eyes as she looked him straight in the face.

"I surely would not! I'd give years of my life to catch him! But I can't help you; I can only say what I said at the inquest – I don't believe Bill had a thing in his mind when he started off that morning for Empton. Mrs. Yates and that daughter of hers, besides his lordship, talked of his being in high spirits owing to his promotion being likely. Well, there was nothing o' that when he left me, and if he talked like that to his lordship and sundry, ain't it likely he'd ha' said something of it to his lawful wife? No," as her visitor rose, "if he heard anything, as you say, it was something he learnt that morning after he'd left and before he saw Mrs. Yates at the lodge. You can take it from me."

"I suppose I must, and thank you. There'll be a bit of a pension for you, Mrs. Mayer – the superintendent was killed while doing his duty. Not much, I'm afraid, but it's all to the good."

"Thank you, inspector," she replied quietly, "but I'm not worrying about that. His lordship'll see to it – Bill having died inside of his own gates, so to speak. He isn't one to let a poor woman suffer, even though my family is out in the world and all. Still a bit of pension will be all to the good."

The inspector nodded. "If anything should turn up you'll know where to find me," he said kindly and left, cudgelling his brains for a solution to what appeared to be now an insoluble problem.

As the door closed on him Mrs. Mayer glanced round her with a hint of secretiveness in her eyes. She was alone in the house. Her son from Devonshire was to arrive in the evening, her daughter had gone home to put a finishing touch to her own mourning to wear at the funeral. Instead of going back into the kitchen where Betty had left the potatoes for dinner peeled and ready for boiling, she slipped up the short flight of narrow stairs into the bedroom she and her husband had shared for so many happy years, and closed the door softly behind her.

Tiptoeing across the room, although there was no one in the house to hear her, she opened a drawer in an old-fashioned piece of furniture standing against the wall and slipped her hand into the back of it.

At the same moment the door below opened and a footstep crossed the passage. Mrs. Mayer drew her hand back as though it had been stung, closed the drawer as softly as she had opened it, and stood up.

"There's Betty back." She stood still and her eyes filled with tears. "I don't care," she muttered defiantly, "not if it is the law of the land! Not if the King of England was himself to ask on his bended knees. Yes, Betty, coming," she cried in answer to her daughter's voice calling her from below, and with a backward glance to make sure the drawer was safely closed she went downstairs.

"I saw Mrs. Yates in the town, mother," Betty said, divesting herself of hat and coat. "She says she's coming in to see you day after tomorrow."

"So long as she don't bring that daughter of hers with her I shall be glad enough to see Susan Yates," her mother replied without enthusiasm. "When's she coming?"

"I told her to look in somewhere about four o'clock and you'd give her a cup of tea. It'll be early closing and Frank'll be having his afternoon off, so it'll be company for you. Frank'll want me at home."

"You've been very good to me, dearie," Mrs. Mayer said warmly, "but I got to stick it out, I suppose – moving and all that. How I'll do it, God knows! Susan Yates lost her husband a matter of five years ago now, and his lordship let her five on at the lodge. That's the worst of living in a police station – very nice while it lasts, but the widow has to break up her home and clear out when her husband leaves her."

Mrs. Mayer looked round the little room and sighed. It was so familiar, and yet with life turned grey and the pivot of her very existence removed it all looked flat and unresponsive. The clock on the mantelpiece that she and Bill had bought when he got promoted to sergeant still ticked on with the same monotonous perseverance as ever, but it seemed somehow to be telling quite a different story. The chenille table-cloth that she had bought out of savings on the housekeeping one year and been a surprise for her husband who always had an eye for a bit of bright colour; the arm-chair worn almost through to the stuffing where his elbow had rubbed it; the broken bar round the fender which one of them had remarked ought to be mended at least once a week since it had got broken months before – all, everything reminded her of the companion who was gone. Life seemed very empty.

When Mrs. Yates paid the promised visit two days later she found her old acquaintance a trifle more settled in her mind. The funeral was over. It had been well attended, for Superintendent Mayer had been respected not only by his companions in the Force, but by the whole countryside. "Very gratifying for you, Mary," her visitor consoled, "on foot and in cars – the mayor and the gentry all turned out to pay respect to poor Bill's memory; and not more than they should do, either. He died doing his duty, and what can a man do more?"

The platitude seemed to bring comfort of a sort. Mrs. Mayer nodded and poured out the tea with a hand that shook pitifully.

"Hard on you having to move. I was lucky that way," the other went on. "Seems like tearing you up by the roots. Have you got a place to go to yet, Mary? Perhaps Betty'll take you for a bit while you have a look round?"

Mrs. Mayer shook her head. "I don't hold with plumping yourself down on other people – maybe where you're not wanted. There's a cottage belonging to his lordship on the edge of Holford Common he's offered me – rent free too – and I'm to move in soon as I can."

"Is the new superintendent appointed yet?"

"I don't know, but he will be almost at once, and I must get out of this," Mrs. Mayer said drearily.

"You poor thing! Well, I know what you're suffering. I felt just like that when my Tom was took. Mighty bad it is, whatever way you look at it."

There was silence for a moment. Mrs. Mayer cut her guest another slice from the loaf and pushed the butter towards her.

"Your girl's with you, isn't she?" she asked after a pause. "Funny her being married like that and you not knowing. To that Mr. Saunderson too – and he murdered."

"They don't seem getting on much about who murdered him," Susan Yates remarked. "I don't understand Mary Ann.

You'd think she was taking it to heart the way she goes on, and yet I know she isn't – not because she was fond of him, that is."

"She'll get a good bit of money, won't she?" the other asked curiously. "Bill told me as how it didn't seem there was a Will – died intestinal don't they call it? – and the wife'll get most of what's going."

But Mrs. Yates felt herself to be on thin ice and disinclined to discuss the point. Mary Ann had done nothing so far as she knew to establish her claims as Saunderson's widow, and, with a slippery customer such as he had been, there was no saying whether the form of marriage gone through at the Marylebone Register Office might not prove to have been a sham. Saunderson himself had said it was, but Mary Ann had not believed him. At any further reference to the subject her daughter turned crusty and said there was time enough to go into the rights and wrongs of it later on.

"She shuts herself up in her room and won't see anybody," Mrs. Yates went on evasively, "and goes white if you so much as mention the police. She's talked too free to the police as it is, in my opinion, and I told her so, and ever since she keeps her mouth shut like a mouse-trap and won't speak."

"That's a sight better than talking too much," Mrs. Mayer replied with the wisdom born of many years' close contact with a member of His Majesty's police force.

"Truth is, if you ask me," the other observed, "I believe she's frightened, and it was I that did it. There's a lot of talk about motive these days, and if it comes to motive – who's going to benefit by Saunderson's death more than his wife?" She glanced over her shoulder and lowered her voice. "That's what I says to her. She'll have to face it all in the long run. It's no sort of use trying to keep anything from the police – within reason, that's to say."

Mrs. Mayer turned scared eyes on her visitor.

"Not keep anything from the police!" she echoed in a voice that had turned shrill. "Depends what it is," with a note of defiance in her manner. "If it don't do anybody any harm –"

"They'll find it out sooner or later," Mrs. Yates put in, "bound to, and then where are you?"

Mrs. Mayer lowered her eyes and with nervous fingers rolled her handkerchief into a tight ball under the shelter of the table-cloth.

"Wouldn't you keep anything from the police, Susan?" she asked earnestly.

Mrs. Yates hesitated.

"Tom kept something back once – nothing to matter, nothing he'd done himself – but they found it out. They always find out, Mary."

Mrs. Mayer glanced about her nervously.

"There's things," she said in a thin, high voice again, "that don't hurt anybody – I wouldn't tell the police, not for all you could offer me!"

The other looked at her in astonishment.

"And you the widder of a superintendent, Mary!"

"It's because of that I say it," was the enigmatical reply. "And there's things I wouldn't tell the police – not if it was ever so – and I'm not ashamed of it, either!"

CHAPTER XX

Inspector Stoddart, sitting at his desk at Scotland Yard, had decided to confront Lady Medchester with Garwood's statement – that he had seen her in the gardens at Holford on the night and about the time of Robert Saunderson's murder.

He had always had a suspicion she knew more than she had admitted, and congratulated himself on the brain-wave that had prompted the little trap he laid for her, and for which he had invoked Anne's innocent connivance. He had been certain she knew something about those beads; he had discovered by his ruse she did not know so much as she thought she did. She had imagined they belonged to Anne.

The inspector had no love for Lady Medchester. He felt instinctively hers was a mean mind, secretive and vindictive. Where it served her purpose he suspected her to be capable of going to great lengths to gain her own ends: no scruples would be allowed to interfere with their achievement. He could easily understand why she and Anne had never been friends, a fact well known in the neighbourhood; their natures were apart as the poles. He believed Garwood's tale and wondered in his own mind whether it had been she who had made an assignation with Saunderson that night in the summer-house. Somebody had, that was certain, and rumour had been pretty free in coupling their names together.

The definite clues they had to the crime were more or less unsatisfactory and seemed likely to lead to nothing; the slip of paper found in Saunderson's notebook bearing the words, "I accede because I have no choice," was badly written in block letters and paper torn apparently off the end of a half-sheet of so ordinary a type that it might have been bought at any stationer's in any town, and results from it were hardly to be hoped for.

There was also the note signed with the letter M, that Harbord had found in Saunderson's flat. On reading it their minds had simultaneously jumped to Lady Medchester, but so far there was nothing to prove she had written it. It, too, was in non-committal block letters, on very ordinary notepaper. Had the date suggested in it for the proposed assignation coincided with the date of the murder Stoddart might have been justified in taking immediate action. But it did not; the date mentioned was considerably previous to that of the crime, and although that did not preclude the possibility of a second meeting having been, arranged there was nothing to prove it. Saunderson could quite well have met a dozen women, without making his actions any concern of the police, and if Lady Medchester chose to deny authorship of the letter, as she assuredly would, they had no means so far of proving it against her.

His strongest asset in the case lay in her denial of having been out in the gardens that night. Persons with clear consciences don't need to tell lies. She had every right to go out into her own grounds at any time of the day or night, and had she admitted the fact in the first instance and said frankly she had seen nothing, or, if that were not so, had told what she had seen, she would have been believed and there would have been no more trouble about it.

But she had not been frank, and had thereby immediately laid herself open to suspicion. The fact of Lord Medchester being a person of some importance in the county did not simplify matters. Stoddart felt that for his own sake he must tread warily: the authorities strongly objected to becoming embroiled with persons of influence.

He had made up his mind; he would have yet another interview with Lady Medchester, and, without warning, confront her with Garwood's statement about her movements that night. If she could prove an alibi so much the better; but she had made no effort to do so in the first instance, had produced no evidence proving her own assertion of not having left the house, and a belated explanation born of second thoughts would have to be peculiarly unassailable to carry any weight.

Then there was the matter of the beads. He intended to press that point, to force the truth from her. He could quite understand her astonishment at seeing the crystal beads hanging round Anne's neck when she had thought the chain to be broken and in the hands of the police. That was no more than he had expected.

But if she had imagined she recognized Anne's property in the broken necklace found near the scene of the crime, and the three loose beads in the dead man's pocket, why had she shown no surprise when first confronted with them? It would almost seem it had not been a surprise to her. The two necklaces were so much alike there was every reason for her to have been mistaken, but why had she not said – as she believed – the beads belonged to Anne Courtenay when asked?

An instinct told the inspector it was not in order to shield her husband's cousin.

Then there was Miss Delauney's story bringing Lord Gorth and his sister into it. That, too, was, mere chatter – nothing to go upon – and her own assertion of being married to Robert Saunderson, by the registrar in Marylebone had had to be substantiated. Police inquiries had disclosed the fact that Saunderson had been lying when he said the marriage ceremony had been a sham. The record of the marriage was there sure enough; in their own names, and no question about it. Miss Delauney of the halls was Mrs. Saunderson without a doubt. All these threads, apparently leading into blind alleys, had to be followed up, and Garwood's evidence had to be dealt with first.

So about four hours later Inspector Stoddart walked into the first floor sitting-room at the "Medchester Arms," where Harbord, with a cigarette in the corner of his mouth, was writing up a report.

"Ring up the Hall," he said, flinging down his hat, "while I get a bit of something to eat. I caught the train by the skin of my teeth. Find out if Lady Medchester's at home and, if not, when she will be – but don't say why you want to know. I am going to have a word with her, and I'd as soon Lord Medchester was out of the way."

It was six o'clock when a footman informed Lady Medchester that Inspector Stoddart would like to speak to her. She was writing letters at her writing-table, and as the man delivered his message stared straight in front of her without looking round. When she spoke, after a perceptible pause, her face was white to the lips.

"Inspector Stoddart – what does he want?"

"To speak to you, my lady," the man answered stolidly.

"Yes, but what about?" she asked impatiently.

"He didn't say. He's got the other detective – I think his name's Harbord, my lady – with him, and says he would like to see you at once."

"Tell him I can't –" she began; then with a little helpless gesture, "I – suppose it's no good. Where's his lordship?"

"Gone over to East Molton, I believe, to see Mr. Burford."

She turned and faced the man in the doorway for the first time.

"Show the inspector into the library and say I will be with him directly." As the door closed and she was left again alone she flung the pen angrily on the table and rose. "What is it *now*?" she muttered. "Am I never to have any peace? Oh, Dick! – my dear –" She broke off with a sob.

Moving across the room to the mirror over the mantelpiece she drew powder and puff from a vanity-bag hanging at her wrist, and applied it skilfully to eyes and nose. A delicate brush of geranium to cheeks, white for the moment as chalk, and a finishing touch of lipstick made her feel herself again, and with lips firmly set and anything but welcome in her eyes she crossed the wide hall to the library.

The detectives turned as she entered.

"What do you want?" she said abruptly. "I suppose it's more questions about these – these murders? I have already told you all I can – and I have nothing further to add."

Stoddart drew a chair a few feet forward.

"Won't you sit down?" he suggested. "A new development has arisen, and there are one or two questions that must be asked."

Lady Medchester frowned at the implication that the interview might be a long one, and shook her head.

"I prefer to stand, thank you. Surely there is some limit to this continual inquisition on the part of the police! Why should an innocent person be subjected to this sort of thing? It's not my idea of British justice!"

The inspector's eyes scanned her face with so uncompromising a look that her own dropped.

"The innocent?" he said coldly. "But innocence has to be proved – and proved up to the hilt in cases of this sort." He paused – no one knew better than Inspector Stoddart when to give his actions a dramatic setting. "Why did you say you had spent the hours between nine and eleven on the evening of Saunderson's murder in your bedroom, Lady Medchester?" he asked sternly.

She stared at him angrily.

"Because I did. I can't prove it because, as it happens, I was seen by no one between those hours. I was in my bedroom, and my maid –"

Stoddart moved a step forward.

"On the contrary, you were seen – in the garden," he interrupted. "Wait," as she attempted to speak, "don't make matters worse by denying it."

"Who saw me – is supposed to have seen me?" she said with a vehement gesture of denial. "I tell you I was in my room."

"Never mind who saw you; you were seen, that's enough. It's no good denying it; I have my witness. If you knew no more of this affair than you first admitted there would have been no need to resort to subterfuge. Now, Lady Medchester, be frank –

it will be better for you in the long run – and I *know* you were in the garden that night."

Bluff is an excellent servant when applied to certain types of human nature, and it did not fail here. Lady Medchester caught at the back of a chair to steady herself. In spite of powder and paint she looked ten years older than when she came into the room.

"Tell me," Stoddart went on, pressing his opportunity, "was it you who met Saunderson in the summer-house that night?"

The shock of the sudden question broke down her last defence.

"It was not!" she cried emphatically. "I never went into the summer-house at all – at least, not until – not –" dropping helplessly into a chair.

"Oh – damn you!" she cried, losing all control, reverting to type as, in a crisis, is the manner of her kind. "I did not kill Saunderson, if that's what you think – and I don't know who did!" she finished violently.

"Better make a clean breast of it, Lady Medchester," Stoddart said evenly; experience had taught him when to turn the screw and when to ease the strain. "Nothing that does not bear on the case shall go any further."

She stifled a sob with a handkerchief rolled into a small, compact ball, and for a moment silence reigned in the long room from whose walls the painted eyes of her husband's forbears looked down upon this unworthy bearer of the name. Her shoulders shook with the effort to smother her sobs and bring herself to the point of confession.

"Send him away," she said at last, nodding her head in Harbord's direction.

At a signal from the inspector his subordinate went out, closing the door softly behind him. The sight of a soul bared to the world cannot fail to have its effect on the least thinking man or woman.

Stoddart waited in vain for Lady Medchester to speak.

"Why did you go out in the garden that night?" he asked gently.

With a deep sigh she looked up, the rouge on her cheeks riddled with tears.

"I'll tell you all I know," she said slowly. "You won't understand – no man ever would understand – and it doesn't matter," she added desperately. "I did go out that evening, but it was not in order to meet Robert Saunderson."

"Why did you go?"

She sat up and pulled herself together.

"I went into the garden that night to spy on Anne Courtenay – as she was then. I never liked her, perhaps because I knew she did not like me. There was a peculiar touch of careless arrogance towards me in her manner that got through the skin somehow – and I'm not thin-skinned as a rule. It may have been unintentional – I don't know. Anyway, I hated her; and I suspected that when she pleaded headache and went to her room she was up to some game or other. So I slipped out into the gardens and hid among the trees near the summer-house."

The inspector nodded. With a recollection of the rumours concerning her and Saunderson he could read between the lines. Jealousy was writ large all over the page.

"You were seen," he said shortly. "I can describe the exact spot where you stood, if you wish."

Lady Medchester shook her head.

"No need to do that. I am telling the truth – anyhow, this time.

"I had only waited a few minutes," she went on, "when sure enough Anne Courtenay's figure flitted from the shadow of the house into the moonlight and I held my breath. There was no doubt about it, she expected some one to meet her."

"What makes you say that?"

"Because instead of walking calmly into the open she darted from one patch of shadow to another, glancing each side of her in a nervous sort of way quite unlike her. As she came near to where I was standing in the deep shadow her face looked pale and drawn, even in the moonlight, and I saw she was making for the summer-house just beyond the rose garden. At the foot of the steps she hesitated and looked round her again. The moon went behind a cloud, but I could still see her. She mounted slowly and pushed open the summer-house door."

Stoddart listened with breathless attention. Was this going to be the solution of the problem that had worried him by day and interfered with his sleep at night? Somehow, he did not feel all the exultation he would have expected. Anne Courtenay!

"What did you do then?"

"I stood still of course," was the sharp answer. "I wanted to find out whom she expected to meet in the summer-house. She came out again almost immediately and half ran, half tottered down the steps; I thought she was going to fall. She caught at the gate into the rosery to steady herself, and the moon came out again full and I saw her face – horror-stricken, her eyes staring in front of her. Then she ran, flinging caution to the winds, as though all the devils in hell were after her, and disappeared into the house. And that's all I saw."

She ceased abruptly, but the representative of justice had not yet done with her.

"What did you do then, Lady Medchester?" he asked, keeping his eyes steadily fixed upon her face.

The victim of this rigid interrogation wiped her lips with the handkerchief folded and unfolded by her nervous fingers as she talked, and looked round as though hoping for a means of escape. There was none; she knew that well enough. The law had its clutch on her; she was frightened and tired – too tired to care much what happened to her. There was only one thing

– if that could be kept from this tormenting devil he should have the rest.

"I waited a moment to make sure she was not coming back," Lady Medchester resumed, "then I went across the rosery and up the few steps to the summer-house. I *had* to see what Anne Courtenay had seen that had blanched her cheeks and put that look of terror into her eyes. I pushed open the door –" She broke off with a shiver, and for the first time looked Inspector Stoddart straight in the face. "You must believe what I say, for I swear I am telling the truth," she protested.

"What did you find in the summer-house?" he asked, unmoved.

"Robert Saunderson's dead body was lying on the floor," she went on in a hard voice, her manner changing, "and at the sight of it I knew Anne Courtenay was meeting him secretly. It was a shock." Her eyes dropped. "Robert Saunderson and I have been friends – friends," she repeated with emphasis, "for some time, and I had had no idea of it."

"Yet you followed her into the garden?"

"I guessed she was going to meet some one, and I wished to know who it was," was the evasive reply. She covered her eyes as though to screen them from the penetrating gaze of the man opposite her. "I had always hated her, but I think at that moment I could have killed her. I dare say you don't understand – it was the deception –" She broke off.

"I understand perfectly," the inspector interposed. Being man as well as policeman he felt rather embarrassed. It was so easy to read between the lines.

Her hand dropped from her eyes and she continued:

"Self-preservation, I suppose, is the most powerful instinct we have, and even at that moment I knew I mustn't be found alone with Saunderson's dead body at that hour. I looked round hurriedly to see if any weapon could be seen, and my eye was caught by something on the floor between the body and the top of the steps. It was a necklace of crystal beads, shining in the moonlight – broken, as though the wearer might have stooped forward and caught it on the door-handle. I slipped it into my pocket and crept back across the gardens and into the house."

She sank back in the chair as though the narrative had come to an end; but the inspector's questions were not finished.

"Did you hear any shot fired during the interval between the entry of Mrs. Bur ford into the summer-house and her exit?" he asked.

Lady Medchester shook her head. "I am sure no shot was fired, or I should certainly have heard it."

"Are these the beads you found, Lady Medchester?" he asked, producing the broken string from his pocket and holding them up to view.

"Yes."

"Then how was it they were found near the scene of the crime – three of them in the pocket of the dead man?"

A curious look of cunning satisfaction came into her eyes. She gave a harsh little laugh.

"Because in the morning when I examined the beads I thought they were Anne's, and that I had been a fool not to leave them where I found them. Suspicion would have fastened on her quite naturally, and I should have had my –" She pulled herself up abruptly.

Stoddart smiled; there was no need to supply the word.

"But," she went on, eyeing him defiantly, "I didn't see why I shouldn't remedy the evil; there would be no harm in assisting the ends of justice instead of hindering. I determined to put them back."

She wiped her mouth again nervously. Her interrogator waited in silence.

"Of course I know it was wrong of me to have done it for the reason I did, and I'm not sure I am not sorry. But you have no cause to complain, as my intention was to help the law; and as the beads have turned out not to be Anne's there's no harm done. Anyway, I went out as soon as I could leave the house without being noticed, and from my old hiding-place in the trees saw the police were already at work in the summer-house. They came out on to the steps, talking; Wilton, the gardener, was with them and he pointed in the direction of the old barn. Then the three of them walked off and I got my chance."

She paused, and Stoddart noticed tiny beads of perspiration were standing out on her forehead.

"I tore off three of the beads, ran across the rosery and into the summer-house, slipped them hurriedly into Saunderson's pocket and, throwing the remainder of the necklace into the shrubbery, got back to the house without meeting anyone."

She sank back into the chair again and closed her eyes.

Inspector Stoddart looked down at her with an inscrutable expression in his eyes. What will a jealous woman not risk for revenge?

"And as those beads do not belong to Mrs. Burford, whom do you suppose they do belong to?" He shot the question at her suddenly.

"I haven't the least idea," Lady Medchester replied listlessly.

And this time the inspector believed she was speaking the truth.

CHAPTER XXI

Inspector Stoddart left Holford Hall considerably worried.

It looked uncommonly as though Miss Tottie Delauney's story might be true, and that Mrs. Burford had played the star part in this sordid drama. If so, his suspicions that Saunderson and Superintendent Mayer had been murdered by the same hand would have to go. Mrs. Burford might possibly have shot the former, but for the hour during which Mayer had been killed she had an unassailable alibi.

He promised Harbord, who had been waiting for him in the hall, to tell him the main points of the interview later on. He wanted to think, and when he had that object in view had found nothing so efficacious as solitude and a cigarette in the fresh air.

It was a lovely autumn day – one of those days on which it seems good to be alive. He turned his back on the Hall with its old grey walls shining as placidly in the last rays of the setting sun as though no such tragedies as crime and sudden death had been enacted under their shadow; walked through the rosery with the fateful summer-house on his right; glanced as he passed at the shrubbery and woods on the left where Lady Medchester had hidden herself on that evening of tragedy; and passed on towards the boundary of the copse.

What a woman! Experienced as he was in sordid crime and the seamy side of life, he felt as though he needed cleansing after such a contact. A woman without excuses for her mean jealousies, and her indulgence of instincts not far removed from the brute beast.

He walked slowly along the narrow path, worn by the passing of innumerable feet through scrub and undergrowth, under the shadow of beech and oak to a side gate leading to the high road. He was becoming very familiar with the geography of the place, and had purposely avoided the lodge with the possibility of being intercepted by Mrs. Yates or her daughter and forced to talk when he wanted to think. He had the power, so necessary in his profession, of thinking in watertight compartments, of switching off from one aspect of a subject before switching on to another: an invaluable asset and one that many a time had stood him in good stead.

Lady Medchester's confession – for it amounted to no less – had not greatly advanced the case. The problem of why the beads had been found in the murdered man's pocket after Mayer had declared they had not been there when the body was first searched had been solved, and he made a mental note to emphasize that fact when retailing the story to Harbord. He rather congratulated himself on having pulled up the latter for underrating the superintendent's intelligence on that occasion. But they were no nearer their ownership. They were certainly not Anne Burford's; no one would be likely to possess two strings of beads so nearly identical. The weapon still remained a problem. Both murders had been committed by means of a shot, and in neither case was there any trace of the revolver. The bullet that had killed Saunderson had been found lodged in the wooden boards of the back wall of the summer-house. In Mayer's case the bullet had not been found at all; it had quite likely embedded itself in the soft ground among the roots of the undergrowth and never would be found.

But Anne Burford? Was it possible?

He would have been prepared to go bail almost on her straightforwardness. She had given her evidence so unhesitatingly, so simply, with such an air of complete innocence, admitting her presence in the garden that night, but disclaiming all knowledge of any unusual occurrence having taken place. He would have been inclined to doubt Lady Medchester's story – she was capable of any malicious invention that would clear herself and inculpate the girl she hated – if it had not been that Miss Tottie Delauney's evidence pointed in the same direction. Although founded on statement only and not carrying much weight in itself, each story backed the other up.

Why had Anne not admitted her visit to the summer-house? A girl might be shy of an assignation of the sort being discovered, particularly as she was already engaged to Michael Burford, but she might have explained the episode away very plausibly; could have said she drifted in by accident while wandering about the gardens. Women were ingenious at that sort of thing, and from all accounts no one would ever have suspected her of a deliberate arrangement to meet Saunderson secretly.

But she had denied the whole affair, and if she could lie once she could go on lying, unless – Stoddart's mind was suddenly side-tracked along another line – she was shielding some one?

He reached the wicket-gate leading to the high road, and leaning his arms on the top rail stared in front of him. If Anne Burford were shielding some one, it brought Lord Gorth into it good and plenty. That was what Miss Tottie Delauney had said – that Anne Courtenay had killed Saunderson to save her brother, and herself.

Save him from what? Nothing incriminating Harold Courtenay had been found among Saunderson's papers, and he seemed harmless enough, taking him all round; not much brains perhaps – people said he was making a foolish marriage.

Stoddart smiled grimly. All marriages came into that category in his opinion; he intended to remain a bachelor. If, as they said, a woman was at the bottom of all trouble, it was asking for it to marry one of them. But Lord Gorth's dossier would have to be looked into more particularly; and Mrs. Burford's, too, for that matter. She had brought it on herself by her want of frankness.

Lord Gorth lived somewhere in the neighbourhood, not far away. The inspector had never been there, but he had heard it talked about. He decided to ring him up from the Medchester police station. His alibi had never been satisfactory; no alibi at all really. He had been seen that night by one or two of the guests at various times during the evening; that was all it amounted to. There were intervals nobody could swear to, times when he could have slipped away to the summer-house and back again and no one have been the wiser.

The little perpendicular lines between Stoddart's keen grey eyes deepened as his thoughts travelled away from the scene of that first tragedy and strayed to the spot where the superintendent had been murdered. That the two crimes were closely related was certain. He still clung to the theory that both had been committed by the same hand, but if that were the case then Anne Burford and her brother were both innocent. They were far enough away when Superintendent Mayer was killed to be entirely clear of suspicion.

Inspector Stoddart pulled himself up. After many injunctions to juniors not to start a theory and then make the facts fit it, here he was doing it himself! There was nothing to prove the criminal in the one case to have been the criminal in the other. Circumstances pointed that way, and that was all that could be said.

He felt justified in the conjecture that the criminal who fired the shot that killed Mayer had heard him state that he knew who had killed Saunderson. There were three persons of whom that could be said – Mrs. Yates; the self-styled Tottie Delauney, her daughter; and Lord Medchester.

But it was possible Mayer had mentioned it to some one else. He had been in a self-congratulatory mood, finding it difficult to keep this precious discovery to himself, as was evidenced by his confidences to Mrs. Yates and Lord Medchester. He had very nearly blurted out the whole secret to the latter, only restrained by the discipline of his training in the Force.

Had he met anyone on his way to catch the Empton bus? Some one who had given him a clue to the murderer – and who had then, perhaps, regretted it and lain in wait for him on his way back?

These questions raced through Stoddart's brain as he stood leaning on the wooden gate, his eyes gazing across the road at the hedge opposite without consciously seeing it. It was growing dark; a few stray rooks were cawing overhead, and a dove in the recesses of the wood was coo-cooing with gentle persistence. The tall trees beyond the hedge threw the road into shadow.

Stoddart was susceptible to the beauties of nature, and for the moment the man in him outweighed the detective. He could have consigned all criminals to the bottom of the sea. He would like to settle on a farm and till the soil, be done with this everlasting suspicion of his fellow-men that led him into the foul places of the earth, and feel no longer in a perpetual state of warfare.

He lit a cigarette absently and threw the match away; it lay flickering, poised on the long grass bordering the road, as he opened the gate and passed through.

Glancing down, he put his foot on it, but not before something that glittered from among the long, green blades reflected the flame and caught his eye. Instinctively he stooped to pick it up, and laid it on the palm of his hand, shining in the dying light.

It was a crystal bead.

On the instant the detective was again uppermost. He stared at it, surprised. He could: have sworn it was a bead from the broken string that lay among the police exhibits – the string thrown by Lady Medchester into the shrubbery, three of which she had slipped into Saunderson's pocket. What did this mean? Surely she had not strayed so far afield that night –

what would have been her object? Or had this single bead been dropped here by its rightful owner?

Stoddart pushed it impatiently into his pocket. Every new detail that cropped up and might be expected to throw light on the case only seemed to add to its perplexities. He turned to the right, heading for Medchester, then thought better of it and, re-entering the wood through the gate, retraced his steps until he came to a point where the footpath forked. Leaving the track he had come by on his left, he took the other, and skirting the spot where Mayer had been shot came out on the drive close to the lodge gates.

It had struck him it might be as well to find out whether Miss Tottie Delauney had ever owned a string of crystal beads.

In spite of an autumnal nip in the air the window of the front room was open, and, as the detective crossed the plot of grass with the path running up the centre to the front door, voices raised in discussion reached his ears. Mrs. Yates and her daughter were apparently in slight disagreement over something.

"If you can't what the lawyers call substantiate your statements, my advice to you, Mary Ann, is to hold yer tongue," was the injunction that drifted through the window to the inspector's ears. "I don't hold with putting things into a policeman's head. Let them find it out for themselves – that's what I say. I was saying to Mary Mayer when I went to see her in Medchester. 'Mary,' I said, 'it's no manner of use trying to keep anything from the police,' I said; 'you mark my words, they'll find it out sooner or later without your help,' I said, 'and least said soonest mended,' and that's what I say to you –"

"How you do go on, mother!" her daughter's voice broke in. "First you tell me to keep nothing from the police – then you tell me I talk too much. I've got nothing to hide; I told them all I could. If they don't believe me I can't help it. I say Anne Courtenay did my husband in, and I don't care –"

The window was closed suddenly from inside as the inspector knocked at the front door. Mrs. Yates opened it.

"Oh, it's you," she remarked without enthusiasm. "Come in, sir – the inspector from Scotland Yard, isn't it?" She showed him into the front parlour, where Miss Tottie Delauney was lying full length on a cretonne-covered sofa, looking at a picture paper. She sat up at sight of the visitor and nodded.

"I and Inspector Stoddart are old friends," she said graciously.

It was always worth while to cultivate friendship with the mammon of unrighteousness, she had learnt that in her precarious profession; you never knew when a friend in high places mightn't come in useful, and just now she was particularly anxious to placate the authorities.

"Like a cup of tea, inspector?" she invited. "I'll boil a drop of water in no time, and I dare say you've walked a good step one way and another."

"I don't mind if I do, Miss Delauney," was the ready answer.

Mrs. Yates pushed a chair towards him.

"No news yet about who killed poor Bill Mayer?" she asked as her daughter, ready to bestir herself when it came to her own interests, disappeared into the kitchen.

He shook his head. "Nothing to tell the world about; but we're getting on. What a lot of trouble and anxiety we should have been saved if Superintendent Mayer had told you what he knew, Mrs. Yates."

"It wasn't my fault he didn't," Mrs. Yates replied reminiscently, "but he kept his mouth shut as tight as any oyster."

"And Mrs. Mayer can't help us," Stoddart observed tentatively, thinking of the words he had heard through the open window, "not to go by the evidence she gave at the inquest. Never said anything to you, Mrs. Yates, that might lead you to think she knows more than she let on?"

Mrs. Yates, with a memory of certain inscrutable words let drop by her friend at their last meeting, flushed scarlet and turned her face away.

"Never," she replied loyally. "I don't believe Mary Mayer knows anything more than you or I do. She'd have told it quick enough if it would help to find out who'd murdered her husband."

The rattle of tray and cup and saucer preceded Miss Delauney's reappearance; she had taken advantage of her temporary retirement to remedy the day's wear and tear with powder and lipstick, and it was the Tottie Delauney familiar to the music-hall world that smiled at him over the homely tea-tray. But she kept a wary eye on him as she poured out the cup of tea and supplied him with milk and sugar.

"I was in hopes you'd got news for us," she said brightly. "You thought Bob Saunderson was speaking truth when he said our marriage was a sham, but I bet you know better by now. I'm an honest woman, I am – and I mean to have my rights."

"Certainly you'll have your rights. Every one in this case will get their rights in the end, no doubt. What we have to find out is – what are their rights?"

"Well, I know what mine are, anyway," Miss Delauney replied with a toss of her henna-dyed head. "I shall be entitled to the half of all poor Bob left as his wife, as there aren't any children to provide for, and there are those who'll see I get it."

"Did you know he had made no Will?" The inspector shot the question at her.

Miss Delauney dropped her eyes.

"No, I didn't," she replied after a perceptible pause. "I knew he hadn't made a Will up to the time we parted company, but how was I to know what he'd done since? I knew nothing about his affairs. When I heard of the murder I came here to – to look round as it were. Why shouldn't I? A wife couldn't do no less in my opinion." In moments of excitement Miss Delauney was apt to revert to the diction natural to her. "If you've come here to be asking questions again I'm sorry I gave you a cup of tea, that I am!" she cried, chin in air, hand on hip, a pose he felt sure had met with much applause on many a music-hall stage.

"Bob Saunderson mayn't have been a pattern husband," she went on before either of the others could speak, "but he wasn't a bad sort take him all round, and I'll thank you police to find out who did him in!"

"Now, now, go easy, Mirandy," her mother murmured uneasily.

Stoddart smiled. "We shall have to find out who had a motive for doing so," he said smoothly, and Miss Delauney subsided on the edge of a chair, a scared look creeping into her eyes. "But I didn't come here to talk about the murder" – he put a hand in his pocket – "as a matter of fact, I looked in to see if either of you ladies ever had a string of beads like this?"

He placed the crystal bead on the table, "Where did you find it?" Mrs. Yates asked after a pause during which both she and her daughter glanced at it furtively as though suspecting a trap.

"At the edge of the wood."

"Not mine," Mrs. Yates said curtly. "I don't hold with those sort of gewgaws. Waste of money, I call them."

"I am sure," the inspector suggested persuasively, "Miss Tottie Delauney's admirers don't share that opinion, Mrs. Yates," and he looked expectantly at her daughter.

"Mirandy likes a bit of colour," Mrs. Yates put in hastily. "She had some beads like that only they was red as rubies and –"

"I'm not answering any more questions, mother," the other said sullenly, "and I'll thank you to keep your mouth shut too."

"Well, somebody's missing it," the detective remarked, replacing the bead in his pocket.

Having got as much – or as little – information from the two women as he had hoped for, he walked off towards Medchester, not much the wiser for his pains.

He was greeted at the hotel door by Harbord.

"There's a man asking for you," he informed him; "wouldn't talk to me – said he wanted the top boss of this here murder case. He's to call again first thing tomorrow morning."

"What sort of a man?"

"Tramp, if you ask me. Three days' growth on his chin, and looks as though he wouldn't recognize a piece of soap if he saw it."

"Umph," the inspector muttered, and added under his breath, "What I want to meet is somebody who'll tell me whom those beads belong to."

CHAPTER XXII

Inspector Stoddart's visit left an atmosphere of uneasiness at the lodge.

Miss Delauney's antagonism to His Majesty's police force, developed during a career that had more than once been within bowing acquaintance with the Law Courts, was instinctive and ineradicable. She distrusted policemen, from the man on point duty to the Chief of the C.I.D. In her opinion they were a prying, meddling crowd, making a still more difficult problem of life, which Providence, or some other potent authority, had already made sufficiently complicated.

It might have afforded her a modicum of consolation had she known that she had puzzled the inspector. It was true she had not claimed ownership of the vagrant bead, but neither had she denied it. His knowledge of the subject had remained exactly where it was. On comparison it was found to match the police "exhibit" in every particular, and was without doubt a part of the necklace thrown by Lady Medchester into the shrubbery under the erroneous impression that it belonged to Anne Courtenay. When he laid it on the table in full view Miss Delauney had not flickered so much as an eyelash – he had watched her carefully. It appeared to convey nothing to her at all; nor to her mother, who was presumably less experienced in histronic display.

However, it was not through the question direct he hoped to get the coveted information; although the clue of the bead necklace had been kept from public knowledge, guilt would be on its guard, and it would be by some side-track that the owner would be detected.

From small beginnings great results may arise.

Is there a more trite observation than that in the English language? But like other similar axioms it is none the less true, and if Inspector Stoddart could have foreseen what was to result from the fact that Harbord spent the following night wide awake, owing to an aching tooth, he would have received that information with more interest when it was offered to him in the morning by the sufferer.

As it was, although not wanting in sympathy, after suggesting an early visit to a dentist in Medchester, he considered the situation adequately dealt with and proceeded to other business, including the promised visit from the tramp overnight. When by eleven o'clock the man had failed to appear, the inspector, deciding with indifference he had changed his mind, settled down to deal with certain reports, and saw his colleague depart in search of relief from one of the most cruel torments to which human flesh is heir.

In the meantime trouble had been going on at the Hall.

Lord Medchester had put his foot down. In spite of persuasion amounting almost to tears on the part of his wife he absolutely refused to have a wedding-party at Holford. If Mr. Maurice Stainer was not in a position to give his sister a suitable send-off, then let Harold himself do it from Gorth, of which he was now sole master.

"But," Lady Medchester remonstrated, "it's unheard of for the bride to be married from the bridegroom's house!"

"It will also be unheard of that she is married from mine – because she won't be," his lordship replied grimly, and chuckled at his own retort. "'Pon my soul – not so bad – what?" he laughed again. "But I mean it, Min," he added, sobering down. "I won't have Miss Sybil Stainer playing the star part in any show under my roof. And that's that!"

He left the room, followed by Lady Medchester's despairing eyes, until the door, sharply banged, hid him from view. She sat for a moment as though turned to stone.

The door reopened to admit the new Lord Gorth. He was scarcely recognizable as the former Harold Courtenay. In appearance ten years older, his face was white and drawn, his eyes dull, the sparkle of youth in them faded. Little lines showed at the corners of his eyes and his hands moved restlessly. He walked listlessly across the room and dropped into a chair.

"Dick says he won't have the wedding here, Harold," Lady Medchester said, looking at him anxiously, "and I'm afraid it's final. Do you think you could persuade Sybil to be married quietly, here at the village church, or even at a London Register Office? And I suppose I may go as far as to promise a wedding cake and a glass of champagne here after it. Surely as long as she is married she needn't care how the ceremony is performed?" Her voice was bitter, but Harold did not seem to notice it. "I suppose Anne wouldn't let the marriage –" she began tentatively, but broke off as Harold's eyes suddenly lost their apathy and flamed into indignation.

"I won't have Anne asked. My God! hasn't she done enough?" he began furiously; then pulling himself together at the surprise in Lady Medchester's face, "Anne has suffered more than you think – dragged into all this muck. I dare say she would have the wedding from her house if I asked her; but I am not going to ask her." He went on more quietly, "I'll speak to Sybil. If she understands that Cousin Dick definitely refuses I dare say she'll be reasonable."

Lady Medchester looked as though she hardly agreed with him.

"Life plays funny tricks sometimes," he went on after a pause. "I suppose it's one's own fault."

"You shouldn't be saying that, with the world at your feet – money, title, marriage – what more do you want?" She smiled ironically. "A veritable fairy dream, the world would say."

"A damnable nightmare!" he retorted.

"Then why are you doing it?" she asked curiously.

He looked at her uneasily and rose to his feet.

"Why are you trying to persuade Cousin Dick to have the wedding from here?" he asked abruptly. "You don't want it. You don't like Sybil."

The colour faded from his cousin's face.

"We have to do things we don't want to do sometimes," she replied evasively. "But you must speak to Sybil and persuade her to give up the idea of a big show. She shall stay here if she likes and you can be quietly married at Holford Church, and go straight away for the honeymoon after we've drunk your health. Dick can't object to that."

Harold nodded gloomily.

"Her marriage will then have the seal of our approval," she went on, "which, after all, is what she wants – and her brother can give her away."

He moved towards the door. "Needs must when the devil drives, I suppose. I only hope I may get Sybil to see it. If she'll be reasonable I'll marry her in three weeks if she likes, instead of sticking out for the two months I bargained for." And he flung out of the room before his cousin had time to remark on the un-bridegroom-like remark.

For some time there had been a tacit understanding between these two; although not comprehending the other's secret, the mutual knowledge that neither was any longer a free agent had established a link between them of a sort.

Minnie Medchester smiled rather grimly as she resumed the letter-writing at which she had been engaged when interrupted by her husband's ultimatum. Harold's task of persuading his ladylove into what he had called a reasonable frame of mind was not going to be a light one. She had had more than one experience of Miss Stainer's tantrums when things went wrong, and she did not envy him his mission. It had become a sort of *idée fixe* with Sybil, this godmothering of her by the Medchesters. It was odd she should have sufficient intelligence to realize her prospective neighbours in the county were not likely to hail her with enthusiasm as a suitable wife for Lord Gorth, and yet should fail to understand that the seal of Holford Hall's approval would never be sufficient to outweigh her own shortcomings. The county would probably have none of her in any case, though all the Medchesters in the world were to take her by the hand.

But this was hardly a line of argument possible for the man who was going to marry her to adopt, and Harold quailed, as many a better man has quailed, at the prospect of tackling an angry woman.

His fears proved to have been unnecessary. Either a fragment of common sense had penetrated the thick skin of her self-esteem or the desire for publicity on her wedding day had evaporated.

"I'm sick of Minnie's waverings this way and that – one day assuring me she has that husband of hers on the end of a string, and the next that he has put his foot down and isn't taking it up again. What does it matter, anyway? Once I'm Lady Gorth it's me who'll be calling the tune" – grammar was not Sybil Stainer's long suit – "and they'll be ready enough to dance when I tell them. And I'll make 'em dance too!" she added viciously, while the man listening to her shivered inwardly at the crude vulgarity of her outlook.

Through his own manoeuvring they were standing on the lawn in full view of the house; no lover-like demonstrations could be expected of him out in the open.

"We'll be married just as soon as you can get a licence," she went on.

To strike while the iron was hot had always been her idea when dealing with her own interests, and this suggestion of Harold's had its advantages. Less chance of slip 'twixt cup and lip, perhaps, and a speedy marriage would bring Anne to her bearings. No use to kick against the pricks then.

"We'll be married at the church here, as Minnie says, and go away from the Hall afterwards. No Register Office for me – church is better style, and if you get a special licence no banns need be called. So get a move on, Harold. I'll go up to town for a few days – must see the last of old Maurice and get a bit of shopping done.

"Buck up!" she added. "Not much of the impatient bridegroom about you, I must say!"

"Played out nowadays, that sort of thing," he answered apathetically. "I think you're wise to take Lady Medchester's offer –"

She glanced at him sharply. "No need to swallow the poker," she put in. "'Lady Medchester,' indeed! She'll be my cousin as well as yours when we're married!"

"It will save trouble in the long run – a quiet wedding," he went on as though she had not spoken, "and come to the same thing in the end."

"Now look here, Harold," Miss Stainer admonished, "understand I am not going to take any nonsense from you lying down. I know what I know – and there's others'll know it too if you don't behave yourself. Once I'm your wife it'll be different –"

"Oh, I know all that," he interrupted wearily. "What more do you want? We'll be married whenever you like, I tell you. You had better go and tell – Minnie" – he brought the name out with a gulp – "you accept her offer. She'll bet glad to have it settled – one way or the other – and I'll see about the licence."

He strode off, glad to have got it over without a "scene." Sybil Stainer rather enjoyed scenes; she said it cleared the air and gave an opportunity for getting in a home-truth or two.

She also knew when she was beaten, and it had been dawning upon her for some days that, although for certain reasons she could put the screw on Lady Medchester when she liked, it was a different matter when dealing with Lord Medchester, and she had no idea of losing the bird in her hand because she could glimpse a bigger one in the bush; that is to say, she would never allow the unsubstantial glories of a large and fashionable wedding to endanger seriously the wedding itself.

Before Harold broached the subject to her she had already decided that, as Medchester was making such an unholy fuss about it, it would be politic to give way with regard to the manner of it and get on with the business itself. Life, in her experience, was so essentially a matter of ups and downs, it was foolish to tempt Fate by asking too much.

As Harold drove off after his interview with Sybil Stainer, he passed Harbord walking into Medchester in search of a dentist. He recognized him as one of the detectives engaged on the unravelling of the murders in which they all seemed to have become involved, and suppressed a first kindly impulse to offer him a lift. The man might make use of the opportunity to ask questions – questions Harold did not want to answer. So far as that unpleasant bill with Robert Saunderson's signature on it was concerned, that had been settled; it had been easy enough to raise the money when he had come into the Gorth properties and, with the principal witness dead, there was no one to bring up awkward questions about the signature. The name had been forged very cleverly, and Messrs. Usher & Snell, the money-lenders in whose office it had been left, had apparently never suspected its genuineness. Saunderson would never have let on about the forgery. He would want to keep all the cards in his own hand till the right time came. Circumstances, accidental or otherwise, had certainly played into Harold's hands as far as that was concerned.

So he professed not to see Harbord, who, he hoped, had possibly not seen him, little thinking that each step taken by Scotland Yard's emissary was a step nearer the solution of the problem that was causing them all so much distress.

Who is to say how far we can exercise free will, and how far we are the puppets of an arbitrary fate? What impulse is it that makes us choose this road or that: one perhaps leading to goals big with opportunity; the other dwindling into an arid, barren *cul-de-sac*, pitted with futile footsteps that never get any further? They may both have looked fair enough at the start. What influence lies behind the final decision?

There were three dentists, it appeared, in Medchester. Harbord learnt so much from a local directory and, knowing nothing about any of them, chose one at random. He did not suppose there was much the matter, and the least efficient member of the dentist's craft should be able to give him something to stay the pain till he could get back to London.

He missed the first because he disliked the name – Le Mouette. He distrusted flowery names, and it sounded foreign. So he chose the second, bearing the simple and familiar name of Howard, and a few minutes later was knocking at his door.

Mr. Howard was in but engaged; if the gentleman had no engagement he might have to wait a little. Would he take a seat in the waiting-room, and the maid assured him she would let Mr. Howard know the case was urgent.

Harbord found himself sharing the cheerful little waiting-room with two other unfortunates who presumably would be attended to before his turn came. If he had not been reluctant to face another sleepless night he might have been tempted to return to Holford forthwith; but having got so far it seemed foolish to give way to impatience.

A natural instinct, further developed by training, to observe what was going on round him caused him to take stock of his fellow-victims. Not much of interest to be gained there! A young woman, nursing a swelled face, and keeping a pair of scared eyes fixed on the door, as a lost soul might wait a summons to the Inferno; and an elderly man deeply immersed in the pages of a financial paper probably some days old.

Harbord turned to the table upon which papers old and new and a magazine or two lay scattered in untidy profusion. He drew up a chair and selected one at random, and had absently turned over a few leaves before discovering it was a railway guide to the best hotels in the North of England. He dropped it and picked up another. The door opened, the young woman rose and followed the beckoning finger into the Unknown – so Harbord imagined it to be from the expression on her face.

One step nearer to his own turn.

The paper he had chanced on was the "Bysphere," and hardly knowing what he was doing he turned the pages idly, stared at portraits with names under them, of men in tweeds carrying golf clubs, ladies notorious in society or stageland, a picture of the river crowded with boats, Japanese parasols, girls with bare arms in punts, with "Henley Regatta" beneath. This made him glance up at the date; the paper was an issue of months ago, but it served as well as anything else, and at that moment the maid reappeared and, the elderly gentleman obeying the call, Harbord was left in sole possession of the waiting-room. Anyhow it would be his turn next now, so there would not be so much longer to wait.

He continued to turn over the leaves of the ancient weekly, but his thoughts were elsewhere. He had seen Lord Gorth drive past him outside Medchester; it had set him wondering again, in spite of the pain he was suffering, whether that young gentleman and his sister were really involved, entangled in the knotted threads of this sinister problem. Things were beginning to look bad for Mrs. Burford; he, with Stoddart, would have been almost ready to vouch for her innocence, and yet here she was, telling lies like the rest of them, and he was sorry –

His thoughts came to an end in an audible exclamation.

He bent over the page before him, every sense suddenly alert and attentive. He stared at it, turning it this way and that; took it to the window and scanned it in the better light, holding it close to his eyes to examine it in detail. Muttered "Good God!" as visions of a rapid rise in his profession rose before him.

Then returning to the table he flattened out the paper and, with an anxious glance at the door, which might admit a witness at any moment, he took out a penknife and rapidly detached the entire page neatly from the rest; folded it carefully and slipped it into the breast pocket of his coat.

This done, he wiped his forehead, upon which tiny beads of perspiration stood out as the result of unusual excitement, and realized that every trace of the pain in his tooth had disappeared! He seized his hat, opened the door softly, and tiptoed along the entrance passage, through the front door, into the street.

Half an hour later Inspector Stoddart, still busy over his reports, was startled by the sudden and somewhat violent entrance of his colleague.

"What the devil?" he began, annoyed at the interruption; but at the sight of the other's face the words died on his lips.

"Sorry, sir," Harbord said, "but I've got news for you!"

The inspector raised his eyebrows. "Well – had the tooth out?" he asked sardonically.

"Damn the tooth!" the other replied without emotion; then lowering his voice, "I can tell you who the crystal beads belong to!" and with a glance behind him to make sure the door was closed, he drew the page he had cut out of the "Bysphere" from his pocket and laid it on the table.

CHAPTER XXIII

Mrs. Yates was setting out the breakfast things for herself and her daughter on the morning following Harbord's remarkable recovery in the dentist's waiting-room, and grumbling to herself as she did it.

Devoted mother as she was, she was growing tired of doing the work while Miss Tottie Delauney reaped the benefit, lolling in idle self-indulgence while her mother washed up or swept the floors. At the moment she was still lying in bed in the room above, while Mrs. Yates had already been up and about for an hour or two; as she set teacups and saucers on the kitchen table, neatly covered for the meal by a red and white checked cloth, she was conscious that even a mother's devotion might peter out, and had a curious sense of futility and a wish to sit down and cry her eyes out.

The year was dying slowly. A thin drizzle blurred the outlines of bush and hedge round the lodge, the big iron gates barring the way to visitors, ghostly in the grip of the wet mist. The road shone dark and grey, reflecting as clearly as a river the trees and posts that bordered it. Every twig dripped moisture, the reds and yellows of autumn that had glowed so vividly in the sunshine looked dead and lifeless, and the quacking of a string of ducks waddling across the road in single file, to discover what treasure the little rill running under the far hedge might yield, added to the general melancholy of the dismal day.

Mrs. Yates, having opened the window when she first came downstairs to give the place an airing, shut it again with a jerk. It was letting in more damp than air; she shivered as she put the kettle on the fire. She was not going to wait any longer for that lie-abed daughter of hers, nor was she going to pander to her lazy habits by carrying a cup of tea up to her room. She had done so at first, but now she was tired of it. There was still a draught from somewhere, and urged by an ever-present dread, rheumatism, she went back to the window and made sure it was properly closed.

As she glanced through the small, leaded panes, a figure came into view on the road outside, looming dimly into sight through the driving mist: the figure of a man, evidently a gentleman of the road, walking slowly with steps that lagged, and reflected full length by the hard, wet ground at his feet. He limped a little; his shock of flaming red hair, with no hat to shelter it, made a bright blot of colour against the grey hedge beyond.

Mrs. Yates stared through the glass pane, her hand arrested half-way to the latch of the casement. She had seen that red head before, and the rather vacant features it surmounted. But where?

Before the man had reached the centre of her field of vision she remembered. He had passed along the road – she had seen him from the gate – on the morning poor Bill Mayer had been shot. She had never given him a thought since, but the sight of him shuffling along stirred her memory, and she distinctly remembered seeing him on that previous occasion. It was before Mayer himself had come along; he was going towards Medchester while Mayer was coming away from it, and what with seeing the superintendent and hearing all he had to say, and then the disturbing news of his death, the tramp had passed entirely from her mind. Not that it could matter much, but the sight of him brought back the tragic circumstances of that day with sudden poignancy.

She was a kind-hearted woman and the slowly moving figure appealed so eloquently as a bit of human flotsam and jetsam, drifting past through the murk of the autumn morning, that she impulsively threw the window open and called to him as he passed. He was not the sort to be invited into a spotlessly kept kitchen, especially with the possibility of a sudden descent on the part of the fastidious lady of the music-halls upstairs, but a cup of hot tea passed through the window could hurt nobody. He imbibed it greedily.

"Thank 'ee kindly," he said, returning it, "puts a bit o' life into you on a morning like this. Las' time I was 'ere –" He looked round curiously, but the closed gates barred the view into the drive beyond, and a curtailed vision of grey, dripping branches and a hedge already shorn of its summer foliage was all that could be seen.

The man moved nearer to the window and dropped his voice.

"There was a murder near 'ere, wasn't there? A nark 'e was, wasn't 'e – policeman I mean?" he asked in a hoarse whisper. "'Appened the very day I was 'ere las'. I seed it in a picture paper wot somebody had dropped in the road just this side o'

Mapsdale. Well, missis" – he wiped his mouth with the back of his stumpy fingers – "they do say 'tis an ill wind wot blows nobody no good, and maybe there's a bit waitin' for services done. Leastways there's no 'arm in tryin'."

"What do you know about it?" Mrs. Yates asked sharply.

A sudden caution looked out through a pair of cunning little eyes.

"I'll deliver the goods to the proper party, missis. I ain't a-givin' nothin' away. Not me! Thank 'ee kindly for the tea." And, jerking a finger towards a lock of red hair drooping disconsolately over one eye, he shuffled off to be swallowed up immediately by the wreathing mists.

Stoddart and his colleague were finishing a late breakfast when Mrs. Marlow knocked at their sitting-room door later on in the morning.

"A man to see you, sir, and never in my life did I see a redder head of hair – carrots and pillarboxes are fools to it, and that's a fact," she said volubly, her hand round the edge of the door, her body somewhere in the background. "I said as how you were busy eating your breakfast, and he said he'd wait – and, if you ask me, he means it – looks as if he'd wait till the last day and then wait some," she added thoughtfully, "though I told him –"

"That's all right, Mrs. Marlow," the inspector interrupted.

"The man who called before probably," Harbord muttered.

"Clear away these things and then show him up," Stoddart finished.

Considerably more bedraggled than when enjoying Mrs. Yates's hospitality outside the lodge, the red-haired tramp entered the room and, touching his forelock, stood awkwardly by the door.

"Are you the man who called the day before yesterday?" the inspector asked curtly.

His visitor nodded assent, finding it difficult perhaps to find his voice in so august a presence.

"What's your name?"

"Ted Watson."

"Why didn't you come here yesterday?"

The man swallowed twice, and Stoddart continued:

"Never mind; it doesn't matter. What do you want?"

The nearest publican could probably furnish the answer.

The tramp looked nervously from one to the other of the men before whom he was arraigned, and then apparently plucked up courage.

"It's this way, mister," he began. "There was a man shot about here not so long ago, though I don't mind the date" – Stoddart, suddenly alive to the possibility that the man might know something, nodded encouragement – "a police constable seemingly – done in 'e was – name of Mayer –"

"How do you know what his name was?" the inspector snapped.

"Saw it in the papers – it was coz of what I sees in the papers I'm 'ere now. I knows what I knows" – the cunning in his eyes increased and he edged nearer to where the two detectives sat by the table – "and I'll tell what I knows, when I knows what I'll get for it, see? That's fair."

The inspector looked at him sternly. "You don't make bargains with the police, my man. What you know you'll tell, or it will be the worse for you."

The man stared back truculently. "When you 'appen to ha' got summat another party wants –" he began.

Stoddart tapped authoritatively on the table.

"Lock the door," he said to his assistant.

Harbord rose and made a step forward. The bluff acted like magic: the red-haired man subsided.

"Now, mister, no offence," he cringed. "I'll tell what I know, but I may tell 'ee the cop what was called Mayer promised me, 'e did –"

The two detectives exchanged a rapid glance.

"Tell us what you know," the inspector urged more gently. "You won't lose by it if it's worth listening to. A jug of beer, Alfred, from Mrs. Marlow – it's dry work talking."

The visitor appeared to find the prospect of beer encouraging. He grinned broadly and plunged forthwith into his story.

On the night when so much tragedy had been staged at Holford Hall – the night of Saunderson's murder, though he hadn't known then there'd been a murder – it seemed he had been on the road, making his way to Medchester through the village of Holford. It had been a warmish day and a bad one – that was to say, he had had no luck on the road, and was both tired and hungry. But he wanted to get to Medchester before night, and that evening some time after dark – he couldn't tell what time exactly – he found himself where the road was overshadowed by trees, and where a little gate led into what he now knew to be Holford woods.

As he was about to pass on the figure of a woman appeared suddenly on the other side of the gate, and he instinctively drew back into the shadow on the far side of the road. For a moment the moon shone full on her face and he would know her again anywhere. She fumbled with the latch, glancing up and down the road nervously, but never noticing the man cowering in the ditch opposite. Having got the gate open, she came through, closed it softly behind her, and went off at a run along the road.

Stoddart here called a halt for refreshment, and when Mrs. Marlow's ale had been disposed of asked in which direction the woman had run, and the tramp resumed his story.

The woman had run along the road towards Medchester, which went past the lodge, and he had crept out of the shadows and followed her. But she had stopped suddenly, so suddenly that he had only just time to fling himself flat in the long grass beside the road or she would have seen him. She stood in the middle of the road, passing her hand over her neck and shoulders and peering on the ground as if she'd lost something. She shook her dress and the bag she had in her hand, and came a step or two back along the road – stopped again and took a step or two in the direction she had come.

Then she seemed to make up her mind, turned again and went off along the road round a comer and out of sight.

"Towards the lodge?" Stoddart asked.

Yes, towards the lodge, or it might be Medchester, or there was a short cut he had heard tell across the park to Holford village – he couldn't say where she went. He got on to his feet and followed, and when he arrived at the spot where she had hesitated and turned round he saw something white lying on the road close to where she had been standing.

He picked it up. It was a bit of paper with something written on it; not being a scholar, and the moon having gone behind a cloud, he couldn't tell what it was – looked like marriage lines or something – and he hastened after the woman, thinking he might get a shilling or two for giving it back to her. But he couldn't catch up with her, and never saw her again.

"And so you've brought the paper here?" the inspector remarked. "And time, too, considering weeks have gone by. Why didn't you take it at once to the police?"

"I ain't brought it with me, coz I ain't got it," the man replied sulkily, "and if you be kind enough to listen to me, mister, you'll 'ear as 'ow I did take it to the police."

"Go on," Stoddart said shortly, with a glance at Harbord; were they going to know at last what it was Mayer had learnt that had cost him so great a price?

The man threw a suggestive glance at the empty beer jug and continued.

Not catching up with the woman he had slipped the paper into his pocket, spent the night under a convenient haystack, and resumed his tramp in the morning; not very early because he had overslept himself. He put the paper in his pocket and forgot all about it.

Having tramped the country for he didn't remember how long, he found himself back at Holford, heard of the murder of a bloke called Saunderson, and thought of the slip of paper still lying forgotten in his pocket. The police might be willing to give him a bit for it; anyway, it was worth trying.

He had passed the lodge, which he knew pretty well by this time, by about half a mile when he met a policeman walking along the road from the direction of Medchester. A bit of a boss he was, with a cap instead of a helmet and a bit of braid about him. He had never seen him before, didn't – begging their pardons – see more of the police than he was obliged to, but had learnt since the officer's name was Mayer.

Thinking to save himself a visit to the police station, he had stopped the officer and handed it over to him, with the request that if it should prove to be of any value he wouldn't be forgotten. It was just as well, he went on, to stand in with the police when you didn't do yourself any harm by it, a remark that had brought a grin to Stoddart's lips.

"What then?" the inspector asked shortly. "Did it seem to be of any importance?"

The man nodded.

"He seemed all dithery-like when he'd read it."

"What did he say?"

"He said, 'Well, I be damned!' twice over – very slow."

Stoddart moved impatiently. "Was that all he said? Get on, man!"

"There ain't nothin' more to tell – leastways 'e told me to report myself at the station at Medchester next mornin' at ten o'clock and I'd probably 'ear o' something to my advantage."

"And did you do so?"

The tramp drew the back of his hand across his mouth.

"Not me! By evenin' it was all over the place that a man 'ad been murdered – and a policeman at that – close to the 'Olford lodge, near where we'd been talkin' in the mornin', so I makes myself scarce. 'Tweren't no manner o' use gettin' mixed up in a murder case – and havin' awkward questions asked. So I 'ops it, and let any reward for the findin' of the paper that might be comin' to me go 'ang."

There was a pause; the pair of cunning little eyes wandered vaguely round the room to come again to a halt at the beer jug. But nobody took the hint.

"What have you been doing with yourself since?" Stoddart asked.

"Trampin' the country – and doin' no 'arm," was the defiant reply.

"Umph?" the detective looked doubtful. "Why have you come here now?"

The flamboyantly red head leaned forward confidentially.

"I picked up a noospaper lying in the road as I was trampin' into Mapsdale and there I reads about the inquest. 'Twas an old noospaper – days and days. That was last Wednesday. There I sees the policeman's name was Mayer, and as 'ow 'e'd told the lady at the lodge 'e'd got a line on summat an' no one knew 'ow 'e'd got it. So I thinks to meself –" He hesitated, looking doubtfully at his interrogator. "You'll play fair, you gentlemen," he whined, "you won't let nothink I say be used agin me? I needn't ha' come 'ere if I 'adn't wanted to –"

"Tell us all you know and you'll be none the worse for it," Stoddart said curtly.

"Well," he drew back with an air of relief, "I come 'ere now because I could see I 'ad a bit o' information and thought it might be worth a bit o' money. Nobody knows I met the cop 'cept 'im and me, and if you put 'im out of it there's only me – and if you arsk me, I tell yer I believe he got a bit o' vallyble information out o' that there bit o' paper."

"What did he do with the bit of paper?" Both detectives bent forward eagerly.

The tramp shook his head.

"I can't tell yer that, gentlemen, for I knows no more than the babe unborn. When I left 'im 'e was standin' in the middle of the road a-readin' of it over again. I went my ways, and when I 'ears about the murder I 'ooks it, and never 'eard no more till I picked up the noospaper in the road outside o' Mapsdale."

Stoddart muttered a strong word under his breath.

"You didn't see him put it in his pocket? Think," he urged, signing to Harbord to get the beer jug replenished.

"I didn't stop to see what 'e done with it. I tell 'ee – 'e was a-standin' in the middle o' the road 'oldin' the paper in 'is 'and – like so." He held up both hands in front of him as if grasping a visionary slip of paper. "I turned my back to 'im, a-walkin' along the road towards Medchester, and I went round a corner and didn't see 'im no more. Then when I 'ears about the murder –"

The inspector held up his hand. "We know all that," he said curtly, "you 'opped it. Would you know the woman again who came through the little gate?"

"Ay, that I would. I seed 'er face plain enough in the moonlight."

Stoddart drew the page his colleague had cut from the illustrated paper from his pocket and laid it on the table before him.

"Anything like that?" he asked, spreading it out flat.

The man pushed his red-crowned head forward and studied the picture; frowned, put his head on one side and pulled the sheet nearer to him.

"That's 'er," he said shortly, "that's the face I saw in the moonlight."

"You're certain?" the inspector pressed.

He nodded. "That's 'er all right," and added thoughtfully, "so 'elp me, Gawd."

CHAPTER XXIV

The two detectives, having got rid of their visitor for the time being, looked at one another with raised brows.

"Well," Stoddart remarked, "that's that. Pretty exasperating about that paper, but we've got something definite to go on at last. I'd like to know what that bit of paper was about, and whether poor Mayer was shot for the sake of it. Seems to me, Alfred, our theory looks like holding good – the same hand fired both shots. Mayer knew too much."

He paused a moment lost in thought.

"I rang up Mrs. Burford," he went on, "while you were away in Medchester and said I should like another bit of a talk with her, but I'm not sure after this that I want it, not straight off. You might ring up and cry off for me. The story wants a bit of thinking out, and the sooner we get on to it the better – and keep a line on Mr. Ted Watson."

The message had found Anne nearly at the end of her tether.

It is one thing to face a dramatic moment with calmness and fortitude; it is quite another to face life day in day out, week by week, the sword of Damocles suspended by the slenderest of threads, and yet to keep up a brave, unflinching attitude towards a world that will certainly judge you through its head rather than its heart.

For Anne could gauge the situation into which by her own act she had precipitated herself fairly accurately. Judged on the merits of the case, to put it colloquially, she hadn't a leg to stand upon; she was well aware of that, even though ignorant of the fact that owing to Lady Medchester's evidence the police knew she had been in the summer-house that night. If she stood firm in her refusal to admit her brother's part in the meeting arranged between herself and Saunderson – and she had every intention of doing so – her assignation, were she to admit it, would bear inevitably a sinister interpretation, would connect her with his death in a manner more sinister still.

Over and over, round and round her brain, every conceivable aspect of the affair revolved. Night and day she got no peace; her last thought at night, it greeted her when she opened her eyes in the morning; and adding the last straw to the burden was Harold's coldness, his curt, unsympathetic message sent through a woman he knew she detested, and, worst of all, his continued absence. Considering all the circumstances and the supreme sacrifice she had been prepared to make for him and for the sake of the family name, dragged by his action through the mud, it seemed unbelievable that he should stand aloof now that she was in trouble.

Not even to her husband had she divulged the true circumstances of that night. He knew as much as she had told the police – no more. It would be part of the reward of the trials she had faced that her brother and the family name should go unscathed, especially in the eyes of the man who had stood by her and whom she loved with all her heart. Her loyalty had withstood every temptation, but when the message came that Inspector Stoddart proposed to pay her another inquisitorial visit she found herself at breaking point, and in something approaching panic had flung herself into her husband's study where he was busy over the day's correspondence, and to his surprise and distress burst into tears.

"Michael," she sobbed, "I can't stand it! That inspector is coming again, and I know I shall – shall go mad – and say something I don't mean – and" – as he drew her on to a low seat in the window beside him – "which probably won't be true!"

He slipped a protective arm round her. "Why should you mind?" he soothed. "Whatever others may think, *we* know Harold is innocent and, knowing that, nothing you say is likely to incriminate him."

But Anne remained silent, desperately undecided whether to make a clean breast of it to him or not. She was so passionately anxious to keep her brother's character unstained in the eyes of the man who had so generously joined his fortunes with her own in the moment of her trouble. If she told him half the truth only, how explain her presence in the summer-house that night? She was torn two ways, shaken by slow sobs as her husband, not understanding, tried to calm her obvious terror of being raked by the fire of Scotland Yard methods again.

The truth was he himself was a little puzzled. Harold's attitude with regard to his marriage was not the attitude of a happy bridegroom; still less that of a man whose actions were free and independent. He seemed rather in the position of a man forced to do something against his will, and, although Anne continued to reiterate her faith in his innocence, her husband found himself subconsciously adding a question mark whenever the subject was mentioned. There was something behind it all he did not understand, and Michael Burford hated mysteries.

But the immediate necessity was to comfort Anne and soothe her fears, and patiently he recapitulated the arguments in favour of her brother's innocence, Anne knowing all the time he was in possession of only half the facts, and therefore quite unaware of the motive that might have spurred Harold into a criminal act.

In that lay the difficulty of her position. It was so hard that now Harold had made good, had, as she knew privately, redeemed the incriminating paper the moment his heritage as Lord Gorth enabled him to raise sufficient money for the purpose, her tongue must still remain tied as to her motive for arranging the meeting with Saunderson that evening. The fact still remained that Harold's misdemeanour had forced her into consenting to marry a man she hated, and that her brother had accepted the sacrifice; further, a knowledge of all the facts would certainly justify the police in regarding Harold with the gravest suspicion.

It amounted to this, that if she were to tell Michael of her visit to the summer-house, she must suppress the reason, and leave it to his generosity to put upon it an innocent interpretation.

And now, here were her nerves giving way when she wanted all the backing they could give, and she sobbed incoherent phrases into her husband's broad shoulder while he silently breathed fire and brimstone against the Yard and all its ways, and determined to pay the detective a visit on his own account and extort from him an explanation of his conduct and suspicions.

Then, at breaking point, Stoddart's second message came through, and Anne, in an ecstasy of relief, was in danger of being overcome by an attack of hysterical laughter. With the resilience of youth the hope once more reasserted itself that, if only the real murderer could be found, Harold's forgery of Saunderson's name, and her own assignation with him might never transpire, but lie, buried between them, till the day when according to general belief no secrets will be hid. Such secrets, she thought optimistically, might not loom so large in a world where all cupboards will be opened and skeletons invited to walk out. Some of them, at all events, might be overlooked in the crowd.

Anyway, it was a respite, and, to her husband's relief, Anne dried her eyes and joyfully accepted his offer to drive her into Medchester in the car.

It was a radiant autumn day, the glowing tints of beech and elm, the more vivid for the deep blue background of an almost cloudless sky, and in the reaction from her black hour Anne felt almost happy as she slipped in beside Michael and pulled the door of the car to after her. There is an exhilaration in rapid motion that will dislodge dull care from most shoulders, and the colour began to creep back into Anne's cheeks, the life into her eyes.

At the corner where the roads from East Molton and from Holford to Medchester forked, they met the bus heading for Holford. Anne glanced at it indifferently, little thinking that it carried with it the key to the riddle they had all been so vainly trying to solve, and upon which hung so much of vital importance to her own future and to that of her brother.

Anne Burford was not the only woman in the neighbourhood who had been fighting her way through an emotional storm that day, the main difference in the situation being that whereas the one found herself almost submerged by circumstances brought about by no fault of her own, the other had brought them on herself, and was in addition therefore confronted by remorse and a sense of ill-doing.

It had been Mrs. Mayer's last day at her home in Medchester police station. The new superintendent had proved to be unmarried and, being of a kindly disposition, had begged her not to hurry herself, but to transport herself and her belongings to other quarters at her own convenience. So she had packed at her leisure, and it was not until she had emptied the drawers in the old-fashioned bureau, standing against the wall in her bedroom, of their contents that she made an overwhelming discovery.

In the first flush of it she had stood, rigid, gazing into space, her eyes filled with dismay, fear, and a sense of right struggling for mastery. Then, coming to a sudden decision, she had closed her lips in a thin, hard line, put on coat and hat, and with a parcel in her hand had caught the bus for Holford.

Inspector Stoddart, having finished lunch at the "Medchester Arms," was on the point of starting for the Hall when he was told by Mrs. Marlow's maid there was some one to see him. He was inclined to be impatient at the interruption.

During the last twenty-four hours events had been shaping themselves more satisfactorily, but the whole case was still too much in the air for any definite action to be taken. Harbord's discovery in the dentist's waiting-room of the ownership of the crystal beads, added to the redhaired tramp's evidence, had given substantial grounds for a well-defined line of inquiry, but there still remained a most important point which would have to be established before proceeding further.

So when it transpired that the some one's name was Mayer, the widow of the murdered superintendent, Stoddart decided to postpone his visit to the Hall and to receive her in their sitting-room, with Harbord in attendance to take notes or bear witness should witness be required.

Mrs. Mayer was ushered in, breathless from her journey and, as she would have said herself, upset, whether through fear or shock it was impossible to say at first sight. She sank into the chair placed for her by Harbord, hugging to her the parcel she was carrying as if loath to part with it.

The inspector gave her time to pull herself together, then he asked gently:

"Is there anything I can do for you, Mrs. Mayer?" He had always felt sorry for the poor woman.

She turned a pair of frightened eyes towards him.

"I didn't mean any harm," she said in a low voice. "I never thought as how it could matter. Believe me," bending forward earnestly, "I wouldn't have done it if I'd known. I knew I didn't ought – not to hide anything from the police – Bill he often said that in my hearing – 'Don't hide anything from the police,' he said – and I never thinking – not knowing as how there'd ever be anything –"

"I dare say it's nothing very serious, Mrs. Mayer," Stoddart said kindly. "You tell us what it is and don't go making yourself unhappy about it before the time. Tell us all about it in your own way."

She sat straight up in the chair and placed the parcel on the table in front of her.

"I've got to make a clean breast of it sooner or later, so I suppose I may as well do it straight off," making a brave effort at self-control. "After all, I didn't mean any harm, and you won't forget that, inspector."

"Don't be afraid," he encouraged, "we shall be glad to hear anything you have to say."

"Well, it was like this. The day after my Bill was" – she hesitated for a word and her lip quivered – "shot, it came over me to go and see the spot – sort of sacred – you understand –"

She paused again.

Stoddart, who was hanging on her words, convinced somehow they were going to get the truth about Mayer's death, nodded in silence.

"So peaceful it looked," she went on, her eyes becoming dreamy, "the tree trunks rising up out of the green moss; the ground strewn with red and yellow leaves – some of them fallen fresh in the night; there was a bird chirruping somewhere – you'd never have thought a man had been killed there. I just looked round, and wished the trees and the bushes could have spoken and told me the name of the coward who'd done it – killed a man doing his duty."

Again she paused, and neither of her hearers seemed inclined to break the silence. She sighed heavily and resumed:

"My eyes fell on something glittering under a bush, and when I went to see what it was I found it was the shiny peak of a cap. I picked it up – my Bill's cap – dropped there, I suppose, and overlooked when they took him away to the Cottage Hospital."

The inspector glanced at the parcel on the table.

"The cap was missed when they went over his clothes, Mrs. Mayer, and a constable went back to look for it next day. Of course he didn't find it."

"I'm sorry, inspector, I am indeed; but it was my Bill's cap, which I'd brushed for him and watched him put on his head when he left me that morning. I just couldn't give it up! I know I oughtn't to have kept it – it belonged to the Government and all that – and I oughtn't to hide anything from the police – and Bill a policeman so to speak himself – but there it was! I kept it and," she added fiercely, "I meant to have kept it till my dying day in spite of all the police in the world!"

Again there was silence.

"And why didn't you?" Stoddart asked gently.

"Providence is inscrutable in His ways, and He made me do the right thing in spite of myself," she said simply. "I took Bill's cap home with me, hid under my jacket, and I went half-way round Medchester and in at the little garden gate at the back of the police station instead of by the front, fearful I'd meet a constable who'd ask me what I'd got hid. Then I wrapped it up in a bit of clean tissue paper what Betty's – that's my daughter – new black hat had come in, and put it away in the drawer of an old bit of furniture that was left to Bill by an old gentleman he'd done a good turn to when burglars got into his house. And

I'd never have told anyone, not the police nor even my own daughter that I'd got it, if it hadn't been for – for what I found out."

"What did you find out, Mrs. Mayer?" Stoddart urged, as patiently as he could. Perhaps it might amount to nothing after all.

She hesitated and drawing the parcel towards her fidgeted with the string.

"It was when I was packing up to come away to-day. I came to tell you at once when I knew," she protested. "I opened the drawer and took out the cap from the back, and I sat down in a chair and held it in my hand and thought of how Bill had put it on that morning, and how glad I was I had got something he had worn the last thing before – before –"

"I am sure you were," the inspector said sympathetically, "and then –?"

"Then I was just passing my fingers over it – loving-like – and I found, slipped into the lining that runs round inside, a bit of paper. I pulled it out and I saw it had something written on it, and in a minute I remembered all the talk and the questions about Bill having learnt something after he'd left me in the morning, and how the coroner and the police had thought that was what he'd been shot for, and how nobody had found out what it was, and there was I hiding the very thing that maybe they were all looking for. It gave me a shock, it did – and I came along here as quick as I could."

"The red-haired tramp! Lord, how the pieces begin to fit in!" Harbord muttered.

With fingers that shook the poor woman unfastened the string, and from the tissue paper produced the peaked uniform cap that had belonged to her husband. She pushed it across the table to the inspector.

"I never so much as looked at it – just let it be as it was," she explained. "I knew it didn't ought to be there, not in an ordinary way like – he never carried anything inside his cap. Didn't I know, as gave it a brush up and put it on his head for him as often as not! So I've brought it along. I am sorry – and a woman can't say more."

Stoddart took the folded slip of paper from the strip of lining and laid the cap back on the table. There was dead silence in the room as he read what was written in rather faded ink. When he had finished he turned to his colleague and for all the expression that appeared on his features they might have been carved in wood.

"Ask Mrs. Marlow to give Mrs. Mayer a cup of tea before she starts back, Alfred," he said.

Harbord disappeared, and Stoddart looked at the woman seated opposite.

"You shouldn't have kept the cap back, you know, Mrs. Mayer. It's Government property and it's a criminal offence to hide anything from the police that may forward the ends of justice."

"I know that," she admitted, "but when a woman has lost – the best man what ever was –"

The words tailed off into a sob.

The inspector gave the cap the slightest push in her direction.

"It's the paper that's wanted," he said with a gruffness assumed possibly to hide a different emotion; turning his back, he stared out of the window.

Mrs. Mayer hesitated, put out a hand, and gathered the cap into the shelter of her coat, safe from prying eyes. Then with a grateful glance at the figure standing by the window she softly left the room.

When Harbord returned his superior was scanning the slip of paper held up in front of him.

"Well?" Harbord asked eagerly.

The other looked up with a grim smile and handed him the slip of paper.

"All we want," he said tersely. "The one link that was missing – the motive!"

"What are you going to do now?"

Stoddart reached for his hat and coat.

"I am going straight off to get a warrant," he said, making for the door.

CHAPTER XXV

"That's the third car from the Hall you've opened the gate for, mother."

Miss Tottie Delauney flattened her nose against the casement window of the lodge and peered out into the fading light of the autumn afternoon.

"What's up at the Hall? And here's another," she added as a raucous hoot outside sent Mrs. Yates trotting through the front door. In a moment she was back again.

"That was Mrs. Baily-Barton," she informed her daughter, breathless from the effort of swinging the heavy gates to and fro. "Her chauffeur is a son of John Nomes's that keeps the tobacco shop in Medchester High Street. Here's another! Mirandy, go and open the gate, there's a good girl. I can't get me breath all in a minute."

"Not me!" was the casual retort. "Let 'em open it themselves. Don't you put yourself out, mother. Chauffeur indeed! Fat and lazy! Why can't he get out and open it himself? The machine won't run away."

But Mrs. Yates was already bustling down the gravel path to the drive, and the creak of a ponderous hinge broke into the soft purr of the big car awaiting her kind offices inside the gates.

"Who was that?"

Mrs. Yates, returning, a hand clasped to her heart, made no reply.

"Why don't you prop it open? There's no sense running in and out like that, and I don't suppose any strays'll get in from the road."

"Blest if I don't next one as comes through. There's bin a tea-party goin' on at the Hall – so Mr. Wilton said when he passed through to the gardens this morning – in honour of young Lord Gorth – Mr. Harold that was – and his young lady."

"She's older than him, I guess, and she's older than that Mrs. Stuck-up Burford with her nose in the air for all that I could tell –" Miss Delauney stopped abruptly.

"You hold your tongue, Mary Ann," her mother interposed hurriedly, "especially when it comes to talking about yer betters. They are going to be married to-morrow, quiet-like in Holford Church. I do hold with going to church – seems kinder asking a blessing – and you want all the help you can get when it comes to husbands. That's what I say. That husband o' yours, Mary Ann –"

"Oh, leave him alone, mother!" was the sharp retort. "What's the good of raking up things best forgot? Let sleeping dogs lie. The less the police mess round the better. I gave 'em a hint and they didn't take it – if they can't see through a stone wall I'm not the one to make a hole in it for them. There's another car! I wouldn't demean myself running out after them," Miss Delauney added as her mother scrambled to her feet, "not if I was you."

"What do you suppose his lordship gives me my house for, rent free?" Mrs Yates threw back at her from the door. "And what do you suppose I should do without it?"

"You wait till I come into me own," Miss Delauney muttered. "I suppose a wife has got her rights."

Having sped the parting guest, Mrs Yates returned to her chair.

"That was Lady Darman, high and haughty she is. I wonder her ladyship asked her. I hear his lordship's going to town and won't be home till the end of the week. Don't hold with the marriage he don't – so Mr. Wilton says – but her ladyship's fair set on it."

It had, however, been by no wish of Lady Medchester's that the neighbourhood had been enjoying the hospitality of Holford Hall that afternoon. Ostensibly with the object of introducing her own acquaintances to the future Lady Gorth, invitations had been sent out; but Lord Medchester had refused to lend his countenance to the entertainment. He had taken himself off to London until it and the subsequent marriage ceremony at the village church should be over. Reluctantly admitting his jurisdiction did not extend to Church matters, and that Miss Stainer was entitled to be married in any church she chose, he could only express his disapproval publicly by absenting himself and advertising the fact to all and sundry who might be interested.

The party brought together with so depressing an atmosphere inspiring it had not been a success. Those among Lady Medchester's neighbours who had accepted the invitation had done so mainly out of curiosity, and finding themselves entertained perfunctorily by an apparently apathetic hostess, and treated with a sort of hostile insolence by the woman who proposed to settle down among them, had departed as quickly as bare politeness permitted, leaving behind them in the large drawing-room used only for receptions of a more or less formal nature, and insisted upon by Miss Stainer on this special occasion, four people in varying degrees of bad temper.

Lady Medchester made no effort to hide her annoyance and humiliation at the performance she had just gone through. She was not accustomed to giving parties that were failures, and she turned to Anne Burford, present more or less under compulsion, with an unspoken appeal for sympathy that was very unusual in her attitude towards her cousin.

Harold sat in a corner frankly in the sulks, and Miss Stainer, the fourth occupant of the room, was trying to put a good face on the situation by humming a tune and standing with assumed nonchalance on the hearth-rug, warming a foot at the fire.

Destiny as often as not seems to set the stage for life's most poignant dramas with a careless hand. No studied grouping of principal actors, no background of significant details, nor play of limelight on the stars of the piece. The scene as the act opens may be commonplace and undistinguished, the position of the players apparently haphazard, until the red light of tragedy transforms the common setting of everyday life into an indelible picture.

Lady Medchester, at the end of her patience, looked irritably across the room at her guest.

"I wish you would stop humming that thing, Sybil," she protested, "it gets on my nerves. You were at it all the afternoon – and out of tune at that!"

Miss Stainer turned sharply, a reply on her lips; but before she could speak the door opened and before anyone realized what was happening, unannounced, Inspector Stoddart and Harbord were standing inside the room.

Lady Medchester, with a suppressed cry of terror, pressed a hand to her heart and fell back in her chair. Anne, suddenly faced with possible danger, crept instinctively to her brother's side; he slipped a protective arm round her and murmured something in her ear.

But Stoddart, his face cold and impassive as Anne had never seen it, took no notice of them. He crossed to the fireplace where Miss Stainer stood, staring at him, eyes wide and desperate, and laid a hand on her shoulder.

"Sybil Stainer, I arrest you in the name of the law for the murder of Robert Saunderson on the twenty-ninth of August last – and I warn you anything you say now may be used in evidence against you!"

There was a moment of tense silence; the movement of a hand as if in search of a handkerchief; a sharp report – and Sybil Stainer dropped limply at Stoddart's feet.

CHAPTER XXVI

Two days later, each with a bit of the story to tell, Inspector Stoddart and his companion were ushered into the library at Holford Hall, where Lord Medchester awaited them.

"I shall be interested to hear how you arrived at your conclusions, inspector," he remarked, motioning them to be seated. "To be quite frank, I never liked the woman – couldn't imagine what the devil my wife saw in her. But it's a bit of a shake-up to have a thing of that sort happen under your own roof – a damn sight worse than the murder, being a woman and all that," he finished vaguely.

"No need for you to go over the threads that led us nowhere," Stoddart began. "We'll follow up the main line of it. It seemed such a precious tangle when we began, bringing us up against a blank wall time and again. Where there was motive we were confronted with a watertight alibi; and where opportunity could be proved the motive was wanting – and murder without motive is a senseless sort of proposition."

Lord Medchester acquiesced. "Give me the salient facts. What put you on to the line eventually?"

"As often as not it's one part grey matter to two parts chance that does the trick; though I will say that if the grey matter were to be entirely absent perhaps the so-called chances wouldn't turn up. Anyway, the first definite pointer we got was because my colleague" – he jerked his head in Harbord's direction – "couldn't sleep one night on account of toothache. And even then there didn't seem to be any motive."

He pulled his chair a few inches nearer to his listeners, and carefully deposited his hat underneath.

"No need to repeat what you know already," he went on, "but I'd better tell you straight away there's one bit of the story will have to come out before the evidence can be pieced together. I'm sorry, Lord Medchester."

And, as considerately as the circumstances permitted, he repeated all that Lady Medchester had told him of her part in the affair, and her presence in the garden that night, while his hearer sat as though turned to stone, unable to refute and loyally reluctant to accept the statement.

"The difficulty all through with which we were faced," the inspector went on hurriedly, glad to get on less delicate ground, "was the ownership of the crystal beads. They were peculiar beads, cut in a peculiar way, not outstandingly unique, but I had noticed that in the broken necklace picked up in the shrubbery one of them was missing, leaving a gap in the chain, and the bead next to the gap was broken. A bit of a signpost that. Miss Stainer never entered into my calculations, and I don't mind confessing now I was taking an interest in Miss Tottie Delauney, Mrs. Yates's daughter, who had kept her presence at the lodge so quiet and was so ready to try and put the crime on some one else's shoulders. But there wasn't enough to go on."

"There would have been opportunity there, with her headquarters at the lodge," Lord Medchester muttered, "and, if she gets his money, motive."

"True enough, especially in poor Mayer's case – to keep his mouth shut. But nobody was forthcoming to testify to her having been near the Hall or in the gardens that night and – well, I've had a good bit of experience, and Miss Delauney wasn't the type that goes so far as a murder – much less two of them. She's more the kind that's nervous of firearms because she doesn't know which end they'll go off at. The motive wasn't so very plain, either. She didn't care for her husband nor his goings-on with other women, and couldn't be sure whether he'd made a Will or not. She confessed as much. She had persuaded him into making her an allowance, and if he had made a Will it was quite possible she might have found herself better off with him alive than dead. That seemed to put her out of court."

Lord Medchester nodded assent. "And how did you get on to Sybil Stainer?"

Stoddart smiled. "That's where this man comes in."

He turned to Harbord, who shook his head, being of a retiring disposition and nothing of a spokesman. The inspector resumed:

"He had toothache one night, as I was telling you" – he indicated his companion – "and went off next morning to see a dentist in Medchester. As no appointment had been made he had to kick his heels in the waiting-room till his turn came. And now this is, we must admit, where chance gave a hand rather than grey matter."

He paused impressively. Inspector Stoddart was not wanting in a sense of the dramatic.

"Harbord picked up one of the papers lying on the table at random: an old one – a date in July. One of those illustrated papers about people in Society. In it he came on a full page portrait and under it was printed – 'Miss Sybil Stainer, one of the stall-holders at the Duchess of Merebank's bazaar.' And" – he paused, to give due effect to the words – "round her neck was hanging the crystal bead necklace, the gap on the chain, the broken bead next to it, hitting you, so to speak, in the eye!"

Lord Medchester, his interest keenly aroused, bent forward eagerly.

"Lord! What a bit of luck! and Harold within an ace of marrying her!" he added under his breath.

"Harbord was so pleased he forgot all about his toothache, made a dash for the door, and a bee-line for me. And that's how we first got on to Miss Sybil Stainer.

"But it was only a first step," he continued. "It proved she had been on the scene of the tragedy that night, but there didn't seem to be any motive."

"How the devil did the woman know Saunderson was to be at Holford that night?" Lord Medchester put in.

For an almost imperceptible moment Stoddart hesitated.

"Might have arranged to meet him there for aught we know," he answered, and turning to Harbord added, "she was on the spot all right, for, if you remember, we took the very rooms at the 'Medchester Arms' she and her brother had vacated that morning – the day after the murder. We knew Robert Saunderson was a bit of a blackmailer, and where that comes in you never know where you are, low-down blackguards that they are! But we searched his papers and not a trace could we find of any transactions with Miss Sybil Stainer."

The inspector added the incident of the finding of the stray bead by the little gate; no doubt it had lodged in her dress or bag when the necklace broke and fell in the road as she passed through the gate.

"But we hadn't seen the tramp then," he added.

"Not justified in making an arrest and didn't want to question her for fear of putting her on her guard?"

"That's so; and while we were hesitating about forcing the situation Providence again played into our hands."

The inspector proceeded to relate the story the red-haired tramp had had to tell, confirming the silent testimony of the crystal beads, that Sybil Stainer had been in the gardens that night; of the paper she had dropped, of how it had lain in his pocket, and of his meeting with Superintendent Mayer on the morning he was shot.

"Then we were up against the problem of what Mayer had done with the slip of paper handed to him by the tramp, and vanished apparently into the blue, the contents of which Mayer had considered too important to be divulged either to you or to Mrs. Yates, and that had sent him posthaste to the nearest telephone. And then," he said slowly, "Mrs. Mayer came on the scene. She came to see me at the 'Medchester Arms.'"

"What had she to say?"

Stoddart smiled whimsically. "She was half out of her mind, poor woman, with grief at the loss of her husband and remorse at having cheated the law. The truth was, she had found poor Mayer's cap lying among the bushes near the spot where he was killed, and taken it home and hidden it, and an hour before she arrived breathless at the 'Medchester Arms' in search of me had discovered there was a bit of paper slipped in behind the strip of lining that goes round inside – without a doubt the paper handed to Mayer by the tramp, and that he must have placed there for safety."

"Good Lord! It's like putting a puzzle together! Get on with the story – what had the paper to do with the murders?"

"It put the lid on the evidence against Miss Stainer. I always said the two murders were done by the same hand. I take it Miss Stainer overheard Mayer talking to you and what he said at the telephone through the open window – you remember you found her brother loafing about outside, though we don't connect him with the crime. She nipped down by the short cut to intercept the superintendent before he reached the lodge, inveigled him into the bushes by pretending to be hurt – any pretext would have done – and shot him with the automatic she carried in her bag, as we now know, for use should any desperate emergency arise. She silenced Mayer, but she didn't allow for the bit of evidence hidden in his cap."

"What was the nature of that bit of evidence?"

"It was a copy of a marriage certificate," the inspector replied, "a marriage that took place about four years ago in South America, between Sybil Stainer and a man called Guido Baruta. He seems to have vanished into the blue, but there is no record of his death – we cabled for information. The certificate is in order right enough, and" – he paused impressively – "the name of Robert Saunderson was on it as witness! That was good enough!"

Lord Medchester stared at the speaker, his slowly working mind labouring to put two and two together.

"*There* was motive, good and plenty!" Stoddart repeated. "Nothing more wanted. Motive enough, with a brilliant marriage hanging in the balance and Saunderson with the game in his hands so far as she was concerned – and motive was all we wanted. A woman who had committed one murder to gain her ends," he finished slowly, "wasn't likely to stick at a second – and Miss Sybil Stainer meant to be Lady Gorth in spite of all the devils in hell! She was that sort of woman."

"There are two points in this case that need never come out, Alfred," Stoddart remarked as they walked down the drive towards the "Medchester Arms." "One of them is – What made Anne Courtenay go to the summer-house that night? Had she an assignation with Saunderson or was it pure accident? Do you remember the bit of paper found on Saunderson's body – 'I accede because I must'? I always thought that was written by Anne Courtenay. But she was shielding that young cub of a brother of hers. I'll bet that was it, though we may never know now. Miss Stainer, of course, got a glimpse of her in the garden, guessed her brother Harold was financially involved with the murdered man, and played one against the other, making each think the other had done it."

"Just so," Harbord agreed, "and neither of them knew how much she knew, and both of them had something to hide." he said thoughtfully. "The truth about that doesn't matter now."

"The other fact about which we may exercise a bit of *suppressio veri*," the inspector went on with the suspicion of a twinkle in his eye, "is the letter from Lady Medchester to Saunderson we found in Miss Stainer's bag, taken no doubt from the dead man's pocket-book when she took the marriage certificate – a letter fit to scorch the hair off your head! No wonder Miss Stainer had the writer of it under her thumb! That need never come out, for Lord Medchester's sake; his wife can tell him her own story. He's had his suspicions about the relations between them all through – he was always nervous what might come out in evidence – anybody could see that."

"Funny what some women will do for money and position, and what chances they'll take!" Harbord remarked thoughtfully. "Then she found herself in a tight place, and took the simplest way out." And he added solemnly, "She paid the price."

THE END

Lightning Source UK Ltd.
Milton Keynes UK
UKOW06f0935191116
288021UK00024B/610/P